# BLOOD MAGIC

WITCH'S BITE SERIES BOOK THREE

STEPHANIE FOXE

STEEL FOX MEDIA LLC

**First edition, September 2017**
**Version 2.0, May 2019**
**ISBN 978-1-950310-06-7**

*It's never easy, but it's always worth it.*

*Thank you to everyone who cheered me on as I wrote this. Your support was indispensable.*

# CONTENTS

1

---

The movers are wearing crisp gray uniforms. They have the truck almost completely packed with boxes. I pull my jacket a little tighter around me; it's chilly this evening.

I'm going to miss this house. It was just a rental, but I had felt like it was home, even if it did have rats under the porch and no central heating or cooling. Having it taken away like this is humiliating. At least I didn't have to pay to fix all the damage. Reilly did that when he broke my lease for me.

I turn and watch the sun disappear in a wash of golds and oranges. It's not quite six pm, according to the clock at least. Daylight Savings Time is such a joke.

The heavy weight of exhaustion that has been bothering me all day dissipates as it sinks below the horizon. Twilight turns to darkness, but I can still see every detail of the trees that surround my house. Javier's magic stirs inside of me with relief.

"Ma'am?" one of the movers asks hesitantly.

I turn around.

"What?" My tone is a little harsh, and the guy

looks nervous, a bead of sweat forming on his forehead.

"Mr. Walsh said you would need to select a week's worth of clothes for us to pack separately. Would you mind doing that now?"

I rub my hands over my face so I don't snap at the mover. His heart is hammering loudly in his chest, and it's distracting, though I am relieved to find I don't have any urge to bite him.

"Sure, lead the way," I say, shoving my hands in my jacket pockets.

He walks back inside, leaving the door open behind him.

I follow slowly. I haven't been inside since I came here with Lydia and found the house was trashed. The graffiti on the outside of the house has already been stripped off and repainted. The smell of bleach and other cleaners burn my nose as I step inside.

The cabinets are empty. The mess of food and glass has been cleaned out of the kitchen. The window in the living room is fixed, and a shiny new AC unit has replaced the old one. The couch and broken coffee table are gone.

The mover stands awkwardly in my bedroom door until I follow him into the room. My clothes are all hanging on a rack. Anything that can't be hung is set in neat piles on the bed. A suitcase is lying open on the floor to my left.

I grab things off the rack and throw them in the suitcase. I barely see what I'm grabbing. My skin is crawling with anger, and my gums ache, fangs pricking at the inside of my lips as my control begins to slip.

I want to set it all on fire and run, but I can't. Reilly would wipe out the clan, and he'd probably kill me too when he inevitably tracked me down. I hate him. I hate someone else having this kind of control over me. I wish I didn't care.

My phone buzzes. I glance at the screen; it's Lydia again. I reject the call and shove the phone in my back pocket.

"So, uh, is that everything you'd like?" the mover asks, his voice quaking.

"Yeah, that's it," I say before turning and stomping out of the room.

Reilly had insisted I come here this morning with no explanation, and while I had wanted to refuse just because he had insisted, I had wanted to say goodbye to this place. I'm not sure it's helping though. It doesn't feel like closure; it feels like I'm losing it all over again.

When I get in the car, I'm tempted all over again to just drive off and never look back. Instead, I drive to the clanhouse. I want to see Patrick before I go. I want to know why he betrayed me.

There is a plain white van parked in the driveway I don't recognize. There isn't any writing on the side. I park Javier's car in the garage, then walk around to the front door and knock loudly.

A moment later, the door opens and Emilio steps aside to let me in without a word. His face is paler than usual, and his mouth is locked in a frown. The house is quiet, as if no one is here tonight.

"Good morning, Emilio," I say out of habit.

He doesn't respond. I shove my hands in my pockets.

"Where is Javier?"

"In his room, recovering," Emilio says, casting an accusing glance at me.

"I wasn't trying to hurt him," I say through gritted teeth.

"But you did," Emilio says, whirling around. "You

hurt him, and now you have taken Leslie from us. The clan is weak because of you."

I step closer to him, my new fangs popping down as rage and hunger stir in my gut. I can practically smell the magic inside of Emilio. It's less powerful than what I took from Javier, but I still want it.

"None of this is my fault," I growl. "If anything, Javier betrayed me."

Emilio growls back and curls his lips up to reveal his own fangs.

"Javier should never have hired you."

"Enough," a voice rasps from above us. I don't think I would have been able to hear it without vampire magic coursing through me. Javier is standing by the banister, shoulders drooping, and his face gaunt like he's been starved. "Olivia, please come upstairs."

I brush past Emilio, keeping my eyes on him until I'm halfway up the stairs. Javier's knuckles are white where he grips the banister, barely able to support himself. He stares at me, something flickering in his eyes I don't understand.

I offer him my arm. He slips his hand through and clings to my bicep as I help him back to his room. The lights are all off, but a fire is flickering in the fireplace in the corner. I've never seen it used before.

He sits down on his bed, panting slightly from the effort of walking.

"I didn't know it would be this bad," I whisper. "In the past, it hasn't—I haven't done this on purpose very often. I'm sorry."

"Don't apologize. You saved Patrick, again, and defended yourself. I would not have let you take my power if I was unwilling to deal with the consequences," Javier says, attempting a cheeky grin.

I walk over to the chair Javier normally sits in and plop down, resting my elbows on my knees. A heavy silence settles between us. I'm not sure if I want to offer more apologies, or accusations.

"How long have you suspected there was something different about me?" I ask.

"Since the day I heard you healed the necker in the cafe," Javier says hoarsely. "On Lydia's advice, I reported it to the council, which has gained me the status I had been looking for. I sold the idea of hiring you to them by saying it was an experiment."

Javier sighs and crosses one leg over the other.

"The news spread surprisingly quickly, and someone from Reilly's clan contacted me within a couple of weeks of your hire date."

"Good to know I had been sold out from the very beginning," I say, my voice thick with exhaustion.

Javier smiles wanly. "There is a lot I misunderstood about your situation. I don't think I would have done anything differently even if I had known though."

I look up sharply. I expected at least some remorse.

"I know you will not, and cannot, accept this right now," Javier says in a whisper. "But there was no one else who would be able to protect you like they will. This will be for the best in the long run."

"For the best?" I sneer. "That's easy for you to say when you aren't the one being forced to serve the whims of a psychotic vampire."

Javier is silent. His heartbeat is still even and quiet. I hate that he isn't as angry as I am.

"Reilly can protect you."

"He's using me," I hiss at Javier. He has barely any magic left in him, but I still want it. My hands curl into fists, and my gums ache. I could rip it all out and wipe that smug expression off his face.

"You're hungry," Javier muses, the ghost of a smile playing at his lips.

"What?"

"You're craving magic like I crave blood." His eyes search my face. "I've sired dozens of vampires. I know the look."

"You don't know anything about what I'm dealing with," I snap. "No one does."

"Perhaps not," Javier says, leaning further back into the pillows. "But Reilly could help you figure it out. Help you control it."

"Reilly is concerned with only one person, and that is himself." I turn and walk toward the door. I don't want to hear anything else from Javier.

"Patrick left because he didn't agree with my co-operation with Reilly. It's part of why we argued."

I stop, my hand gripped tightly around the door-knob, wanting this part to be true.

"He cares about you, Olivia. Very much."

Mr. Muffins pads out of Javier's bathroom. The door handle bites into my palm, and my heart clenches with guilt. I had forgotten about her. Hadn't even considered what would happen to her now that I was leaving.

"I'll take care of her, I promise," Javier says.

I open the door and walk into the hall and slam it behind me. Of course I have to leave behind her too.

Patrick is leaning against the wall by the door. His arms are crossed, and he's staring hard at the floor. I take a few steps past him, then pause. I don't know what to say to Patrick either, but I do know it's nothing like the apologies I offered Javier. I'd rather punch Patrick.

"Reilly already knew what you could do," Patrick says as he stares at his feet. "He said I could either help him learn more about you, or he could just go ahead and kill you."

"Then you should have told me," I say, turning halfway back around to face him. "You could have warned me somehow."

"He was always listening, and if you had disappeared, he would have blamed me whether it was my fault or not. He would have destroyed the entire clan. I couldn't risk them all for—" He bites down on his cheek. "I couldn't risk them all."

"I risked everything for you," I say quietly.

Patrick runs his fingers roughly through his hair.

"I'm sorry," he says, taking a step toward me.

"Don't apologize," I snap. "Don't talk to me ever again."

The coven had threatened me and the clan, and I had risked my greatest secret to protect Patrick. I don't understand how easily they gave up. Reilly isn't all-powerful. In their position, I would have found a way. I should run and let the clan deal with the consequences.

I pause at the top of the stairs and glance back at Patrick. He is slumped down on the floor, his head in his hands. I squeeze my eyes shut for a moment, then go to look for Reilly.

2.

———————————

There are two strange vampires standing on either side of the door to the parlor with their arms crossed. They are wearing matching expensive black suits with a red sigil sewn into the lapel, but other than that, they are a study in opposites.

The one on the right has sandy blond hair tied back at the nape of his neck and looks like a Viking. His broad shoulders are testing the limits of his suit jacket. The one on the left has intricate tattoos that are barely darker than the skin on his face. There is more ink visible than skin, and the designs are in the negative space. It's striking.

They're both staring at me as I approach. The one on the left sniffs the air, then relaxes slightly.

"Mr. Walsh will be done in a moment, Ms. Carter," he says in a deep voice. There is a hint of an accent, but he speaks well and easily.

I come to a stop a few feet away from them.

"Who are you, and why are you here?" I ask, crossing my arms and looking at the door behind them suspiciously.

"We are Reilly's clanmates. He requested that we care for Leslie while he completes his duties."

"Are you taking her somewhere?"

Tattoo inclines his head. "Yes, but you do not need to worry about your friend. She is our clanmate now, she will not be mistreated."

I scoff. "Sure."

The door cracks open, and Reilly slips out, tugging the sleeve of his dark blue button-down shirt back down over his wrist. His suit jacket is slung over his other arm.

"Olivia, I didn't expect you to be done packing so soon," Reilly says with a satisfied smile, his cheeks dimpling. "I thought you might drag your feet."

"Well, here I am," I say drily. "How is Leslie?"

"She is sleeping as her body adapts to the changes. It will be successful though. I was able to turn her in time," he says as he pulls his jacket back on.

I scuff my boot on the ground and release a breath I didn't realize I was holding. "Good."

Reilly nods toward each of his men. "Take Leslie home."

The Viking claps his hand on Reilly's shoulder. "We will keep the new one safe. Good luck on your travels, brother."

Tattoo and Viking go into the room, and Reilly strides toward me.

"We need to leave now, or we won't make it to Phoenix before sunrise."

"We're driving all the way there tonight?" I ask, falling into step beside him.

"Yes, we need to meet up with the JHAPI agents tomorrow. They won't wait for us if we are late."

As we reach the front door, I notice Patrick hovering at the top of the stairs. I ignore him. The betrayal still stings, even if he does claim he was trying to protect me. I hadn't trusted anyone for so long. It figures that as soon as I do, they all turn out to either be terrorists or liars.

I pull the door shut behind me a little more firmly than necessary. Reilly glances back with a raised brow.

"You're in a great mood," he comments.

I roll my eyes at him.

"Of course I am. Why wouldn't I be? I've always wanted to drive to Arizona with a vampire that is blackmailing me into helping him. It was on my bucket list."

"You have a strangely specific bucket list," Reilly says, ignoring my sarcasm.

I shove my hands in my pockets. "Are we going or what?"

He waves his hand toward a sleek, black sedan parked in the driveway. "After you."

I brush past him and yank the front passenger door open. The seats are leather, and it smells like a new car. I pull the door shut behind me and try to find a comfortable position to sit. I don't know how long the drive to Arizona is. It has to be less than eleven hours, or we'll run into the sunrise. Either way, I'm in for a long night.

He puts the car in drive and speeds out of the driveway. I tighten my seatbelt over my lap. His driving hasn't gotten any better.

"You were a bit harsh toward Javier and Patrick," Reilly comments.

I whip my head around to face him. "Are you kidding me right now?"

Reilly shrugs. "No, simply voicing my opinion."

"On a private conversation you had no right to listen to in the first place," I say with clenched teeth.

"I'm not very concerned with your privacy," he says, smiling.

"Ah, of course not," I mutter. "And it's not harsh to be pissed at a friend for betraying you."

"Javier is your employer, not your friend," Reilly says slowly, as if I'm stupid.

"He was both," I say back just as slowly, mocking him. I worked for Javier, but Reilly wasn't there when Javier was begging me for help. Javier cared about me; it just turned out he cared about himself more. Patrick has no excuses at all.

"You weren't in his clan. He doesn't have any obligation to protect you."

I snort. "I didn't have any obligation either, but when it came down to it, I protected him and helped him."

"That's your problem, Olivia. You do more than you need to for people," he says as he shifts into a lower gear to speed around a semi-truck. "You wouldn't have a felony on your record if you hadn't gone back for that hurt cop when you were first arrested. The council wouldn't have found out about your abnormalities if you hadn't healed that necker in the cafe. Javier was using you from the beginning, but you helped him the with NWR issue. Everyone is always trying to use you, and for all your bluster about not letting anyone control you, you do let them."

"I help my friends. Only you could make that sound like a bad thing," I say, settling back into the seat and crossing my arms.

"I'm not trying to talk you out of it," Reilly says with a shrug. "It makes what I have to do so much easier."

I glare at him. The window is down, and his auburn hair is whipping around his face. He looks completely carefree, and I suppose he is. He's getting his way. I'm the one getting screwed.

"And what exactly is it that you want?" I ask. "If you just wanted to hunt down NWR members, there are easier ways. I'm not that much of an asset."

Reilly turns his head just enough to see my face. "I want to see what you can do."

"There are still easier ways," I mutter.

"This way is more efficient," he says, accelerating again. "Besides, you do best under pressure."

An uncomfortable silence falls. I have to be missing something. If he wants to see what I can do, then he has plans for me beyond this. Or even worse, perhaps his sire does.

"Have you attempted to Find Gerard or Maybelle yet?" Reilly asks.

The welts on my arm ache even thinking about it. "No."

"Why not?"

"There's no point. I don't want to know where they are. You'd just use them against me somehow."

Reilly grins. "I guess I can't argue with that."

"Are you going to try to find them somehow?"

"Not if you tell me what Maybelle told you about your birth."

I pinch the bridge of my nose between my thumb and forefinger and take a deep breath to keep from lashing out.

"If you know so much about me, you can just figure it out yourself."

"What about a trade again? Question for a question," Reilly retorts.

"And why should I believe you won't just lie to me?"

"You can tell now," he says, putting his hand on his chest. "I suspect you'll be able to hear it."

"That's bullshit, and you know it."

"Do you want to test it?"

13

I sigh in irritation but nod. Maybe if I prove him wrong, he'll shut up about it.

"Ask me a question. Something obvious so you can hear what it sounds like when I tell the truth. Just remember to listen very carefully to my heartbeat."

I tuck my hair behind my ears and cock my head to the side. I think my hearing must not be quite as good as his because I can barely hear it over the rumble of the engine and the tires flying over the road. It's there though, a faint and steady thump, *ba-thump, ba-thump.*

"Is the sky blue?"

"Yes," he says. His heartbeat stays the same.

"Is it currently nighttime?"

"Yes," he says. *Ba-thump. Ba-thump.*

"Are you a werewolf?"

He chuckles. "No."

"Are you an NWR member?"

"Yes," he says. His heartbeat thumps slightly faster and takes a moment to slow back down. There are no other signs he's telling anything but the truth. He isn't sweating or twitching. There's no reason for him to be nervous though.

"This is too easy. How do I know your heartbeat isn't speeding up because you're amused?"

"So you think I'm an NWR member now?" Reilly asks, grinning as his fangs descend.

"That's not what I mean, and you know it."

"Then you'll just have to trust me."

"Of course." I sigh deeply.

"How did your mother conceive you?"

"Magic," I say, waggling my fingers at him.

He sneers at me. "You're not funny."

"I'm hilarious. Did you already know about my parentage before you came to town?"

"No," he says. His heartbeat ticks faster, just

slightly, but enough to make my stomach twist. He was toying with me from the beginning and taunting me when he forced me to go to the coven.

"I thought you said you weren't going to lie?" I snap.

"I thought you said you didn't believe my heartbeat could give away a lie?"

I consider opening the car door and throwing myself into a ditch. Death isn't so bad. Probably.

"Why are we doing any of this?"

"My sire saw fit to assign me to get as close to shutting down the NWR as possible. The best way to do that is by using the resources already in place to hunt them down. JHAPI was more than happy to accept my help and yours."

"Do they know what I can do?"

"The team lead does. The others will find out. We don't have the luxury of keeping that a secret in the middle of a fight. I did tell you I needed to see what you can do."

"You don't think they're going to want to lock me up?"

"I wouldn't allow them to."

I scoff. "So you're above the law?"

"Absolutely," he agrees. "So keep that in mind if you decide you think they could help you escape our partnership."

The threat steals away the comfort I had slipped into despite the bickering. It's so easy to forget what Reilly is. He's charming and attractive, but he's not my friend or anything else. He's my jailer. His heartbeat is beating slightly faster, but so is mine. It's strange to be able to hear it. He looks calm, but the thump of his heart betrays his irritation.

I tap my hand impatiently against the counter as Reilly checks in. We'll be in an interior room, of course, since Reilly is a vampire.

Most newer hotels have two types of rooms. They'll have the usual rooms, ones with windows and direct outside access, but they'll also have interior rooms with no windows and doors that very carefully block out the light. Twenty-four-hour check-in is also absolutely necessary. They'll let anyone book the interior rooms, no questions asked, but everyone knows they're meant for the vampires.

Reilly hands over a credit card for the reservation.

"How many keys would you like?" the hotel clerk asks. She's smiling at him and blinking so much, she looks like she might be having a seizure.

"Two keys," he says with a flirtatious smile.

The girl glances at me and frowns. I don't think she had noticed I existed before just now.

"Sure thing," she says, her smile returning.

She activates both the cards and hands them to Reilly, who lifts his suitcase and heads toward the elevators. I trail behind him, annoyed that we have to share a room.

The elevator arrives immediately. There aren't many people up this time of the morning.

"You couldn't have gotten me my own room?" I ask as we step inside.

"It's much easier to keep an eye on you this way," Reilly says, unapologetic.

The elevator opens onto the sixth floor. The room is about halfway down the hall. Reilly slips his key card in and opens the door, waving me inside.

There are two beds at least. It's a nicer hotel than I've ever been in. The walls are painted a nice, neutral shade of gray instead of being plastered with dingy wallpaper. The carpet is plush and looks clean.

I toss my bag on the bed farthest from the door and sit on the end. The room smells like people and old socks. I guess no amount of cleaning can get the scent of the last hundred guests out.

I flop back onto the bed, but that only makes the odors waft up around me. I stand up and pull my shirt up over my nose so I can breathe better-smelling air for a moment.

Reilly raises an eyebrow at me. I cross my arms and glare at him.

"It stinks."

He sniffs the air. "It's usually much worse. You'll get used to it. Just ignore it until then."

I stalk toward the bathroom, muttering unkind things about vampires I hope he is listening to. It has a shower and a clawfoot bathtub I'll definitely be taking advantage of tonight.

I glance at my watch. It's only ten minutes until sunrise now. Reilly certainly cut our arrival close. He has proved he can be awake during the day, but I doubt he can stand direct sunlight without burning at least a little. I turn to walk back to my bed and realize he's stripping out of his clothes in the middle of the room without any warning whatsoever. He lays his suit jacket, then shirt on the bed neatly. The muscles in his back ripple as he moves. It's mesmerizing. The scars that crisscross his skin are more interesting though. He turns around slowly, but my eyes don't snap back up to his face until I realize he's unbuckling his belt.

"See something you like?" he asks, smirking.

"No," I say, rolling my eyes. My heart is beating fast enough that I can hear it faintly.

"Lie," Reilly whispers.

I walk quickly past him and grab my bag, then retreat into the bathroom. I hate vampires.

I turn the tap in the bathtub on. The water comes out hot, steam rising as it hits the cool tub. The running water drowns out the rustle of clothes and the quick beat of his heart. I might be attracted to Reilly, but I'm not stupid enough to let it go anywhere. I get suckered by shitty men often enough. I'm not going to start something with someone who is literally out to ruin my life.

I dump my clothes on the floor and climb into the hot water. It makes my feet sting, but I don't wait to adjust to the temperature; I just grit my teeth and sit down. After another few minutes, the bathtub is full and the hot water is slowly relaxing my sore muscles. I still have bruises from getting thrown down the hallway several times by the witches that attacked the clanhouse.

More salve would be great, but I don't have what I need to brew it anymore. I tap my fingers against the edge of the tub. Perhaps I can talk Reilly into acquiring it for me under the guise of seeing what I can do, or whatever it is he's after. It's probably not worth it though.

Lethargy steals over me, and my eyelids slip shut. I shake myself and scoot back up, but I want nothing more than to sleep. Dawn was hard for me yesterday as well. The first couple of hours after sunrise seem to be the worst. It probably doesn't help that I was up half the day and the entire night as well. I grab the soap and scrub my arms down first. As much as I don't want to sleep anywhere near Reilly, I can't afford to exhaust myself. When I get tired, I get stupid, and that's dangerous around him.

I finish bathing and slip down into the water until the only things still sticking out are my eyes and nose. I shut my eyes and listen to myself breathe for a few moments, then sit up, water dripping into my eyes from my hair. I wipe it away and climb out.

It's cold out of the water, so I dry off and redress quickly. I didn't pack any pajamas, so I'll have to sleep in my jeans. I'm not even going to consider the alternative.

I open the door as quietly as I can and peek out. Reilly is lying in bed, perfectly still. He doesn't look up or acknowledge me at all as I pad across the carpet to my bed. I slide between the covers, my legs still slightly damp. I put my back to the door and stare at him. He's facing me as well, his face slack and his breathing slow and even. I wonder, just for a moment, if I could kill him while he slept. His eyes pop open like he can read my mind. I grit my teeth and force myself to shut my own.

## 3

I slap my alarm off and curl into a sitting position, my elbows resting on my knees. The sun is still up, but it's going to set in about twenty minutes. I push the heels of my hands into my eyes, then push the covers back and crawl out of bed. I grab my duffel of clothes and head to the bathroom.

I change into my nicest pair of jeans and a flannel shirt. This is as fancy as I can manage for meeting the JHAPI agents today. I wasn't paying that much attention when I was packing. I yawn and rub my hands up and down my face again. I hate this lethargy. I wish I hadn't taken Javier's magic in moments like this, but I didn't really have a choice at the time. I had no idea how it was going to change me.

I dip my hands under the faucet and splash the ice-cold water on my face. It wakes me up a little more, but I won't feel completely myself until the sun sets. I look up into the mirror and freeze, my heart clenching in my chest.

There's someone standing behind me. I stare at her reflection, afraid to move. My mother is dead. I know that. She can't be here. But she is standing right behind me, staring at me with her finger pressed to her lips like she's quieting me.

The door flies open, the lock splintering. Reilly fills the doorway with his fangs bared and his hands curled into fists. I stumble back, my hands just barely coming up in time to prevent the splintered wood from hitting me in the face.

"What happened?" Reilly demands.

The bathroom is empty other than me. I whirl around and look into the mirror again, but all I see is my own reflection.

"Olivia," Reilly says, his fingers wrapping around my arm. His fangs are still extended, and his grip is too tight. "What is wrong with you?"

I lower my eyes and swallow thickly. "Nothing. I'm fine."

"Liar," he says, his eyes searching for an injury. "Is it the welts hurting again?"

"Just a bad dream, all right?" I say, hurrying past him toward the bathroom. "I'm fine."

"If it was a bad dream, your heart would have been racing when you woke up, not five minutes later," he retorts, following me out of the bathroom.

"Just let it go," I snap as I toss my bag back on the bed.

Reilly rolls his eyes. "You reacted like you were in danger. Something isn't right. You aren't leaving here until you explain what's going on."

"Why do you care?" I ask, hands clenched into fists at my side. "I haven't tried to run away. I'm cooperating. You don't need to know every thought that passes through my head."

"I need to know if you're about to do something stupid so I can talk some sense into you."

I cross my arms, wincing at the sting. "Well, I wasn't about to do anything. So don't worry about it."

Reilly's lip curls up in anger, and he opens his mouth to say something else, but a knock at the door interrupts.

"It's Agent Hawking," Reilly says instead.

I wrench open the door and plaster on a smile. Her suit is slightly rumpled, and her bright blue eyes have bags under them. Her belt buckle is a native Saguaro cactus today.

"Good morning, Hawking," I say with false cheer.

She raises a brow at me. "If you're going to be that perky, I'm going to need coffee immediately."

"Coffee sounds great," I say in a much calmer tone.

"Also, call me Elise," she says. "The whole last name thing annoys me, and we're going to be working together closely."

"Noted," I say.

"You both ready?" Hawking asks, looking at us.

"I have to run an errand before the meeting. I'll see you there," Reilly says dismissively.

I glance back, suspicious. I notice a piece of the door is visible from where we are standing and edge a little to the left to block her view of it. Elise doesn't seem to have noticed though.

Elise nods once, her long hair swinging around her face. "You have the address?"

"Yes," Reilly says.

"All right, let's go get coffee for everyone," Hawking says, patting me on the shoulder.

I follow her out of the room. We walk to the elevators silently, then pause in uncomfortable silence in front of the closed doors. She taps the button and glances at me.

"So, is that a thing?" she asks, twirling her finger between me and the room.

"No," I say sharply before clearing my throat. "Never has been, never will be."

"Is the council just trying to save money on hotel rooms or something?" Hawking asks with a raised brow.

"Something like that," I say as I shove my hands in my pockets.

The skeptical expression stays on her face. I guess she wouldn't make it very far as a JHAPI agent if she couldn't tell those were bullshit answers.

"That's why I'm always stuck in a room with Zachary," she says with a shrug. "He snores so much. I've thought about putting in a request for a new partner just to escape that."

I laugh. "He does snore, and he doesn't think he does, so he won't try to fix it."

The elevator dings, and she steps inside with a groan. "I might smother him one day."

"I'm sure the jury will acquit you," I say solemnly.

The elevator carries us down to the parking garage in the basement, another thing most hotels offer for the vampires. If it can't be in the basement, they always have some kind of completely enclosed parking area.

Elise drives a standard black sedan. I open the door and go to sit down, but there is a pile of paper and old ketchup packets in the passenger seat.

"Oh, just toss all that in the back seat," she says, grabbing a couple of handfuls and throwing them behind her. I scoop up all the rest and move it to the back of the car, which is also a huge mess, before sliding into my seat.

"Have you ever been to Phoenix before?" she asks.

"No, I hadn't ever left Texas before this." I shrug.

"It's too bad we don't have time for sightseeing."

She punches an address into the GPS in the car,

then backs out of the spot. It's a weekday, and the traffic is atrocious. Of course, we're trying to get to a meeting at the same time the rest of the city is trying to get home from work.

"Oh, there's a phone for you in the glovebox," Elise says, pointing at it. "It's nothing fancy, but it has the team's numbers already programmed in, and it's what you should use to communicate with us. No texting any friends about our cases from your personal phone, all right?"

"Don't worry, I don't have any friends," I say as I open the glovebox and fish out the phone. It's not a smartphone; just an old-fashioned flip phone. "Wow, I didn't think they even made these anymore. JHAPI makes you share hotel rooms and use antiques?"

Elise snorts and pulls her phone out of her pocket. It's the same as mine. "They're cheap as hell."

"We're paying for the coffee ourselves, aren't we?" I ask.

"You're a fast learner," Elise says with a toothy grin. "I tried to expense it my first week here, and the damn accounting department went on about how coffee is a privilege, not a necessity."

She rolls her eyes dramatically, then punches on the accelerator to make it through a yellow light.

"Coffee is absolutely a necessity, especially when you keep the random hours we do," she says with a sharp nod of her head.

My stomach growls. "Breakfast is also going to be a necessity."

"Oh, don't worry, I never forget breakfast either," she says with a smile.

She turns into a packed parking lot. We have to wait for a car that is backing out, but it snags us a spot right in front of the door to the coffee shop. The amazing scent of sausage and peppers wafts through the air as soon as I open the car door. Right next door to the coffee shop is a Mexican restaurant selling breakfast tacos.

"This place is great, and the tacos are only a dollar, as tacos should be," Elise says as we climb out. "Let's get the food first so we have something to eat while we wait for them to make this huge list of coffee."

"Sounds good to me," I say as I follow her inside.

Elise orders four tacos just for herself. I order two, my mouth already watering. I'm glad they're cheap because I realize I have no idea how much money I have. It's been a while since I checked my bank account, and I don't exactly have a job anymore. I swipe my card with a little sigh. So much for my savings goals.

We don't have to wait long for our orders to be ready. Elise grabs two little white bags from the counter and hands me the smaller one.

It's a brief but chilly walk next door to the coffee shop. I snag us a table while Elise goes to submit our coffee order.

I get out my chorizo and egg taco first and lay out a couple of napkins. The first bite is heaven. It's barely on the right side of greasy, as chorizo tends to be.

Elise plops down in the chair across from me and devours her first taco in three bites. I swallow my second bite and raise a brow at her.

"What? I'm hungry," she says around another mouthful.

I chuckle and shove the last of my taco into my mouth. It takes two napkins to mop up the grease from my knuckles. I'm glad the other taco I got is just potato and egg.

We chew in silence for a bit, but I can see her

looking at me, working up to some kind of question. I avoid her gaze as best I can, focusing on my food instead, which I finish far too quickly.

"So, you're working with the vampires," Elise says before taking a big bite of her last taco. She chews slowly, watching my face the whole time. "I was surprised. You and Reilly didn't seem to get along that well."

I shrug, but I wish I could get her to drop this line of questioning.

"Nobody really gets along with their boss. It's no big deal as long as they keep paying me," I lie. If only I was getting paid for this.

The barista calls our name. I drop my crumpled, greasy napkin on the table and hurry over to the counter. Nine cups of coffee in two trays looks right. One of them is just wedged in the center of a tray between the other cups.

Elise wolfs down the rest of her taco, then gathers our trash off the table. We meet at the door, and she leads me back to the car.

Nerves are churning in my stomach. Or perhaps it's just the grease. Either way, I'm not looking forward to sitting at a table of JHAPI agents. The fact that they'll be finding out what I can do, if not what I am, makes it that much worse. I hate being exposed like this. It's been a secret for so long, and I've never considered what it would be like to tell people the truth.

I tap my foot against the floorboard the entire drive to the local headquarters. The building isn't much to look at. It's not even the tallest building on the block. It is square and beige, with JHAPI in big black letters over the main entrance. Hawking drives past that and around to the back and parks in the employee parking area.

I hand her one of the coffee carriers, and we head inside. The inside is just as dingy as the outside. Beige linoleum and plain white walls. The ceilings are dotted with fluorescent lights that throw a harsh glow over everything.

A few people nod as we walk down the hall, apparently recognizing Elise. She leads me to the desk near the front entrance.

"Sorry, I forgot you need an ID card," Elise says before turning to the young man peering at us from the desk in a crisp blue uniform. "I need a visitor pass for Olivia Carter. She should be on Agent Stocke's list."

"Yes, ma'am," the man says, his fingers flying over the keyboard. He scans his screen for a moment before nodding. "I'll get that printed immediately."

He taps a few more keys and slips a blank card into a little machine on his left.

"Please stand on that X for your picture," he says, pointing at a black X on the floor to my right.

I grimace but step on it and face him. He doesn't wait for me to be ready or give me a countdown; he just snaps the picture.

"All right, that will work," he says, clicking on his computer screen again. The printer whirs, then he pulls the card out and slips it onto a lanyard.

"Please wear this at all times while you're in the building. And try to keep the picture facing out," he says, handing it to me with a smile.

"Sure thing," I say, looking at the ID. The picture is awful. I'm squinting, and I have bags under my eyes.

Elise leans over to look at it and laughs.

"Oh, that is perfect," she says, clapping a hand on my shoulder and pushing me in the direction we need to go.

## 4

The meeting room is on the top floor. The far wall is taken up by a large window that overlooks a decent portion of the city. Of course, there's not much to see right now since it's now completely dark outside. The lights of the city aren't as bright as the one I grew up in, but overall I think I like this place. It's not so different.

Elise takes a seat on the side of the table that faces the door. I turn away from the window reluctantly and sit down on her right side.

"I'm surprised we're the first ones here," I comment.

Elise shrugs. "I thought it'd be better to do it this way. Didn't want you to have to walk into a room full of agents."

"That would have been a little intimidating I guess," I say, pulling the stopper out of my coffee and taking a sip. I grimace and suck at my lip; it's still too hot. "Where's Brunson?"

"Doing something for Stocke. He'll be here in a bit." Elise takes a long drink of coffee, then turns to face me. "By the way, I don't think he hates you anymore."

"That's, uh, nice, I guess?" I say hesitantly.

The door swings open without a knock, and a woman with dark skin and a short tapered haircut walks in. She's wearing a crisp black suit that looks both trendy and professional. The suit and white shirt underneath are completely free of wrinkles and fit perfectly.

Walking close behind her is a woman with wavy, reddish-brown hair that drapes over her shoulders. She's wearing a suit as well, but the jacket is unbuttoned and the shirt underneath is silk. She has a long necklace with an amber stone around her neck. She smells like magic.

Something hungry shifts inside of me. I bite down on the inside of my cheek to distract myself. The craving startles me. I've always wanted other people's magic, but never like this. Damn vampire magic is making everything more intense.

"Agent Ivy Andreas," the first woman says, stepping forward with her hand outstretched. I stand and shake it.

"Olivia Carter." Her grip is firm but not overbearing.

"Corinne Davidson," her partner says with a gentle smile. She takes my hand gently and covers it with her other as we shake.

Elise pushes a pair of coffees across the table toward them, which they take gratefully. The two women take the seats across from me and Elise.

Corinne leans back in her chair, a pleasant smile on her face, while Ivy sits with perfect posture. She seems to be the one who takes the lead in their partnership even though she is the human.

"You're the witch the vampire council has brought in, correct?" Ivy asks.

"Yep," I say before taking a long drink of coffee. I

didn't sleep well with Reilly so close to me. Elise seems to be in the same boat I'm in, judging by the way she's also sucking down her coffee. Adjusting to a night schedule isn't easy for anyone. I'm surprised the team was willing to do it just to work with the vampires.

"I've never heard of a witch working with the vampire council before," Ivy comments. Her dark brown eyes scan my face for answers.

I shrug. "First time for everything, I guess."

The door opens again, and a tall man with light brown hair walks in. He looks like a clean cut, all-American jock. Skin tanned from spending all his free time outdoors, muscles, and a sharp jawline. I groan internally; guys like this always seem to have a mean streak.

"Dude, I'm serious, football is really nuanced once you start paying attention," the jock says, looking back over his shoulder.

I wonder if he realizes how much of a stereotype he is.

The man behind him chuckles. "I'm still not watching it."

"Andreas, Davidson," the jock says with a big grin. "I had no idea you two were in on this."

An Asian man with a stocky build walks up beside him. His black hair is short on the sides and slightly longer on the top. It's styled neatly, nothing flashy, but the red and orange flash of tattoos that peek out of his collar make it look like fire is crawling up his neck.

"You know I'd never pass up an assignment like this, Cook. Who'd you have to bribe to get something this good?" Ivy asks, leaning back in her chair as she turns toward the two men.

"Bribe? You wound me," Cook says, playfully

clutching at his chest. "Brunson requested me and Hu personally."

Ivy snorts. "Of course he did. Good ol' boys club hard at work."

"We're not all that bad to work with," the Asian man objects.

"You're great, Peter," Ivy says with a snort. "This idiot is going to drive me insane before we're done though."

Cook just grins at her insult, unaffected. The two men seem to finally notice me.

"Who do we have here?" Cook asks, sauntering toward the table.

"Olivia Carter," I say without getting up.

The smile falls off his face, and he looks me up and down, appearing unimpressed.

"The one and only Olivia," he says with a sneer. "Brunson didn't mention that you were going to be on the team."

I raise a brow at him but don't ask. It sounds like he knows Brunson well. I have no interest in knowing what Zachary might have told him about me, or why he didn't tell him I was going to be here.

"Peter Hu," his partner says, leaning across the table to shake my hand.

"Nice to meet you, Peter," I say as I stand and shake his hand.

Cook crosses his arms and continues glaring at me until Ivy kicks a chair into his leg.

"Sit down and stop making us look bad," she says sternly.

Cook and Peter sit down next to each other. Peter seems perfectly at ease, obviously not affected by his partner's dislike of me.

"Where is Brunson?" Peter asks Elise.

"He's with Stocke. They should be here soon," she says with a yawn.

The door opens again, and a woman walks in. She has mousy brown hair pulled back into a bun and thick-framed black glasses that are too big for her face. She's wearing a black skirt and a blazer over a white blouse. Her thick heels clunk against the floor as she walks to the head of the table and sets down the stack of files she is carrying.

"Good evening, everyone," she says with a stiff smile. A chorus of responses goes around the table, but no one seems overjoyed to see her.

She walks toward me and stretches out her hand.

"Olivia Carter, I am Agent Staci Young. I'm Agent Stocke's partner."

I stand and shake her hand, already tired of the up and down.

"Nice to meet you," I say with a nod before plopping back down in my chair. She straightens her jacket with a sharp tug on the hem and walks back to the seat next to the head of the table. She sits down and folds her hands in front of her.

"Agent Stocke will be here in a few minutes," she says quietly.

"Thank you, Staci," Corinne says with a warm smile. Staci straightens a little, seeming pleased that someone actually responded.

Cook turns back to Ivy, and everyone chats about unimportant things as we wait. I tilt my head back and stare at the ceiling. I feel out of place here. I've never been on this side of the law before. The thought makes me smile. If only Detective Brunson could see me now. He would have wanted me to join something like this. He loved the idea of humans and paranormals working together to protect both sides.

He always said that ignorance breeds fear, and cooperation kills ignorance.

The door opens again, and I hear a familiar voice; Zachary has arrived. The person who walks in first though is a slender woman in her forties with curly blonde hair that is pulled back into a barely contained ponytail. She has a no-nonsense air about her. She walks to the head of the table while Zachary heads to his seat on the other side of Elise with a brief nod in my direction.

"Where is Mr. Walsh?" the woman asks me.

I glance at the empty chair to my right and shrug. "I have no idea. He asked Elise to bring me here and said he would join us later."

She sighs and checks her watch.

"I'm not waiting for him," she decides. She grabs the top file from the stack and flips it open.

"Earlier this month, there was an attack in a small town in Texas where the NWR attempted to frame the local vampire clan for the murders of several humans. The clan and a pack in the area cooperated to take out this cell since the local police department refused to offer support. It was later discovered this was because the department had been infiltrated by the NWR."

She taps a button on the table I hadn't noticed before, and a screen lowers from the ceiling. A face appears on it, one I despise. His smug, handsome features bring back the memory of sitting across from him at the diner. The flirting makes me sick to think about now. He's not so handsome anymore though. There's no way to heal the kind of burns I left him with without magic, which he'd never resort to using.

"Jason Martinez has used a number of aliases over the years, which are listed in his file. He is most likely using another identity at this point, but we are looking for him under all of these names."

Stocke grabs a small black remote control and clicks to the next picture. A map with several red points dotted across the country is displayed.

"This map shows all NWR attacks carried out in the last year."

She clicks the remote again, and the map changes. A large number of the red points turn blue.

"The points marked in blue are all the attacks that Martinez is believed to have been involved with on some level. He appears to be an idea man," Stocke says, spreading her hands. "He has been personally involved with only a quarter of these attacks due to his limited ability to travel previously. Now that he is no longer tied to one location, it is likely that he will become more aggressive with his attacks, and also risk himself in more situations."

She turns back to face her team and crosses her arms, tapping the remote against her bicep.

"We believe the attack in Texas was a test run. They wanted to see if they could manipulate law enforcement and local opinion against the vampire clan. They were mostly successful. The local coven believed the vampires were involved and attempted to help speed along the investigation through unethical and illegal means. If Ms. Carter had not discovered the plot and persuaded the clan to act, it would have succeeded. It was just bad luck for the NWR, and good luck for us, that it turned out how it did."

Agent Stocke nods at the Staci, who stands and passes around the remaining files. One is handed to me as well. I tug the thick file a little closer. The folder is dark brown, and JHAPI's seal is stamped on the front, along with CONFIDENTIAL in bold, red letters.

"Ms. Carter wounded Martinez's pride when she undid his plot. More importantly, however, she took away one of his tools. His face."

Stocke clicks the remote again, and his face appears on the screen again. This picture is blurry, and he appears to be from a security camera in some kind of veterinary office. The left side of his face is blistered and red from the burns I inflicted on him. I can't help the smirk that curls on my lips. I'm glad I left my mark even if I would prefer him dead.

"Martinez had been charming his way around the country. He's going to stand out now. We are working with local police departments and the media to distribute this picture, as well as others. We're going to make him America's most wanted criminal."

Stocke uncrosses her arms and turns the screen off, then sits down. She steeples her fingers and looks around the table. The door opens just as she moves to speak again, and Reilly strolls in.

He is wearing his usual suit. He looks like any other JHAPI agent except for the predatory glint in his eyes and the unnatural grace of his steps. He walks without hurry to the seat next to me.

Cook watches him with narrowed eyes. Even Ivy looks uncomfortable at his entrance. Her shoulders are tense, and she keeps her eyes glued to him.

"Meredith," he says, inclining his head in Agent Stocke's direction.

"Mr. Walsh," Stocke says drily. She turns back to the group, ignoring the interruption. "Martinez is an important target. However, he is not our only target. JHAPI, with the support of the vampire council, intends on taking down NWR once and for all. Whatever resources we need will be provided to us."

Staci sits up and leans forward, an eager look in her eyes.

"Yes, Agent Young, that does mean you can have that cauldron you've been asking for," Stocke says.

I knit my brows together and reassess her. I hadn't even considered that she might be a witch, much less a hedgewitch. I had assumed Agent Stocke was the paranormal in that partnership.

"Taking down the NWR is more than just a difficult task," Ivy says, her posture relaxed once again but her tone slightly disbelieving. "Don't get me wrong, I'm happy to do it, but they've been around longer than this country has in some form or another. We can't stamp out hatred."

"They've never faced opposition like this before. In the past, we have only reacted to their attacks." Stocke taps her finger against the smooth table. "We are going to strike first. We are going to make them fear us."

Cook barks out a laugh. "I like the sound of that."

"So where do we start?" Ivy asks.

"We're going to start here in Phoenix. The files in front of each of you are different cases connected to a local cell, as well as the information we have on their possible location. Agent Davidson, we'll need to start with you. Can you find them?"

Corinne nods, flipping through the file. "I should be able to find one or two."

"Ms. Carter, can you assist her?" Stocke asks, looking at me.

I freeze, my heart racing at her casual question. Everyone turns and looks at me. Zachary pinches his brows together, confused. I don't know what she has told the team, and my instincts can't relax.

I clear my throat and try to ignore the stares of the team.

"I—uh, cannot," I say haltingly.

"She's a hedgewitch, not a Finder," Zachary inter-

STEPHANIE FOXE

jects, looking between us like there must be some confusion.

Stocke smirks and folds her hands in front of her.

"According to Mr. Walsh, that is not actually the case. He informed me that she was a Finder, a hedge-witch, an electric witch, and a healer." She pauses and looks at each agent in turn. "This is obviously unusual, to say the least. As agents, you are all used to dealing with confidential information. This will be no different. The vampire council is lending us their help, and in return we will not betray on their trust, or Olivia's."

Staci frowns in my direction, adjusting her glasses with a nudge from her finger. She looks disapproving.

Cook scoffs. "A witch that can use more than one time of magic? That's ridiculous. I don't buy it."

"Why is it that you cannot help Agent Davidson if you are a Finder?" Stocke asks, ignoring Cook's comment.

I glance back at Reilly, but he just raises a brow at me. I sigh and pull my sleeve up to reveal the welts that have been getting steadily worse. Corinne gasps, her hand flying to her mouth. Stocke simply looks at the red stripes curiously, her head tilting to the side.

"Damn, did you lose a fight with your curling iron or something?" Cook asks.

"I had a little incident," I say as I shove the sleeve back down. "If I use the Finding magic, it knocks me out for several hours."

"Well, we need to get that fixed. What do you need? Salves?"

"No," Corinne interrupts. "None of that would fix it."

"She's right. I've tried all that," I agree with a shrug.

"I can help her with it, but it will take time," Corinne says, directing her response to Agent Stocke rather than me.

"All right, get it handled and keep me updated. I need to know if someone isn't at a hundred percent. Will it affect your performance in any area other than Finding magic?" Stocke asks me.

"No, I can deal with it like I have been," I say, crossing my arms.

"I still don't buy this," Cook interjects again. "No one has ever heard of a witch that can use more than one branch of magic."

"Until now," Reilly says, speaking for the first time since his greeting to Stocke.

"Why should we believe you?" Cook asks, spreading his hands out and raising a brow at Reilly. "She just said she can't use Finding magic, and she obviously can't heal herself."

"Want me to electrocute you?" I snap at Cook, tired of his attitude. Bright electric magic rushes to my fingertips and singes the table where my hands are pressed, white-knuckled, into it. I don't like being called a liar.

Cook leans back in his seat, pretending he's unconcerned. I know he isn't because I can hear his heart beating angrily from here. His fingers twitch like he wants to go for his gun.

"That won't be necessary," Stocke interrupts. "Please keep your magic under control, Olivia. I was assured you wouldn't put this team at risk."

Cook holds my gaze, his jaw clenched in anger. He hates me, though I have no idea why. He could have at least waited for me to give him a good reason.

"I won't put anyone at risk." I push back into my seat and cross my arms.

Stocke pinches the bridge of her nose, then continues with her explanation.

"The vampire council has been instrumental in making this possible. We will extend the same trust and respect to the consultants they have provided us with, that I expect to receive from them."

Her tone is sharp, chastising both me and Cook. I bite down on the impulse to say 'he started it'. She seems like the type of woman who doesn't care.

"Does anyone have any other questions or concerns?" She scans the room, but no one moves.

"All right, everyone get caught up on the case files you have been provided with. Pass them around, make sure everyone gets a chance to read through each file. Agent Davidson, please try to Find at least one of our targets. Everyone needs to have their go bags ready. We will leave as soon as Davidson gives the word."

"Agent Young, we'll need a full range of the usual brews, and you have my permission to brew anything else you think might be useful while we travel."

"All the standard brews are already prepared," Staci says. "I'll start making a list of other brews that will be useful."

"Excellent," Stocke says, nodding toward Staci. "Agent Andreas, please visit the armory and make sure everyone is appropriately armed. Make sure you include protective body gear and gas masks. I foresee us needing both."

"Does everyone include our consultants?" Ivy asks, nodding her head toward Reilly and me.

"Yes," Stocke says with a nod. "Treat them like full members of the team."

"Noted," Ivy says as she pulls out a notepad and scribbles a few things down.

Everyone scatters, and I open the file that was set

in front of me. Martinez's face looks up at me. It's an old picture, he looks young and happy. I have to clench my hand into a fist to keep from scorching the file with the sudden surge of magic that rushes behind my anger.

## 5

I'm reading through a third file when Ivy appears at my elbow.

"What's up?" I ask, turning the chair to face her.

"JHAPI agents are trained on a variety of firearms, but I don't know what kind of experience you have. What can you shoot with accuracy?" she asks, her pen poised over her notepad.

"I can use a pistol, and I'm all right with a rifle, but I've shot those less."

"Have you ever shot an AR-15 before?"

"No, just a basic hunting rifle."

"All right, I'll get you a pistol."

"Sounds good to me," I say with a nod.

Reilly walks up behind me. I stand up and move out from between them. I hate it when he stands behind me like that; it feels predatory.

"Would you like a gun or any other weapon?" Ivy directs to Reilly.

"No, that won't be necessary."

"All right, I'll make sure you have what you need, Olivia." She turns and strides from the room, intent on completing the assignment given to her by Stocke.

Corinne is off by herself, unfolding a series of maps on the table we were just gathered around.

"Did your introduction go well?" Reilly asks quietly, having moved closer to me when I wasn't paying attention.

I snort, my eyes straying toward the scorch marks on the table.

"It went fine."

Reilly looks at the marks as well and raises his brow.

"You have a strange definition of fine."

"No one died," I mutter.

"Not yet at least," he says, clapping his hand on my shoulder before striding toward Zachary and Cook.

I walk over to Corinne and stand a few feet away from her next to the table. Hopefully, I can learn something. I've never actually seen a witch Find someone in person. I'm curious how incorrectly I've been using the magic.

She glances at me but doesn't speak as she finishes arranging her maps. Once they are all where she wants them, she takes a step back and looks them over. The maps cover not only the county we are in, but every surrounding county. Each one has smaller maps showing the main roads in the major cities in that county.

"You tried to Find someone who is dead, didn't you?" Corinne asks without looking at me. She speaks softly enough that the others wouldn't be able to hear her.

I tense and bite the inside of my cheek.

"I wasn't sure," I say quietly, glancing at Reilly. "I thought my mother was dead, but then I had reason to believe she wasn't and—well, it doesn't matter."

Corinne smiles gently, her brown eyes soft as they scan my face. "We all do it eventually. The lucky ones have someone with them to help and protect them. You weren't trained, were you?"

I shake my head. She doesn't know the whole story, of course. It's hard to get training when you've stolen someone's magic.

"Not surprising if you've had to hide your abilities. We'll fix that though. Can't have someone on the team with untapped potential."

"I would appreciate it. Do you mind if I watch?" I ask, suddenly unsure if I'm intruding.

"Not at all," Corinne says, sweeping the soft waves hanging around her face up into a ponytail. "I have to search for them one at a time. I'll be looking for this guy first. He was spotted in town a week ago."

She taps her finger against one of the open files. It's a younger guy. It's one of the files I read. He was a chemical engineering student, but his girlfriend dumped him for a witch. He flunked out and fell into a downward spiral that included drug charges and assault. The NWR recruited him while he was in jail.

She cracks her knuckles and extends her hands over the maps. Her shoulders drop as she relaxes all the muscles in her body one by one. Magic hums in the air. For the first time, I can smell it as well as taste it. Her magic is different from anything I've felt before. It's warm, which I expected, but not nearly as hot as my own.

Red lines of magic unfurl from her fingers and twist through the air until they stretch over the entire table. A hush falls over the room, and the group stops talking, all turning to watch her work.

Every welt covering my body responds to the magic. I take a step back, but it doesn't help the dull ache, so I grit my teeth and try to ignore it and the hunger that is growing inside of me with every moment. I don't want to miss any of this.

The magic hovers above the table, each line writhing with eagerness. She extends them down onto the maps in a wave from left to right. The magic grows warmer and brighter as each line digs into the map, searching. A line on the left disappears with a pop that makes me jump. Another follows, then another and another moving in the same direction she lowered them.

Only one tenuous line remains when the pops of magic finally cease. It extends from her left pointer finger to a spot in the city. Corinne walks toward the map, lowering her hand toward the point. The magic grows narrower, but brighter, as though she's focusing in on the person's exact spot.

She pauses and stares off into the distance with unfocused eyes. She exhales slowly and presses her finger to the map. A wave of magic rushes out from her. I shiver in pain and hunger as it brushes past me. Everyone else in the room takes an involuntary step back.

"I Found him," Corinne says, still staring at something no one else can see.

"Can you pinpoint his location?" Stocke asks, flipping through the file.

"I need a more detailed map, but I'll be able to tell you what block they're on. I won't be able to say what building until I get closer," Corinne replies after a moment of consideration.

"All right," Stocke says, scanning the information in the file. "Brunson, get a better map for Corinne and set up surveillance so we can figure out where exactly these people are hiding out. I want everyone ready to go tomorrow evening. We'll go in just after the sun sets if we can."

Everyone scatters, grabbing their things from the table, but Corinne taps my elbow.

"We need to try to fix these as soon as possible. I know they make it impossible for you to use your Finding magic, and I'm not sure what else they might affect as they get worse."

I nod, pressing my hand against my forearm. They still ache just from being around her magic.

"Yeah, fixing this would be great. As soon as we have time."

"Be careful, try to avoid using magic tomorrow if you can, all right?" I nod, and she walks over to see Ivy.

Zachary slips up beside me, startling me slightly.

"So, you can use multiple types of magic?" he asks, his brows furrowed.

Cook is frowning at us from the corner of the room, his arms crossed in front of him. I turn more toward Zachary so I don't have to see him.

"Yes," I say with a tense smile. "But you've known that. The healing magic and the brewing."

"If you had been able to use Finding magic back then, you wouldn't have had such a hard time finding your mom," he says hesitantly.

I grit my teeth and stare at my shoes. I'm not going to offer up information. He needs to either ask his question or leave me alone.

"So, you're just going to stand there? You aren't going explain anything?" he asks, irritation slipping into his voice.

"I'm not sure what you want me to say." I cross my arms and look up at him.

"You got this magic somehow, and recently," Zachary says, mirroring my posture.

"All right," I say with a shrug. "And?"

Zachary looks at me like I've lost my mind and throws his hands in the air. "And? Seriously? That should be impossible. How are you doing it?"

"None of your business," I say. I turn to walk away, but he grabs my arm. I glare at his hand, then at him, and jerk my arm out of his grip. "If you think you *need* more information, go ask Stocke. I don't want to talk about it."

"If you are putting anyone in danger by keeping this secret—"

"Zachary, stop it," I snap, trying to keep my voice quiet, but not doing a great job of it. "I'm not putting anyone in danger, and it's insulting that you think I would. The how and why of what I can do isn't important, and it isn't anyone's business but mine. Stocke wouldn't have allowed me to work with any of you if I was a danger. Use your head."

He takes a step back, his jaw clenched tight. Half the room is watching us, the other half is studiously pretending it's not obvious we're arguing.

"Gerard and Maybelle disappeared. Are you going to try to Find them? To run again?"

I chuckle humorlessly. "No, I'm not."

"That'd be a first," Zachary says, his voice low enough to be a whisper.

Magic sparks at my fingertips again. "I guess Elise was wrong."

"About what?"

"She said you didn't hate me anymore."

I turn on my heel and walk toward Reilly, who is waiting for me by the door. The level of anger that's coursing through me is an overreaction. I know it is. Yet, I still want to rip Zachary apart. My skin is crawling with rage and barely controlled electric magic.

---

I splash cold water on my face and stare into the sink.

I don't want to look in the mirror again, in case she's there. Watching me.

I'm also hungry. The anger and the sparks of magic and being surrounded by so many paranormals today is harder than I expected. I can feel Reilly's presence in the room next door, taunting me. I dig my fingers into the cold porcelain, but my hands won't stop shaking.

"Olivia," Reilly says quietly from behind me. "What the hell is wrong with you?"

A low growl bubbles out of my throat, and my fangs press against my bottom lip as my mouth curls into a snarl.

"Nothing," I rasp.

Reilly moves fast. I shouldn't be able to track it, but the vampire magic is coursing through me like a cold wind. I can't dodge him though, and his hand wraps around my throat as he shoves me against the wall next to the sink.

"Another lie," he snaps in my face.

His eyes are dark and dangerous, and his body is hot against mine. That's not what I want though, even if it is tempting. I want the magic and the blood inside of him.

"You're hungry, aren't you?" he asks, his hand relaxing, but not moving from my throat.

I don't respond. I don't want to admit it. I hate it.

His thumb strokes my pulse point, up, down, up, down, in time with my heartbeat. It's soothing, in an odd way. My breathing slows, and some of the anger fades, curling into a different kind of heat. His thigh is pushed between my legs, and his arm is pressed against my chest. Every point of contact is electric.

"You are going to have to feed, or you are going to lose control," he whispers, his breath skating across my cheek.

"It's not just blood I need," I say, my voice hoarse. "It's magic. I can't get that from some necker."

"How much?" he asks.

"I don't know. Not much, I think. It's never been like this before. It wasn't like this until Javier."

"You're going to feed from me—"

I start to object, but Reilly presses down on my throat and shushes me.

"You will take the absolute minimum you need to maintain control," he says, his face serious, not a dimple in sight.

"Why?" I ask quietly.

"Because I have invested time and money in you, and I need you to keep it together. After tonight, I will find another way. But you are too close to being out of control, and you have to be ready to go tomorrow."

I clench my teeth tightly together but nod. As much as I hate it, he's not wrong.

Reilly lifts his hand from my neck and offers me his wrist. I open my mouth, my gums aching in anticipation of the bite.

I close my teeth and lips around the edge of his wrist. My tongue flicks out, sampling his skin, and I almost moan at the taste. My teeth sink into his flesh like a knife through butter, and hot, sweet blood spills over my tongue. Not just blood though. His magic seeps into me from every point of contact, and the rush from that is almost overwhelming. I want to take it all.

I shove him away as hard as I can, and he stumbles backward, slamming into the bathroom wall. He leans against the wall, breathing just as hard as I am, watching me with a heated gaze.

"Fuck," I say, running my hands through my hair.

"If you want," he says, his cheeks dimpling.

"That line is getting old," I say, rolling my eyes.

"One day, you'll take me up on it." He straightens and adjusts his jacket. "Take a shower and order some room service. I imagine you need human food as well."

"Yeah, I do," I say, pressing a hand to my stomach. It's been quite a while since I had the tacos.

"Don't let it get this bad again," he says, his tone hard.

I look at the floor and bite the inside of my cheek. I can still taste his blood in my mouth.

"I don't intend to."

"I have another errand to run. Don't do anything stupid while I'm gone."

He strides from the room, and I slide down the wall, my legs suddenly weak. I press my hand to my mouth and stare straight ahead, not really seeing anything at all.

## 6

"What do we know?" Stocke asks, leaning back in her chair.

Brunson has the remote this time, and he clicks it, pulling up a map on the projector.

"Agent Davidson was able to narrow down the suspect's location to this city block," Zachary says, pointing at the street highlighted in red. "Surveillance was able to confirm that the suspect is there and was seen entering this building."

The slide changes, showing a plain building set back from the street. It looks a little run down and definitely abandoned. A lone figure is walking across the parking lot toward a side entrance.

"There have been four other people observed entering and exiting the building, but we have not been able to identify them," Zachary says.

Commander Benjamin Driver leans forward and clasps his hands. He's an unassuming man with white hair and a soft, round face. He looks like the sort of man who enjoys mowing his lawn and putting up Christmas lights.

"They've all kept their faces hidden," he says, tapping his thumbs together. "They don't park anywhere near the building, except for one van which drove into the parking lot around seven am this morning."

"So we have no way of knowing how many people might be in that building?" Stocke asks.

"We can estimate five to ten suspects," Driver says, spreading his hands. "But ultimately, that's just a guess."

"Since this is the NWR, we have to assume there will be booby traps and that the suspects will be heavily armed. Commander Driver confirmed for me yesterday that we will have SWAT backup, but that will not make this easy," Stocke says as she looks around the table. "All of you have been on raids before, and you understand the risk we're taking."

I guess you can call the fight that went down at Chevy's bar a raid, but I'm hoping whatever we do tonight will be better organized. And have fewer casualties.

"Now, our goal is to arrest the NWR members, not assassinate them. However, you do what you have to in order to make sure that you, and your team members, come back alive," Stocke says, her tone allowing for no argument. "Brunson, please walk us through the tactical plan."

Zachary stands up and walks to the front of the room. The slide changes to an overhead view of the building. Several points are highlighted, including the street across from the front of the building, and three entrances on the building itself.

"Officers with the City of Phoenix's Homeland Defense Bureau will secure a perimeter around the building. The streets will be blocked here," he points to the main street leading past the building, "and here," he points at the side street east of the building.

He clicks the remote, and the slide changes, zooming in on the building itself.

"We do not have any information on the internal layout of the building; however, we have identified three entrance points which you can see highlighted in red, yellow, and blue. We will have three teams, one for each. Hu and Cook will be Red Team, Davidson and Andreas, you two are Yellow Team, Hawking, Walsh, Carter, and myself will be Blue Team. I have already gone over this with Commander Driver, who is coordinating with the SWAT team for us. They will be with us through the initial entry and attempt to secure the immediate area, and our teams will push into the building."

Stocke turns back around. "Does anyone have any questions?"

The team stays silent.

"The suspects have no idea we are coming, which is a benefit of organizing these raids so quickly. Let's all go downstairs and get prepped. SWAT will be driving us to the location."

Everyone stands and heads out into the hall. We don't all fit on the first elevator, and I end up waiting with Reilly, Cook, and Hu for the second one.

I shift restlessly on my feet. I hate the anticipation of a fight. Everything that can go wrong runs through your mind over and over until you can't see how something terrible won't happen. I follow Reilly onto the elevator and cross my arms tightly over my chest. At least I'm not going into this fight alone.

The elevator carries us down the basement, and I follow the group into the parking garage. There are three armored vehicles lined up, waiting for us.

Ivy gets my attention, and I walk over to her.

"Body armor," she says, handing me a black vest with a patch that reads JHAPI velcroed to the front and back. "And pistol."

The pistol is strapped into a holster attached to a

black belt. I take the gun as well, and she hurries over to Agent Stocke. I tuck the gun between my legs and pull the body armor on over my shirt. It's heavier than I expected, and it feels like putting on a new shoe for the first time. It fits, but it definitely needs to be broken in.

Cook steps up beside me.

"You're on Brunson's team," he comments, his voice low, so no one else can hear.

"Yep," I say, popping my lips on the 'p'.

"If you do something to get him hurt or killed, I will bury you," he says, stepping into my personal space.

I hold my ground and look up at him, tilting my head to the side.

"What exactly is it you think I did to him? Or would do to him?"

He laughs in my face. "Don't act like you don't know you broke his heart."

I stare at him, confused, then roll my eyes.

"It's been five years. I've grown up; maybe you should too. I'm here to do a job, not deal with high school drama."

Cook walks away, shaking his head. Whatever his issues are with me, they're going to have to wait until another time. I tighten the belt around my waist and adjust the pistol until it isn't poking me in the stomach.

Reilly is waiting for me by the last vehicle. I tug at the uncomfortable vest one more time, then walk over to join him. Time to get this over with.

---

The earpiece is too big for my ear canal. Having something in my ear makes my breathing seem louder too, and I can't hear everyone's heartbeats, which makes me feel weirdly off balance. I hadn't realized how quickly I'd come to depend on that for knowing where everyone is in the room. I readjust the body armor again, but there's no making it comfortable.

The gas mask is even worse. It smells like plastic and someone else's sweat. Each puff of my breath makes my face hot and the inside of the mask humid. I tug at the strap on the back of my head and try to adjust where it sits under my chin. All my senses are muffled. I don't know how anyone is expected to fight like this.

Elise's hand appears on my shoulder, and she gives me an irritated look.

"Quit fidgeting," she whispers.

I mouth back *sorry* and try to hold myself still. The waiting is making me nervous though. Storming in without thinking is more my style.

Elise, Zachary, Reilly, and I are entering behind the local SWAT team through a side entrance. The rest of the JHAPI agents, excluding Agent Stocke and Staci, are divided up between two other entrances. The building isn't very large. It's nestled in-between two much larger structures, and it's the kind of place you'd never think twice about.

The front is plain stucco, with minimal windows and no signs. A fairly large parking lot obscures the view of the building from the road. The parking lot is generally used by people who live in the apartments next door and overflow from the roofing business on the other side.

"Red Team is a go," Stocke's voice says in my ear.

The SWAT member in front motions forward, and the two men behind him swing their battering ram against the door, which instantly gives way. In the midst of the splinters of the door, I see the glint of silver.

Two canisters are tossed through the open doorway, gas pouring from the spout. Our group pushes forward, and I follow Elise, my left hand resting lightly on her shoulder while my right hand grips my pistol tightly. I keep my trigger finger carefully indexed. I'm grateful for the night vision the magic I stole from Javier gives me because it is dark as sin inside the building.

My breaths puff loudly inside the mask as I scan the heavy fog of gas for movement. I can barely make out the silhouette of the SWAT member who entered first.

"Two doors to the left. Staircase straight ahead," an unfamiliar male voice sounds in my earpiece.

The team splits up with two of the SWAT members and Zachary peeling off toward the closest door on the left. Three others advance to the door just past it. Reilly stops the second team at the door, crouching down to listen to something the others can't hear.

The gas has cleared just enough since we came in that I can see the staircase that stretches up into pitch black ahead of us. One SWAT member heads toward it, and Elise follows. I hesitate for a moment, then go after Elise.

We reach the top of the staircase and spread out quietly. There are double doors in front of us, and two smaller rooms to the left. One door is half-open, the other is shut. There is a short wall that lines the opening of the staircase.

The SWAT guy approaches the open door cautiously and pushes it all the way open as he enters the room. Elise follows close behind. I'm a few paces behind, my eyes glued to the double doors, all the hairs on my arm standing on end. I'm a beat too slow, and the door slams shut behind them, trapping them inside and me outside.

The double doors fly open, and I lunge for the wall that lines the stairwell. There's a bulky, decorative chrome planter with a fake tree sticking out of it at the corner that I squeeze behind. Bullets fly over my head, and there is muffled shouting in my earpiece, along with more gunfire. I guess the fight is on now.

A man in a mask and camo pants steps around the wall, holding a shotgun, and I lift my pistol and fire three times. The bullets go wide because my hands are shaking, but he falls back.

I scramble backward and take a deep breath as electric magic rushes through me. Right now, they think I'm human. I won't use my magic unless I have to, and definitely not before I can use the element of surprise to my advantage.

The door Elise and the SWAT member went into rattles violently, like someone was thrown into it. At the same time, gunfire echoes up the stairwell. It finally registers that someone is shouting my name in the earpiece. I tap it three times, the code I was told to let the team know I was still alive but unable to respond.

The men in front of me don't try to advance again, but they do shoot every few seconds to keep me from moving. I tighten my hands around my pistol and try to think. I can stay here for a while, but I don't know if Elise is okay, and I'm not willing to leave her in that room forever. She hasn't shifted, which worries me.

I can't breathe right or see, so I rip the gas mask off. A symphony of smells assaults me. Gunpowder. Blood. Silver. Vomit. The welts on my arms twinge unexpectedly, and I see movement in my reflection in the planter. I lean a little closer and see my mother looking back at me. My heart jumps into overdrive. I cannot be hallucinating right now.

She points behind me and holds up two fingers, then disappears. I push my back up against the planter just in time to see the second door fly open and a man step out, his gun pointed right at me. I shoot first, and my bullets thud into his chest. He falls forward, blood spreading across his shirt, but there's another man behind him. I feel, more than hear, the planter shatter as a bullet strikes near my shoulder.

I push forward onto my knees and fire again. I hit him in the arm and halt his advance. My gun clicks, and I realize the slide is locked back. I drop the magazine and scramble for another, but he's already lifting his gun again.

I pull on the magic inside of me and rush forward faster than any human would be able to move. In the time it takes his heart to beat once, I close the distance between us and my fist collides with his jaw.

He falls, unconscious, and I pivot and lunge for the other door as gunfire explodes from my right. A bullet punches into my body armor, and it feels like I was just hit by a baseball bat, but my momentum carries me through the door.

Elise is hunched in a corner over the SWAT guy who isn't moving. Her lip is bleeding, and she is half-shifted. Her hands are curled into claws, and fur is creeping across her face. There are three men standing in front of her; one is holding some kind of taser, the other two have nightsticks. There is shouting in my earpiece. I rip it out. I need to be able to hear.

Elise lunges forward, taking advantage of the distraction my entrance has caused. She hits the man on the far right, one hand wrapping around the night-stick, the other landing in his stomach.

I lift my hands toward the man with the taser and push out a burst of electrical energy. It crackles across the room like a lightning bolt and strikes him in the chest. He flies backward and hits the sheetrock with a thud.

The other man runs toward me. I slip to the left to avoid his first strike. There is gunfire outside the room, and I vaguely hear what sounds like Zachary shouting from downstairs.

A howl erupts to my right, and out of the corner of my eye I see that Elise has finally shifted. She locks her jaws around the throat of the man she was fighting and twists her head violently. He struggles, his hands clawing at her face.

I drop under another swing and punch upwards, catching the man in the stomach along with a surge of electricity. His body goes tense, and he falls.

I try to stand but find myself unable to. The welts on my arms twist in pain, and my vision swims. Elise runs for the door, pausing to glance back at me. I nod, and she races out.

This cannot be happening. I didn't try to use my Finding magic, so there's no reason the welts should be reacting like this. I push to my feet with a pained grunt and stumble toward the door. My senses are still buzzing on overload. Everything is sharp and clear despite the dim lighting. There are clusters of heartbeats all around the building, all racing with fear and adrenaline.

*Olivia*, I hear Reilly say, his voice cutting through all the chaos. *Put your fucking earpiece back in.*

I roll my eyes but fumble for it nonetheless.

"Carter here," I say, my voice shaking to an embarrassing extent.

"Olivia, stay put," Brunson responds. "We have them cornered, but if you come out of that room, you may get caught in the crossfire."

"Is Hawking with you?" I ask. "She ran out of here just a moment ago."

There is a pause. "No."

A howl echoes through the building, and I hear Zachary curse. I edge around the corner of the doorway and look outside. The team is advancing up the stairs. The double doors are still wide open, and I can see Elise facing off against three men. She's holding her own against them, but there is a fourth coming up behind her she doesn't seem to have noticed.

"Don't shoot me," I say into the mic before charging out. The welts ache, but I push through the pain and pull on the vampire magic inside of me. I have to be fast.

## 7

I sense Reilly coming up the stairs behind me and put on a burst of speed to stay ahead of him. The fourth man lifts his gun. I tackle as he fires, and we both go flying. I reach for the gun as he's trying to turn it towards me, but I'm faster. I squeeze his wrist, and the small bones give way with a crunch. He screams in pain, and the gun falls. There is gunfire behind me as the team enters the room.

The man struggles against my grip. I rear back and punch him hard in the jaw with my left hand. It's an awkward angle, but I'm stronger than I normally would be, and he goes limp.

I flip around, ready for another threat, but the men Elise was fighting are face down on the ground. One of the SWAT members is cuffing two of them. The third appears to be dead.

Reilly steps out of the shadows on the far wall and sets Elise, who is still shifted down. She shakes from snout to tail, then licks his hand gratefully. He must have grabbed her and gotten her out of the way.

Zachary rips out his earpiece and storms toward me, his lips curled into a sneer.

"What the hell were you thinking? I told you to stay put!" he shouts.

I stand upright, even though the movement makes me want to vomit. I desperately need something to dull the pain shooting through the welts.

"He had a gun pointed at Elise. There was no time to wait for you to enter the room," I shout, pointing at the unconscious man behind me.

Zachary clenches his jaw and glances back at Elise, who is limping towards us as she shifts back into human form. Reilly is looking me up and down, his nose twitching as he checks for injuries.

"Stop yelling at her, Zach," Elise says quietly. "I ran in here on my own and shouldn't have. She's right, he would have shot me. The bullet grazed my leg as it is."

Zachary's face changes from angry to worried in an instant. "How bad is it?"

Elise rolls her eyes. "It'll be fine, but it burns. There was silver in that bullet."

"I can fix it," I say, taking a step forward. My knees buckle, and the room spins. I don't realize I'm tipping forward until I face plant into Reilly's chest.

"You're not using any more magic tonight," Reilly says as he swings me up into his arms.

"You're not using any—any magic," I slur. Everything is buzzing, and my vision is foggy.

Elise walks closer and peers down at me.

"You're naked," I comment helpfully.

She raises a brow and looks back up at Reilly. "Is she all right?"

"She'll be fine," Reilly says, but his heartbeat thumps uncertainly.

"Lie," I mutter, slapping my hand against his chest. "He doesn't know."

"Get her out of here. Staci probably has something that will help her," Zachary says. His brows are pinched together in unexpected concern.

Reilly carries me out of the room. I distantly hear Elise shouting for someone to bring her some clothes.

I blink, and we're at the bottom of the stairs. I'm not sure if Reilly moved vampire fast, or if I just passed out for a minute. I can smell the magic inside of him, and if I had any strength left, I'd try to take it.

"You need to feed again, don't you?" he asks.

I nod slowly, my cheek sliding against his rough body armor. "Not gonna lose control, but the vampire magic, I think it took from me while I was using it."

I let go of the magic as much as I can. The sounds fade into the background, and the overbearing scents stop making my nose itch.

Reilly lowers my feet to the ground and helps me stand. I blink and look around. We're outside now by the van. No one else is around, but I can see Agent Stocke talking to Ivy and Commander Driver near the entrance.

"It really is a curse." A laugh bubbles up in my throat, and I bite my lips to try to keep from losing it. "I never thought I'd be made weaker by stealing magic from someone."

"It's not making you weaker," Reilly says. "You just don't have any control. You dump all of your energy into every move."

"I did what I had to—"

"That's not the point I'm trying to make," Reilly interrupts. "You need to be trained. You're using magic you weren't born with. You've never been taught how to control it or channel it. Anyone, even a vampire, can wear themselves out like this. You understood that with your healing magic, why did you think this would be any different?"

I sit down on the edge of the van. "It was easier to feel my limits with that. I also hadn't taken much of the magic. I thought that was why it was so hard to use."

"What you did today was stupid," Reilly chastises. His heart is thumping with annoyance.

"I don't need a lecture," I snap. "You're the one who wanted to test my limits under pressure. Guess we just found out."

"I meant running in after Hawking. I didn't bring you into this to have you get killed because you're reckless."

I stand abruptly. "I wasn't going to watch her die. The risk was minimal anyhow. I took that guy completely by surprise."

"You had no idea who else was in that room, and you could have gotten shot by your own team members," Reilly says, shoving his finger in my face.

I slap it away. "You ran right in after me."

"Because I protect my investments."

Staci rounds the front of the van, then stops at the expression on our faces.

"I was told you needed me?" she asks, adjusting her glasses primly.

"You were told wrong. I'm fine," I say.

"You look like you're about to keel over and die, but if you say so," Staci says with a tight smile before turning and walking away toward Agent Stocke.

"What a bitch," I mutter.

"You're going to feed tonight," Reilly says quietly.

"You offering your wrist up again?" I ask, hunger swirling in my gut.

Reilly crosses his arms. "No, but I have found a volunteer."

"An actual volunteer, or someone who has no idea what they're getting themselves into and has no choice in the matter?" I ask.

"He'll be in the hotel room at five-fifteen a.m. Don't use any more magic before then."

"Fine," I mutter, wrapping my arms around myself.

Reilly stalks off, but Elise comes and finds me after a few minutes.

"Are you going to be all right to join us for dinner? Or an early breakfast, I'm not sure what to call it when you're eating at two a.m.," she asks.

I'm still shaky, and my mind is scattered, but food does sound good. I don't know what else I'll do for the next few hours if I don't join them, so I nod.

"Sure, I'll be fine."

"All right," Elise says, clearly skeptical. "Let's go. I'll drive you."

---

"It's tradition," Ivy says as she pushes a plate toward me. She's the only person still dressed in her suit. She seems comfortable in it though, like it's just how she prefers to be. "I started it in the Academy, back when I was with the FBI. Eating together, especially after a night like this, helps."

I grab the plate and pile a few pieces of pizza on it. "So, this is meant to be family bonding or something?"

Ivy shrugs. "Sure, but it's practical too. We need to discuss what was found and clean our weapons."

I sit down next to Elise. She's the only person here I am even remotely comfortable with. She's on her fourth piece of pizza already. I guess the shift really does increase a were's appetite.

Everyone else is already settled in. Hu and Corinne are discussing something about an upcoming council summit. I don't pay attention to what the councils get up to, and I don't care to start, so I tune them out.

"How's your leg?" I ask.

Elise shrugs. "I think there's still a speck of silver in there somewhere, but it's healing, so it'll work itself out tonight."

"If it doesn't, let me know. I can get it out," I say, taking a bite of my pizza before it gets cold.

"So you really can heal?" she asks.

"Yeah, nothing like what a real healer could do, but simple stuff like that is easy enough."

"You definitely packed a punch with that electric magic," she says with a short laugh and a shake of her head. "To be honest, I was kind of doubting whether or not you could actually use that kind of magic until I saw it."

"Well, I'm obviously not great with it."

"You moved really damn fast too. Is that some kind of physical magic? It wasn't part of what Stocke mentioned."

Elise has a way of asking not-so-innocent questions out of nowhere. I chew the bite of pizza in my mouth and swallow uncomfortably. Cook is staring at us from across the table, not even pretending not to be listening in.

"Um, yeah. Some kind." I shrug and grab another piece of pepperoni and jalapeño from the box. "I've never tried this combination on pizza before, but whoever ordered this was a genius. I'll never order anything else."

"I am, indeed, a genius," Hu says from the end of the table, toasting me with his own slice of pizza.

Agent Stocke walks in, and the conversation dies

down. She's dressed down as well in a long-sleeved blouse and jeans. Her curly blonde hair is out of its bun. She grabs a plate and some pizza, then sits down at the head of the table.

"Tonight, we arrested three members of the NWR. A few were killed instead of being captured," Stocke says before taking a bite of pizza. "The raid didn't go perfectly, but everyone made it home, and no one on our side was seriously injured. Good job."

"Hell yeah," Elise says, lifting her can of soda in a toast. Everyone lifts whatever they're holding, pizza or drink, and sounds their agreement.

"Now, this particular cell seems to be relatively new. From what we found, it seems to confirm they were more of a recruitment center than anything else. We did, however, find bomb-making materials and information on several targets around the city. The suspects who were arrested are being interrogated, but none of them are offering up any information yet," Stocke says.

"Was there any information on their computers?" Hu asks.

Stocke shakes her head. "They were able to destroy the hard drives before we got to them."

"What's next?" Ivy asks.

"We have a flight to catch tomorrow evening. We're headed to Las Vegas," Stocke says.

"Vegas?" Cook asks, perking up.

Stocke nods. "We received a tip that Martinez may be in the city sometime in the next week or two."

"Any other information?" I ask, leaning forward, my heartbeat kicking into overdrive.

Stocke shakes her head. "Not on Martinez. You can look through all the intelligence we have on NWR activity in Las Vegas on the flight."

I hadn't thought there was any chance we might catch him quickly, but if we already know what city he's in, maybe there is hope. I stand to throw my plate away, and Elise hands me her plate as well, leaning back in her seat and patting her stomach in satisfaction.

I throw the trash away but have to pause at the unexpected jolt of pain that runs through my arm at the movement. It's been a couple of days since I've been able to apply the salve to my welts. I need something tonight; this is getting ridiculous.

"You gonna pass out on us again, Carter?" Cook asks from across the room. His tone suggests he hopes I do.

I roll my eyes and walk back to my chair, ignoring the slight dizziness that accompanies the movement.

"It's not a permanent fix, but Staci does have some salves that can help with the pain," Corinne says, her eyes full of concern.

"The traditional salve will help for now, but I need something stronger to really make a difference, and I don't have anything to brew what I need," I say, wiping some grease I had missed off my fingers.

"Can Olivia just borrow Staci's cauldron and brew whatever she needs?" Hu asks as he pops the trigger pin out of his gun.

"No."

"Absolutely not," Staci and I say in unison. I turn and glare at her, and she's frowning at me like it was my idea.

"She's not touching my cauldrons," Staci bites out like the idea disgusts her. I absolutely understand because I wouldn't let another witch near my cauldrons either, but her tone is a little much.

Hu looks at us, clearly amused. "Sorry I suggested it."

"I do have a basic healing salve with me," Staci says, patting her napkin on her mouth before standing and walking over to her briefcase. She unzips it and picks up a blue tub that is neatly labeled. "This should last you a couple of days. I'll make more once we are at our next location."

I walk over and take the tub. Staci looks smug about it, and I'm tempted to throw it back in her face, but this is one of those moments where it's really not worth it to let my pride get in the way.

"Thanks," I say with a flat expression.

"No problem," Staci says with a smile as she walks back to the table.

Once it's clear everyone is done eating, the remaining pizza gets cleared away. We pull out our guns, carefully clearing and checking them before laying them on the table.

Ivy had given me a cleaning kit along with the pistol. I grab it and go through the familiar motions of disassembling the Glock and laying out each piece. The minty smell of the lubricant takes me back five years.

I had spent most Sunday afternoons with Brunson and his father at the shooting range, always followed by cleaning the guns, then the family dinner. It was their version of church.

I look up to find Zachary staring at me, and I pause, brush in hand. It takes him a moment to turn back to his gun. I'm sure he's reliving the same memories I am. It's bittersweet for me, I have no idea what it means to him anymore.

8

My hands are trembling as I pack up my gun and cleaning supplies. It's just past five am. I don't have long to get back to the room, and honestly, the feeding can't come soon enough. The pizza helped with some of the dizziness, but I still feel completely drained.

I try to slip out of the room unnoticed, but Corinne follows me into the hallway.

"We need to talk soon, about what's going on," she says quietly.

"I know, there's just nothing I can do about it today. I need to rest," I say, taking another couple of steps toward the elevator so she doesn't think I'm willing to linger.

"Then we talk as soon as we get to Vegas, all right?"

"Sounds like a plan."

The elevator dings and opens. I turn away and hurry inside, punching the button for floor six. Corinne stands in the hallway, watching me as the doors slide shut. I slump back against the wall and put my face in my hands. The welts are hurting more than I want to admit.

The elevator arrives at the sixth floor, and I step out but pause in the hallway. I don't know who I'm going to be meeting tonight, but I don't want to go in there this weak.

I slip out of my jacket and crack open the little container. I can smell the sweet, light scent of aloe and some kind of mint. It's nothing like my healing salve, but as I dip my fingers in the cool cream, I can sense there is magic brewed into it.

The first swipe of the cream cools the welt considerably, but then it and the skin around it start to go numb. I sigh; if she had brewed the healing salve properly, it wouldn't need to numb anything. It would just *heal* it.

I spread it across my hands and up my arms regardless. I can't reach everything without undressing in the hallway, but the pain has already eased considerably. I feel a little cold and a little sticky now, but it's a welcome change from the constant aching.

I pull my jacket back on carefully and shove the tub in the pocket. The room is a short walk down the hall, but far enough for the nerves to settle in. I don't know what I'm going to do if the poor sap Reilly has in there is afraid or begs me not to feed from them.

The door swings open as I'm pulling out my keycard, and Reilly stands in the doorway, arms crossed.

"You're late," he says before sniffing carefully, then frowning. "Why do you smell like you bathed in toothpaste?"

"Because Staci is a shitty hedgewitch," I say, crossing my arms self-consciously.

Reilly raises a brow but steps aside and waves me into the room. I can smell the volunteer as soon as I step in and hear a slow and steady heartbeat. Whoever it is, they're not nervous like I feared. At least not yet.

A man about the same height as Reilly, but with short black hair, is currently leaning against the far wall, watching me. He is a bit pretty for a man, but he holds himself with an easy confidence. He has light hazel eyes that are currently working their way up to my face from my feet and cheekbones that could cut glass. The light stubble across his jaw keeps him from looking too feminine, but he wouldn't be out of place on a catwalk.

"Olivia, it's lovely to meet you," he says, strolling toward me with a predatory smile. "I'm Damien Black."

For someone who's about to be food, he's doing a good job of acting like he's in control of the situation.

"Is that your real name, or did you change it to try to sound like you're in a bad vampire romance novel?" I ask as I reach out to shake the hand he has held out.

His smile falters, but his handshake does not.

"You'll have to blame my mother for that one, perhaps she had bad taste in books."

"Be nice, Olivia," Reilly chastises.

I smile at Damien, but that doesn't seem to help exactly.

"Reilly said you required my assistance, and while I am happy to help," he pauses, his eyes flicking down to my lips, "in any way, what exactly did you have in mind?"

That explains the lack of nerves. I turn to Reilly and cross my arms.

"Seriously?"

Reilly ignores me and looks at Damien. "I'm calling in your debt."

Damien's face pales, and he swallows once. "In what manner?"

"You will allow Olivia to feed from you and take

75

as much as she needs. You will speak of this to no one, not even your sire."

Damien's expression morphs into confusion, his brows knitting together.

"Feed from me? She smells like a witch."

"Your sense of smell must be severely lacking," Reilly says as he slips his hands into his pockets and leans back against the desk. "She's a vampire."

I force my fangs out and smile at him in lieu of further explanations. Damien looks at me carefully, taking in my jeans, wrinkled T-shirt, pale face, and the small fangs pressing against my lower lip.

"I can hardly object to the attention of a beautiful woman," Damien says with a smile. "Where would you like to feed from?"

He tilts his head to the side in offer.

I snort. "Your wrist is fine."

Damien unbuttons the sleeve of his jacket while holding my gaze. His movements are slow, and his eyes keep straying to my lips. I suspect he might be doing it to wind up Reilly, and oddly, it seems to be working. Reilly's jaw clenches and unclenches slowly as he watches us.

"As requested," Damien says, lifting his now bared wrist in my direction.

I step forward and inhale, breathing in the light scent of leather that clings to Damien. I wrap my hand gently around his forearm and lean in, my mouth practically watering now that he's so close.

There is the slightest tremor in his hand. It's not visible, but I can feel it. It makes my stomach twist. He's afraid of me, of what I might take from him. It must be odd for a vampire to be fed from like this. Then again, anyone would be scared to not have a choice. I know it scares me.

I hesitate, my mouth hovering over his bared skin,

as my hunger wars with my conscience. I glance up and see he is staring at me.

"It's all right, Olivia," he says, pushing his wrist toward me.

His heartbeat stays, elevated but steady, and something untwists inside of me. I bite down, and warm blood rushes into my mouth. The magic inside of Damien is stronger than I expected. Whoever he is, he is older and more powerful than Javier. He still isn't as strong as Reilly though. I pull and feel the cold strength pour into me.

Damien gasps, his eyes going wide. He can feel it already then, the strange pull from deep inside that's more than any normal feeding should take. He leans away slightly, but my grip on his wrist is unyielding. I can feel his pulse quickening with each tug on his magic.

The dizziness and pain I've felt since the raid fades away. My senses sharpen, and I can practically smell Damien's fear growing. I can hear people walking through the hall two floors down. I can hear Reilly's heartbeat thumping away in irritation.

I don't need to take any more blood or magic, but I don't want to stop. It feels too good. I hold Damien's gaze, but there is no heat to it anymore. His face is tight, and he keeps glancing at Reilly as if asking when this will be over. I bite down harder, my teeth bruising his skin around my fangs. He should be asking me, not Reilly. I'm the one taking, I'm the one who gets to decide, I'm—

The hunger is overwhelming. Taking magic like this makes it even worse. I have to stop this, or I'll take too much. Reilly blackmailed Damien into this, and I can't leave him vulnerable and drained like I did Javier.

I tear my fangs out of his wrist and press the back

of my hand to my lips as I swallow the last of the blood in my mouth. I'm panting like I just ran a mile. I take a step backward so I don't grab Damien again.

"What the hell was that?" Damien asks, breathing almost as hard as I am.

"You can consider the debt paid in full. However, if I find out you have spoken of this to anyone, I will personally put you in a coffin," Reilly says, his arms still crossed.

Damien straightens, trying to force his face back into indifference but failing.

"Business as usual, then," he says.

I step out of his way and sit on the end of my bed.

Damien hurries toward the door, staying as far away from me as he can, and I flop back. The door opens and shuts, and an awkward silence settles between me and Reilly.

My body is buzzing with magic, but mentally, I'm exhausted.

"I don't want to do that again," I say, staring at the ceiling.

"You may have to if you exhaust yourself like that again. You have to maintain control, and you have to recover," Reilly says.

"I know, but I'm not going to take from someone unwilling like that again. I shouldn't have done it this time."

Reilly is silent for a moment. "You need to be practical. It's going to be hard, if not impossible, to find someone willing to let you feed on their magic."

I roll over onto my side, putting my back to him.

"I don't care."

All I can think about is the tremor in Damien's hand. It's the same way my hands shook when I realized Reilly knew what I was and was going to use it against me. I can't do that to someone else.

Reilly sighs deeply but doesn't argue farther. Exhaustion steals over me, and I realize the sun must have just risen. I squeeze my eyes shut and slip into sleep.

9

F or some reason, I had been expecting some kind of private plane, not an economy class ticket on a generic airline. The flight had been noisy, there were two bachelorette parties on board, and there hadn't been any leg room. The plane landed around one a.m., and we took a cab to the hotel, which isn't even on the Strip. The rest of Vegas looks sadly normal compared to the glitz and glam you expect from Sin City.

The hotel we're staying at is nice though, so I can't really complain. I dunk my head under the spray again and rinse out the conditioner. The JHAPI agents are all busy chasing down information on the alleged sighting of Martinez. My only assignment for the evening is to meet with Corinne and work on fixing the effects of my stupidity with the Finding magic.

I shut off the water and climb out. The heat is starting to irritate the welts, so I don't want to linger. I wrap myself up in the oversized towel and reach for the tub of salve but don't pick it up. They are irritated but aren't hurting that badly right now, and I'd like to make sure I can tell if anything changes while

I'm with Corinne tonight. I don't want to be numbed at all.

I get ready quickly and without putting in too much effort. My hair goes up in a loose bun, and I wear a loose T-shirt and my most comfortable pair of jeans.

When I walk out of the bathroom, Reilly is sitting in the chair at the desk, waiting for me.

"You're going to see Corinne?" he asks.

"Yes." I wrap my hand around my forearm. "I need to try to fix this."

He nods. "Don't overdo it today."

"I'm not going to," I say in exasperation. "Do you think I'm an idiot? I don't want a repeat of last night."

"Come directly back here when you are done. I expect to see you before sunrise," he says, ignoring my outburst.

"Sure thing, *Dad*," I say sarcastically.

Reilly grins. "I always suspected you had daddy issues."

"Oh, shut up," I snap.

The phone Elise gave me back in Phoenix buzzes once. I flip it open angrily and see a text from Corinne; she's on her way. I'm impressed this old thing can even send and receive texts.

She had insisted on coming to fetch me from my room. I'm starting to think the team has a pact with Reilly to help monitor me twenty-four/seven.

Reilly looks at his watch and stands. "I'll be back in a couple of hours. Don't make me come find you."

I roll my eyes and scoff, pulling on a sock.

"Or you'll be grounded," he says.

I glare at him, but he's grinning, his dimples on full display like they're trying to disguise the fact that he's an asshole.

"I hope you get staked," I mutter.

He clasps his hands over his heart in mock agony.

"So cruel," he says with a laugh as he walks toward the door.

I focus intently on my other sock until I hear him open and close the door. I listen to his footsteps disappear down the hall, then, once he's far enough away, I throw myself back on the bed and curse him soundly.

It takes a few deep breaths, but I pull myself together and sit up. I pull on one shoe, then hear a knock at the door. I go answer it, the other shoe in hand. I peek through the peephole, just to be sure it's Corinne, but when I see it is her, I open the door and wave her inside.

"I'm almost ready," I say in lieu of a hello. "Come on in."

"No problem," Corinne says with her ever-ready smile as she steps through the doorway.

"Do I need to bring anything?" I ask as I sit down and pull on my other shoe.

"No, just yourself and an open mind," she says, looking around the room curiously. My clothes are strewn around my bags and bed. I've always found that when living out of a suitcase, my clothes have a way of ending up all over the place.

"Where are we going anyhow?" I ask.

"The room Ivy and I are staying in," Corinne says. "I just thought the walk would give us a few minutes to chat and get comfortable."

I chuckle. "Okay."

"I know, I'm kind of a hippie," Corinne says with a smile. "My coven is very unorthodox, which is part of why I even ended up in JHAPI. Most covens wouldn't allow it."

"I was surprised to hear there was a Finder on the

team. You could be earning a lot more money doing private work."

Corinne nods. "It wouldn't be as fulfilling. I do take the occasional private commission, but most of the work I do outside of JHAPI is charitable. I make enough to pay my bills. I'm not concerned about becoming rich, and my coven is supportive of that."

"Must be nice," I say, standing. "I've never heard of a coven like that."

"You aren't part of a coven are you?"

"Nope." I shake my head decisively. "And I never will be."

Corinne nods without argument.

Most witches lose their shit when I say something like that. Covens are part-protection, part-employment, and part-family. Usually highly dysfunctional families, but witches are still very loyal. Most will stay with the coven they are born into unless they are courted away somehow. Everyone understands moving to a better coven for reasons like money or power, just as long as you don't turn into a coven hopper.

"Are you ready?" she asks.

"Yes." I grab my key card and wallet and follow her out the door. Their room is a floor up, but luckily the elevator doors open as soon as she presses the button.

"So, were you able to Find people from a young age? Or did you discover it on accident somehow?" Corinne asks as we step inside. She fiddles with her necklace, rolling the crystal back and forth between her fingers.

"It's more of a recent, uh, acquisition," I say hesitantly. Stocke didn't explain how I was able to use more than one type of magic, and I'm not eager to get into the details. The elevator doors open, and we head down the hall.

"After the raid, you seemed like you were hurt, and possibly upset?"

"I was just exhausted, magically. The welts started bothering me."

She slips her key card into the door and opens it, waving me inside first. Her room is exactly the same as the one Reilly and I are staying in. There is a simple, black suitcase next to the bed closest to the door, and then two bright red bags next to the other. I assume that must be Corinne's bed.

"You didn't seem upset about being shot at though," she says as she walks over to the desk that sits to the right of the television. She grabs an electric kettle and heads toward the bathroom.

I pace toward her bed and sit down on the edge since there is only one chair, and I'm not sure where else to sit.

"I guess I wasn't, really. I was relieved no one was seriously hurt," I say with a shrug.

"Have you been shot at before?" she asks.

"Yes."

"That's pretty unusual outside of law enforcement." She walks back into the main area and plugs her kettle into an outlet underneath the desk.

"Not as unusual for witches outside of a coven."

"I didn't realize that," she says thoughtfully, finger tapping against her chin. "I don't know that I've ever met a covenless witch before."

"I imagine you haven't," I say with a sharp laugh. "You seem like a nice lady."

She shrugs. "You seem like a nice lady too."

"I suppose I am now. For the most part."

"Did you know that in the past, Finders didn't use

maps when working their magic?" Corinne asks, changing the subject abruptly.

"I'd never thought about it. I guess there weren't always maps, definitely not as detailed as we have now, were there?"

"No, and back then, your types of injuries were much more common. Being a Finder was dangerous. They're rare now because so many families lost their sons and daughters to the magic, and their lines ended."

I had studied magical history as a child, but it hadn't interested me at the time, and I don't remember much of it. The kettle beeps behind her, and she pours the hot water into one of the paper cups. She drops in a teabag and stirs a packet of sugar into her tea, then takes a sip to test it. She nods contentedly and sits in the chair behind her, the cup cradled in her hands.

"How did they use it at all without a map?"

"Finding magic, at its most basic level, is trying to guide you to the living thing you are trying to find. It uses whatever tools you provide. A witching rod. A map. Or nothing more than your magic itself. That's the most dangerous way to use it, of course, because the farther away you are from your target, the more of your magic it needs."

"Is that why the rule is to not try to Find someone who you can't guarantee will be on the map in front of you?" I ask.

Corinne nods. "We follow all these safety rules now, and people forget why. I think they're overly limiting, but I also think the only people who should be bending them are advanced users with a deep understanding of magical theory."

"That sounds a lot like people's attitudes toward brewing. Safety first. Don't experiment." I shake my head. "Brewing without experimentation is just—chemistry. It's not even magic anymore."

Corinne laughs. "It somehow doesn't surprise me you think that."

I shrug, unapologetic. She lifts her necklace, and the crystal spins a little, back and forth, from the sudden movement.

"This is actually a sort of witching rod. It's an old pendulum that's been in my family for so long, no one actually knows when it was acquired," she says, her eyes following the movement of the crystal. "I've used it several times in particularly difficult cases. I think it helps me channel my magic, to keep it from getting away from me."

I lean forward to see it better. From a distance, it just looks like any old amber crystal, but I realize it's not that at all.

"Is that carnelian?" I ask.

"Yes," Corinne says with a grin. "I think you may need to get something like this when you can. It can be hard to find something that will work, and there are things you need to learn before you even attempt to use one, but it might help you."

"What do I need to learn first?"

She drops the necklace and leans forward, clasping her hands together. "You are going to Find me."

I raise my brow. "You're right in front of me."

"Exactly," she says, pointing at me. "You won't have to strain your magic at all, and you can practice not only controlling it, but really feeling it. I get the impression that every time you've used it has been in a sort of panic."

I shrug. "You're not wrong."

"One of the ways my mother taught me was by playing hide and seek with me as a child, except I had to use my magic to Find her. It was a simple game, but it worked well. I learned how to listen to my magic."

"I didn't realize it could work with the person right in front of you."

Corinne nods. "It does. Are you willing to try it tonight?"

I hesitate. I don't want to overdo it and have to feed again, but I have to be able to fix this. The welts are only going to get worse if I don't.

"How much magic will this use? I can't overdo it, or I'll be comatose for almost eight hours," I say finally.

"Hardly any. I doubt it will be anything more than uncomfortable. Of course, this is magic; I can't guarantee anything."

"All right, then. Let's do this," I say, standing. I'm worried, and a little scared of how this might go, but that's never stopped me before.

Corinne grins. "First, I'm going to blindfold you and have you put on these earmuffs. Then, I want you to Find me. What you're looking for is that tug in your gut that tells you where I am in relation to you. You'll point left or right, then let go of the magic, and we'll do it again."

She hands me a pair of black earmuffs that smells like it came straight out of her gun cleaning kit, then a fluffy eye mask. I take them and hold them hesitantly.

"How, exactly, do I Find you without a map?"

"I suggest starting by using your hands like a witching rod. You do something similar when using Finding magic with a map. Let them point me out like this room is one big map," Corinne says, spreading her arms wide.

I take a deep breath and mentally shake off the nerves.

"All right, I guess I'll just try it."

Corinne moves to stand directly in front of me. "Remember, once you Find me, just point left or right, then let it go."

I nod, then pull on the eye mask, followed by the earmuffs. I can hear the sound of my own breathing, but nothing else. I shake my hands out, then clasp them tightly together.

The Finding magic is responsive as soon as I tug on it. My arms burn immediately as well, but not bad enough that I'm worried. It's more like what I felt when Corinne was using her magic at that first meeting.

I picture Corinne as she looks right now. Simple green blouse, jeans, and her wavy hair loose around her face. The magic moves through me like a wave and pushes out into the room. It's an odd sensation. In the past, it has been directed toward the map. This makes me feel off-balance, like all of my senses are focused outside of my body.

I squint even though I can't see and try to sort out what exactly I'm sensing. I can feel the shape of the room as the magic searches with invisible fingers. I extend my hands cautiously and feel a pull that grows stronger and stronger to my left. My magic slides around Corinne like water.

There's a flash of an image in my mind. It's of me with my hands outstretched. My lips are turned down into a frown, and my brows are furrowed tightly together. The image disappears as quickly as it arrived, but I'm left trembling and drained.

"Left," I gasp out as I begin pulling the Finding magic back into myself. I rip off the earmuffs and the eye mask and toss them on the bed beside me. My hands are shaking, and the welts are burning enough that I have to grit my teeth to keep from groaning.

"Are you okay?" Corinne asks, hurrying to my side.

"It took too much. I think I saw something—" I stop, struggling for words with the pain coursing through my arms.

"Another hallucination?"

"No," I say, shaking my head fervently. "It wasn't like that at all. I saw me. I think I was seeing what you were seeing."

Corinne sits back on her heels and looks at me with wide eyes.

"You don't do anything by halves, do you?" she asks with a laugh.

I stare at her, wondering if she's lost her mind. "I'm glad you find this funny."

"It's not that," she says, shaking her head fervently. "Your ability to focus is excellent. Perhaps too good. I think it's what got you in trouble when you tried to Find your mother."

"I don't understand."

"You have a lot of power and raw talent, and you can easily hone in on what you are trying to Find. Someone as inexperienced as you shouldn't be able to Find someone who is no longer living, much less get their magic so entangled that they can't undo it. It should just have failed."

I put my head in my hands. "Double-edged sword, then."

"Pretty much," Corinne agrees.

"Do you believe in ghosts?" I ask. It's been bothering me since the first time I saw her, and I figure now is as good a time to ask as any.

"Ghosts?" she asks, tilting her head to the side. "No."

She leans back against the desk and crosses her arms, looking at me critically.

"Are you asking because you have seen what you assume is a ghost?"

I shift on the bed, leaning forward to rest my elbows on my knees.

"I've seen her more than once. My mother," I say quietly. "It's like she's haunting me ever since I tried to Find her."

"Where and when have you seen her?" she asks, tucking her hair behind her ears.

"The first time was in the hotel, the morning we arrived. I saw her in the mirror. The second time was during the raid. I saw her in this chrome planter. She pointed behind me, and that's when I realized someone was sneaking up on me. She saved my life."

"Hmm, that is an interesting manifestation," Corinne says.

"Interesting how?" I ask, twisting my hands together. I want her to respond, to tell me I'm not crazy. Or that I am but she can fix it.

"Well, for one, there's no such thing as ghosts. Superstitious human nonsense. You did find a sort of echo though. It's like you're being haunted by her memory," Corinne says, picking up her tea and taking a long drink. "The magic searched everywhere to find her, and because you cannot let her go, your magic is tied up in making these hallucinations manifest. It's the most basic thing we teach Finders, but of course, you were never taught."

I gnaw at the inside of my cheek. On the one hand, I'm glad I'm not being haunted by the ghost of my mother, but it had felt so real. Part of me doesn't want to give up being able to see her.

"And the warning? Is that just a memory too?"

Corinne shrugs. "A memory, your magic protecting you, perhaps."

Her answer is underwhelming, perhaps because I wanted it to mean something more. I take a deep breath and press the heel of my hands into my eyes for a moment, then look up.

"So what now?"

She sets her tea down and walks over to me, pushing up my sleeve. She traces one of the welts on my arm with a feather-light touch.

"This will never fade until you can untangle your magic and let go."

"Let go of what, exactly?"

"This kind of thing happens when the person using the Finding magic is obsessed with Finding someone. You may have tried to end the spell, but you didn't. You are burning yourself up with the magic, and the only way to stop it is to let go. You have to accept that you will never Find her. That she's gone."

I grit my teeth and dig my nails into my palms.

"I know she's gone. She's dead."

Corinne smiles gently.

"You know it up here," she says, pointing to her head. "But you need to accept it here." She points to her heart.

"It sounds like you're saying I need to just get over the fact that my mom is dead."

"That's not what I'm saying at all," Corinne says sharply, her lips pulling into a frown. "I'm saying that you have to accept that she isn't coming back. It's not something you can do overnight either. Until then, it's just going to be difficult."

"No offense, but I really thought you'd be more helpful than this."

Corinne's frown twists up into a smile. "I hear

that a lot. You should have Staci brew you something for those welts."

"I still have enough salve left to last for a few days. I can figure this out before I run out of it," I say, tugging my sleeve back down over my forearm.

Corinne presses her lips together, her face skeptical, but she doesn't argue.

"I should just get some sleep," I say, standing. I head toward the door, wishing I could just be alone for a few hours. Maybe I can hide out in the bathroom for a while.

"I'm sorry, Olivia," Corinne says as I turn the door handle. "For your loss. It's awful, and you'll always miss her."

I pull the door open and walk out without responding. My feet lead me to the elevators, but I hit the button for the first floor. I can't go back to the room yet.

The elevator is empty and carries me swiftly to the ground floor. The sun will be rising soon, and I want to see it. I push through the double doors that lead out of the hotel and step out into the brisk air. The wind is blowing hard, pushing my hair around my face and cooling the hot sting of tears that escaped down my cheeks when I wasn't paying attention.

The buildings here are spaced farther apart in this city than the one I grew up in. They're far enough apart that you can see the sunrise on the horizon between them. They're bathed in reds and golds right now as the sun begins creeping up into the sky.

The vampire magic curls up inside of me like a cat, stealing some of my energy as it goes dormant. The sounds of cars get a little more distant, and the heartbeat of the man hurrying down the sidewalk across the street simply ceases. I feel human for a moment.

With a sigh, I turn to go back inside, but I stop when I see a woman with long brown hair reflected in the hotel door. She's smiling at me, a worn book in her hand. My heart twists all over again, and I realize what Corinne meant. I don't want to stop seeing her.

I yank the door open and stomp inside. It's going to be a long night tomorrow.

# 10

The JHAPI office is located on the outskirts of the city. It's a large, square three-story building. The bottom is red brick, while the top two stories are white brick, making it look like someone stacked two different buildings on top of each other. A large archway stands in front of the building. There are three pillars in the archway representing the three tenets of JHAPI. Fidelity, Bravery, and Integrity, something borrowed from the FBI since JHAPI was originally just another department within that organization.

We step out of the car, and I pull my jacket tighter around me. The temperature dropped fast after the sun went down. Reilly's phone rings as he shuts his door.

"Yes?" Reilly asks as he answers it. There is a pause. "No, I don't want her mingling with the rest of the clan yet."

I glance back at him and pull on the vampire magic, hoping to hear the other side of the conversation.

"—control is excellent, and she had requested a

little more independence," the caller says. It sounds like it might be the tattooed man I met at Javier's.

"I'm glad to hear it, but I know you understand my reasons for wanting to keep her away from the others," Reilly says, sounding annoyed like this isn't the first time he has had this conversation.

"For how long?" the caller asks.

"At least a couple of weeks more. If she's getting too restless, take her out somewhere; just make sure it's away from the clan."

"Yes, sir," the caller says, resignation clear in his tone.

Reilly hangs up the phone and looks at me.

"Was that about Leslie?" I ask.

"Yes," he says as he starts toward the building. I trot after him.

"Is she all right?"

"Yes," he says again.

"Why won't you let her meet the rest of your clan?"

He stops short, and I almost run into his back. He looks back over his shoulder.

"What did Maybelle tell you about how your mother conceived you?" he asks, his eyes scanning my face for the answer. "A question for a question, Olivia. I've already answered two of yours."

I grit my teeth. He can't ever make anything easy. I brush past him, but his hand on my arm stops me.

"You are going to tell me eventually. I've been asking nicely, but I won't do that forever," he says, voice low and his breath on my ear.

I jerk my arm away. "I hate you."

He laughs like that's the best joke he's heard all week. "You sound like a petulant teenager."

I open my mouth to argue with him, but he simply walks around me and heads toward the entrance. I stay where I am for a moment, equal parts angry and frustrated, before following after him. I really do hate him.

Elise and Zachary reach the front door just before I do. Zachary holds the door open and lets me walk in before him.

"I cannot get used to this schedule," Elise says, pressing the back of her hand to her mouth as she yawns.

"It might be easier if you actually went to bed in the mornings instead of watching TV," Zachary mutters.

Elise rolls her eyes. "It'd be easier if you didn't snore."

Zachary glares at her. "I don't snore."

I laugh and try to turn it into a cough, but Zachary has already turned his glare to me.

"I'm sorry, but you definitely snore," I say, stepping back and raising my hands in apology.

Elise claps me on the back. "This is why I like you. Now, we need to get upstairs, or we're going to be late."

Reilly is already in the elevator. He holds the door open for us, and we all squeeze inside. My stomach lurches as it speeds toward the top floor. It stops just as abruptly as it started, and the doors slide open.

The conference room is directly across from the elevators. It's not as nice as the one in Phoenix. There is only one window, and it's not very big, so the room is stuffier and darker. The rest of the team is already there. We grab empty seats at the end of the table, and Corinne slides coffee in our direction.

Stocke stands and looks around the table, making sure she has everyone's attention.

"One of the reasons we're here in Vegas is because of recent disappearances, now believed to be kidnappings or murders. Vampires from five different clans have gone missing. Each clan has only lost a single member, and each clan leader had reason to believe the vampire might have simply run away. However, per clan law, they were still reported as missing to the vampire council." Stocke pulls up a slide with pictures of five vampires, the dates of their disappearances, and their names next to them. "The disappearances caused alarm; there were too many to be a coincidence. The vampire council forwarded this information to JHAPI to investigate. Because of the increased chatter from the NWR in this area and the sighting of Martinez just last week, the case is believed to be related. We will be investigating this until we find the missing vampires, or find proof it is unrelated to terrorism."

"Have any other paranormals gone missing?" Elise asks.

Stocke nods in Elise's direction, looking pleased with her question. "The other councils have not reported any missing persons. However, I would like you to go in person to the local were packs and ask them. Explain that vampires have gone missing and that we are concerned what the NWR is up to. If nothing else, I'd like them to be extra cautious in the coming weeks."

"Sure thing, Boss. I'd like to take Olivia with me if that's all right," Elise says.

"I have no objections," Stocke says with a nod. "Corinne and Hu, I'd like you to do the same with the local covens."

"We'll get started tomorrow morning, bright and early," Hu says with a grin. Corinne nods in agreement.

"Reilly, would you be able to accompany Ivy to speak to the clans that have had a missing vampire?"

Stocke asks, looking toward Reilly at the end of the table.

"Yes." Reilly nods.

"Everyone else will be following up on the Martinez sighting. I want everyone who might have seen him questioned. I want every surveillance tape that might have caught a glimpse of him walking down the street. I want to know who he is talking to, what he is doing, and where he is."

The remaining agents all nod.

"Corinne," Stocke says. "In a couple of days, I'd like you to attempt to Find him. However, we're going to do it by the book and take every safety measure possible. I want to know with certainty that he is close by."

"Yes, ma'am," Corinne says, sitting up straighter. I'm surprised Stocke is being so overly cautious about trying to Find him. I thought it would be one of the first things Corinne did when we got here.

"All right, everyone get to work. Anyone you can't talk to tonight, find a way to see them tomorrow during the day. I want progress updates, and anything of note should be sent to the entire team immediately."

---

I spend the entire night with Elise poring over pack member lists for the two packs in the Las Vegas area. The werewolf council has always refused to report their exact numbers, insisting instead on giving ranges in terms of pack size in certain areas. The lists Elise have been cobbled together from personal knowledge of contacts in the area and whatever information the local police have.

Reilly had disappeared after an hour to go visit

one of the clans since they're actually awake in the middle of the night. I almost wished I could go with him, just to avoid reading any more reports. Luckily, Elise called it quits well before sunrise.

Elise parks the car, and I rub my eyes, only half-awake.

"Thanks for the ride," I mumble as I open the car door.

"Yeah, no problem," she says with a yawn. "I'll see you tomorrow at ten a.m."

"So early," I whine.

"The rest of the world hasn't adapted to the night shift," Elise says as we walk toward the elevators. "Just be glad we get to sleep at all."

We ride the elevator up to our floor silently and head our separate directions with a short wave good-bye. I hope Reilly isn't back yet. It would be nice to fall asleep without feeling watched.

I finally reach the hotel room and dig the key card out of my back pocket. I slip it into the lock, and the light switches to green with a click. I push open the door and stop on the threshold. Reilly is sitting on his bed, and a girl is sitting on him. Her shirt is stretched down over her shoulder, and his fingers are tangled in her hair, pulling her head sharply to one side to expose her neck.

His tongue trails up across a fresh bite. She shudders and moans, but he is looking at me. There's no shame or embarrassment in his face, but I can feel mine heating up.

My fingers tighten on the door as a wave of conflicting emotions crash through me. The first is anger. Then jealousy, which only makes me angrier. Then annoyance, and finally exhaustion. I don't want to deal with whatever this is. I'm not sure if he intended to taunt me, or if he just didn't expect me back so soon. He has to feed; I just expected him to do it anywhere but our room.

I take a step back and pull the door shut, then rub my hands over my face. Elise's room has a couch just like mine. Maybe she won't mind if I sleep on it.

I'm barely three steps from the door when it opens again and Reilly shoos the girl out. I keep walking without looking back. His footsteps get louder instead of quieter though, and I can hear his heartbeat speeding up.

"Olivia, where are you going?" he asks as he wraps his hand around my arm.

"Just finding somewhere to sleep," I say, attempting to tug my arm out of his grip.

"Then come back to the room."

"No, you have company," I say, swaying on my feet slightly.

He frowns at me, eyes scanning my face.

"She's gone, and you're exhausted. Come back to the room."

I sigh deeply and run a hand down my face.

"Don't do that again," I say quietly.

"Do what?" he asks.

"Bring your dinner back to the hotel," I say sharply.

"Why does it bother you?"

"It's just gross. You could have at least put a sock on the door. That's common courtesy."

He smirks. "Were you jealous?"

"No," I say, looking up at him in alarm. "No. Absolutely not."

His smirk widens into a smile, and he presses his hand into my lower back.

"Come get some sleep. It won't happen again."

His heartbeat stays steady. He means it.

## 11

I haven't been awake at noon in well over a week. It's painfully sunny, and the roads are much busier than they are at night. I yawn and squint as I stare out the window. We've driven about twenty minutes north of the city.

Everything immediately around us is flat, including the shrubs and cactus. Nothing seems capable of growing higher than my knee. The mountains on the horizon look like crumbling mounds of dirt. They aren't regal like the mountains I've always seen in pictures with snow on their peaks and trees climbing up the base. Even the sky seems flat here. There are no clouds, just a washed out blue that fades into white at the horizon.

We round a turn, and the first body of water I've seen since we arrived in Nevada appears. It's bordered by dull green grass that's swaying stiffly in the breeze. We've somehow gotten into the hills I had seen in the distance without me realizing it. The river blinks in and out of view between them as we drive.

Elise slows down, then turns left and drives over a small bridge that crosses the river. The pavement doesn't last long, and the car bumps along a gravel road that is mostly designated by the high fence that springs up along either side of us. A mile away from the main highway, we arrive at the main gate.

On each side of the wrought iron gate are pillars of white stone stacked as high as the fence. In front of each pillar is a statue of a wolf. The one on the left is sitting, staring straight ahead. The expression on its face is creepily life-like. The one on the right is howling, its head thrown back and its eyes shut.

Elise comes to a stop in front of the gate and presses a buzzer. Immediately, the gates swing outward. We drive in slowly, but I can't help glancing back at the wolf on the left after we pass through. I almost expect it to have turned around to watch us somehow.

The road winds through more low hills for a quarter of a mile before it opens up to about twenty acres of flat land, neat lawns, and cookie cutter houses. The road we're on goes down the center of the subdivision. At the end of it is a huge stone house that looks like a castle. A watchtower extends up from the middle of the structure. I wonder if the architect didn't realize how phallic it looked, or if that was the point.

Elise pulls over to the side of the street just before the first house and parks the car. There is a man sitting in a rocking chair on the porch. His hands are folded in his lap like he's relaxed, but I can see the coiled tension in his body. He pushes the chair back and forth in a steady rhythm as he watches us. There is no one else to be seen, but I'm sure they're hiding somewhere.

Elise opens her door, and we both climb out of the car. The man stands up and walks down the front steps, coming to a stop at the edge of the yard. His shoulders are wide, and the muscles in his arms are straining against the fabric of his sleeves, but he walks with an easy grace you don't expect of a bigger man.

I tuck my hands into my pockets and wait for Elise to approach before I walk after her. She stops a few yards from the man, who I assume is the alpha of this pack, and pulls out her badge.

I pull on the vampire magic as well as I can in the middle of the day. It's sluggish, but it does respond. The fact that I can't see anyone else makes me nervous. I don't think this is an ambush, but I'd like to be able to hear and smell everything I can.

There are three more heartbeats in the house behind the pack leader. The scent of werewolf is overwhelmingly strong, like they've marked the place. I can't smell anything else, and I'm regretting being able to smell that at all.

"Pack Leader Miller, I spoke with your secretary yesterday evening about meeting with you. My name is Elise Hawking. I'm an agent with JHAPI."

The man purses his lips and nods. "Yes, you are here to investigate the NWR. I can assure you we aren't harboring any of them."

Elise laughs and puts away her badge. "That's good to know. However, that's not what brought me here today."

"Who is this with you?" Miller asks, looking past her at me.

Elise looks back as well and waves me forward. I come to stand beside her.

"This is Olivia Carter. She is working with JHAPI at the request of the council," Elise says, carefully leaving off *vampire* council, probably hoping he'll assume I'm a witch based on my scent.

Miller looks at me for a long moment, inhaling

deeply, then turns back to Elise. "What does bring you here today, if not searching for NWR members on my lands?"

"Missing persons," Elise says.

Miller doesn't seem surprised, or concerned, at her proclamation. "No one is missing."

Lie.

Elise tilts her head. "Five vampires have gone missing. All from different clans, all high flight risks. The only reason anyone noticed is that the clans all reported them missing, and the council noticed the trend. Is it possible that's happening with the local packs?"

Miller shakes his head. "There are only two packs around here. It would be noticed by us."

Not a lie.

"Noticed, but not necessarily reported?" Elise prods.

"My pack will always do its duty to the council," Miller says, his tone going hard.

Not a lie. I hear movement inside the house and glance at the window. The curtain is swaying slightly, like someone just moved it.

Elise pulls her card out of her pocket. "If you do hear or see anything suspicious, please call me. I'd also recommend caution over the next couple of weeks. We're not sure what the NWR is planning, but there has been increased activity in the area."

Miller steps forward and takes the card from Elise, shoving it in his pocket. I'm sure it will be thrown away as soon as we leave.

"Thank you for your time. I hope to hear from you soon," Elise says. She turns and walks straight back to the car, but I take a few steps backward first. I don't want to turn my back on Miller. I don't think he would attack me, not really, but the primal part of my brain recognizes that he's a serious threat.

Miller turns and walks back inside before I even get back to the car. I slip in and slam the door shut.

"He was lying," I say, glaring at the curtain that is swaying again.

"Yes, he was," Elise says, her nostrils flaring in irritation. "He knew we could both tell, and he lied to our faces."

"Why would they do that?" I ask.

"They're telling us to back off. That it's a pack issue and they don't want our dirty, JHAPI help." Elise throws the car into drive and whips the car around. "Stupid, overly traditional, dumb assholes."

"It shouldn't surprise me. I could see a coven doing the same thing," I say with a sigh.

Elise rubs her hands roughly over her mouth. "I get their hesitation, it just frustrates me. JHAPI has done really good work over the last five years, but we could have done so much more if the paranormal community actually trusted us."

"Do you think there's any chance he'll call?" I ask.

Elise shakes her head. "Not really. I just have to try."

The gate opens, and Elise pulls onto the highway.

"That whole thing where everyone was watching us, but no one else was outside was creepy as hell. Just for the record," I say.

Elise laughs. "I guess it is. I've been on the other side before, which takes away a lot of the intimidation factor. I know they have all the kids in there, giggling and daring each other to peek out."

I smile. "That does make it less intimidating."

"You're training with Hu this afternoon, right?" she asks.

I nod. "Yeah, apparently sleep isn't necessary."

"Coffee is all you need," Elise says solemnly. "You'll come to accept that soon."

I shake my head. "Coffee can only help so much."

---

The gym is in the basement. There are way more fluorescent lights than necessary, filling the whole room with a harsh lighting. There is a rack of weights on the back wall, which is also lined with mirrors. To the right is an MMA style octagon cage, and to the left are five punching bags hung in a row. The floor is wooden, except for two matted areas by the cage and the bags.

Hu is at the punching bags, and he is frighteningly strong. He cuts across the front of the bag and throws a left hook punch. His fist connects with a deep, resounding smack that shakes the bag on the chain. He punches with the other hand, then slides backward with a quick jab. He's a fast and powerful striker. I hope he isn't expecting me to spar with him.

He's wearing a tight black tank that clings to the muscles in his back. I can see more of the tattoo that is always peeking out of his collar. My first impression that it is fire was wrong. It's the tip of a vibrant red and orange wing that disappears into his shirt. He circles around the bag, striking faster and faster, stopping only when he spots me.

"Hey, Olivia," he says, leaving the bag swinging and jogging toward me.

"Hey," I say, mustering a smile. He is helping me in his free time, so I'm going to try to be as pleasant as possible even if I have been forced to get up before the sun has set and I feel like shit.

"I'm glad we found time to do this today," Hu says. "Have you received any training at all for this magic? Or has it always been something you hid?"

"No training," I say uncomfortably.

"All right," he says. "Well, let's get started with this."

Hu jogs over to the corner and drags a training dummy over to the empty area between the punching bags and the door. It's the torso and head of a man, no arms, on a black stand. This sort of dummy is normally used for kicking practice. This particular one looks like it has seen better days. The head is lopsided, and there are random gouges and a stain that looks suspiciously like blood.

"This thing is getting thrown away after today," Hu says, rubbing his hands together. "So I was able to talk them into letting us use it for a little practice."

"What kind of practice, exactly?" I ask.

"I want you to show me an attack. Use your electric magic," Hu says as he walks over to stand beside me.

"Okay, so just..." I gesture at it and make an explosion noise.

"Keep it on the lighter side. I'd just like to see what you know." Hu steps back a few steps behind me and nods in encouragement.

I face the dummy, hands on my hips. I don't really know anything about how to use this type of magic, but I don't want to admit that just yet. The things I have done have been on instinct, and they were effective. Maybe I can do this.

I take a deep breath and let the electric magic buzz through me. The hair on my arms stands on end, and some of the hair on my head floats up like someone rubbed it with a balloon. I lift my hands, and a sparking ball of light and electricity hurtles from my palms toward the dummy.

It hits it with a flash and a sound like thunder that makes me flinch. The center of the dummy is melted and twisted, and the lopsided head is now hanging off the side, connected by one lumpy strip.

I clear my throat and smooth down the flyaway hairs that are still floating around me. I feel staticky. With one final breath, I turn around to face Hu.

He has his chin in his hand, and he is staring at the smoldering remains of the practice dummy. He starts to say something, then shakes his head.

"What?" I ask, crossing my arms and looking back at it self-consciously.

"That was very—powerful," he says haltingly. "I'm glad you didn't actually follow through on your threat to Cook in the meeting room the other day. I'd have ended up scorched too."

I smirk at the mental image of Cook looking like the practice dummy. It's harder to be smug without a head. Or a chest.

"As great as that sounds, I wouldn't have done all that to him," I say, waving a hand at it dismissively.

"Are you sure about that?" Hu asks.

I shrug. "Yes?"

"Show me a light attack," he says, waving at the dummy and stepping back a couple of paces.

I frown. He's being dramatic. I can do a light attack. I just didn't understand how light he wanted that last one to be. It's probably easier than putting all my power into it anyhow.

I lift my hands again and pool the magic in my palms. The electricity streaks across the space, a bolt this time, and slams into the dummy, knocking it backward and splitting the base in half. I drop my hands and swallow uncomfortably.

"OK, so I might have a problem with controlling this," I say as I look down at my still tingling fingers.

"Yes," Hu says, striding toward the wall and grabbing a fire extinguisher. He sprays down the dummy but keeps the extinguisher as he walks over to me. "Let's start with something a lot more basic."

I rub my hands against my sweats and nod in agreement. "Right. Basic."

"When using offensive magic, you have two options. A big, powerful attack," he says, gesturing at the dummy. "Or a precise, focused attack that uses less magic and requires less strength."

He lifts his right arm, and fire snakes down it, leaps from his fingers and cracks in the air right in front of my face like a whip. I stumble backward even though I'm a breath too late to avoid it.

"Way to give me a heart attack," I mutter.

Hu laughs. "Sorry, just thought a demonstration would be more impactful."

"Consider it successful."

He snaps his fingers, and a flame jumps up, then stretches out and curls around his hand in a spiral. He slowly builds the size of the flame until I can feel the heat from where I'm standing.

"This was one of the first exercises my mom taught me," he explains, lifting his arm. "The point of it was to keep my magic small and contained, and going exactly where I want it. Electric magic is a little different in execution, but the same concept applies.

What I want you to do is take that wild energy you normally throw at people and contain it in your hand."

"That's it? Just keep a little ball of electricity in my hand?" I ask, crossing my arms.

"That's it," he says with a shrug. "It's simple and something you can practice pretty much anywhere. Once you master that, we'll talk about the next step."

"Okay." I sit down on the floor and cross my legs. Hu comes and sits across from me, keeping the extinguisher within reach.

When I'm brewing, the magic isn't trying to escape or control me like the electric magic does. It's just part of me. I don't remember struggling against it even as a child. Even the healing magic was never this hard to control. I did have to learn quickly not use too much of it, but it was gentle. I always thought of it as a faucet. I could turn the flow up or down, but it wasn't much more complicated than that.

Controlling this magic is like holding a pit bull on a leash. Once I pull on it, it starts pulling on me. It was especially difficult to control at the beginning whenever I got angry. Hell, it's still hard to keep under wraps when I get angry.

"Does your magic respond to your emotions?" I ask, staring at my hands. "I feel like it's always trying to escape when I get angry or frustrated."

"Yes," Hu says with a nod. "When I was younger, it was difficult. However, I had been meditating from a young age, and I knew what to expect. Fire witches are known for their tempers, and some of us use that as an excuse. My mother didn't believe in accepting weakness like that."

"So it is possible to control it?" I ask.

"Yes."

I nod and take a deep breath. If it's just a matter of

being more stubborn than the magic, then I've got this. There's no way I'm going to let the magic I stole control me.

The crackling energy is still pounding in my chest, ready to be used. I tug on it, and the magic sparks along my fingertips. I stop thinking about an attack and simply wiggle my fingers, trying to coax the magic to the surface. A bright blue arc leaps up from my palm. I keep pulling on it, and another crackles across my fingers, then my wrist, then another from my thumb.

The magic is unruly, and asking me to contain something like that in the palm of my hand seems impossible. I grit my teeth and pull harder on the magic until my entire arm is crawling with visible electricity. I look like a Tesla coil. My hand starts to shake with the effort of holding back, then the electricity surges. My hair lifts all at once, and the magic that has been crawling up my arm surges and a bolt shoots toward the floor, scorching it.

Hu is spraying the area before I have a chance to blink, and I cough as the cold fog blows up into my face. I let the magic go and scramble backward.

"I see this is going well," Reilly says from behind us.

I stand up and turn around, still dusting the chalky powder off my side. Reilly is wearing a loose-fitting black tank and dark gray sweatpants. I've never seen him dressed down like this before. He almost looks like a normal person. Except for the drool-worthy muscles, that's something you don't see every day.

"It was a good start, actually. If she had gotten it perfectly on her first try, I would have been a little annoyed that it was that easy for her," Hu says with a chuckle.

"I wouldn't have minded," I say, staring at the mess on the floor, and then the mutilated dummy.

Hu shrugs. "Oh, Elise wanted me to invite you out tonight. We're headed to some club on the Strip around eleven."

"She'll kill me if I don't go, won't she?" I ask.

Hu grins. "She wouldn't kill you, but she might kidnap you. She's aggressive about her friends enjoying themselves."

It occurs to me that while a club isn't necessarily my scene, there will be tequila there. I plaster on a smile.

"I'll come. It'll be a nice break."

"Awesome," Hu says.

"And I can clean up all this," I say, gesturing at the mess from the fire extinguisher.

"That's good because I'm actually running late. Ivy is expecting me in a half-hour to go visit another local coven, and I still need to shower. I'll see you tonight." Hu leaves with a wave.

I turn to Reilly, who is staring at the dummy with a grin on his face.

"Anger issues?" he asks.

I roll my eyes. "Can we just move on to the part where you show me how to not exhaust myself and skip the small talk?"

"Your wish is my command," Reilly says with a mock bow.

The electric magic tingles at the edges of my fingertips. It would be so easy just to lose control and throw everything I have at him. The only thing stopping me is knowing he could probably dodge the attack. He's unreasonably fast. Faster than anyone else I've seen.

"You move insanely fast," I say, trying to nudge him to get to the point. "How do you do that?"

"Well, the strength and speed of a vampire are based on two things," Reilly says, rolling his head in a circle as he stretches his arms out in front of him. "Their sire and age."

"Why the sire?" I ask.

"Strength begets strength. The original clans all have different advantages they are known for. Tenebris is known for our speed. Familia de Sangre are known for their strength. Ānjìng De Sĭwán seem almost immune to the sun; even their younger vampires can wake during the day."

"So your sire's strengths are passed down to you?" I ask.

Reilly nods. "And sometimes their weaknesses. The most effective sires have the best control as well."

I wonder if my sire would be my father, or if it would be Javier. Or now that I've fed from Damien and Reilly if I've somehow taken on their talents and weaknesses as well.

"That explains that half. I've always known that older vampires are stronger, but not why. Witches don't gain actual power as they age, skill maybe, but everyone seems to just have the power they were born with, and nothing more," I say.

"The magic that keeps us alive is different. I remember what it felt like when I was first changed," Reilly says, looking off into the distance. "Every day, with every feeding, I could feel it growing. The potential seems endless sometimes. That's part of the hunger as well; you can feel it making you stronger, and that's addictive all on its own."

I press my hand to my stomach. I can understand that. Sometimes, when I was younger, I thought about all the magic I could steal. I wondered if it could make me invincible.

"So if you drained a hundred neckers, would you become crazy powerful?" I ask.

"No." Reilly shakes his head. "There are limits to the speed at which the magic can develop. I can always feel the point at which I'm tipping over from feeding the magic to simply glutting myself. Some can't, and their lack of control always causes problems eventually."

"This is great and all, but how is this supposed to help me not overuse my magic?" I ask, shifting from foot to foot. I've never had much patience for history lessons or lectures. No one ever just gets to the point.

"The less magic you have, the more sparingly you have to use it. If you dump every ounce of your strength into one punch, then you will have nothing left to dodge their counterattack." Reilly moves without warning. My eyes are barely able to follow he is moving so quickly.

I whirl around, but he's already standing right behind me.

"When I put on a burst of speed, in that brief moment I am engaging my strength, or magic if you want to call it that. Standing here now, though, I'm not still pulling on it."

"So it's about little flashes of magic, and not one constant stream of it?" I ask.

"Yes."

"That's not that complicated. I can do that," I say, squaring off with him.

Reilly grins. "It is simple. It is not easy."

"None of this is easy," I say, raising a brow at him. "I just got done trying to make a lightning bolt fit in the palm of my hand."

"That was amusing to watch," Reilly grins, dimples taunting me.

I yank on the magic inside of me and lunge to the

left, hoping to get around behind him this time. He matches my movement though, and he is faster. I skid to a stop, then trip over the mat as it bunches up from the force of my momentum. I fly a couple of feet before hitting the ground just outside of the matted area with a grunt. Pain shoots through my elbow, and I roll onto my back.

Reilly is laughing unreservedly. There are actual tears of mirth leaking out of his eyes. I push up to a seated position and try to not look like I'm horribly embarrassed. My cheeks are hot though. It irritates me that there's nothing a person can do to stop blushing. It's the ultimate betrayal by your body.

Reilly finally manages to take a breath without laughing and wipes his eyes. "That was a very dramatic start."

"Whatever," I mutter, glaring at the floor.

"You had the right idea," Reilly says, still grinning. "Stopping gracefully is a learned skill."

"Obviously," I say, standing up and just managing not to wince.

"Think of it more like one big step, rather than running," Reilly suggests. "Try it again."

I shake my arms out, irritated by the bruise on my elbow. Using the magic was easy enough, apparently, the struggle will be keeping my body under control. I don't remember having this issue during the raid. I had just moved on instinct without worrying about showing off.

I take a deep breath and dart across the room, ignoring Reilly, ignoring everything but the feeling of movement. I pull back on the magic right before sliding to a stop this time, and my feet glide smoothly across the mat without bunching it. Without pausing, I repeat the movement and stop right in front of Reilly.

I'm a little closer than I intended, but he doesn't flinch.

"Much better," he says.

I can feel his breath on my face. I take a step back to put some space between us.

"I can see how that would quickly be tiring," I say. I'm not exhausted from those two bursts, but I'm not sure how many I could do. The training I did with Hu and using the vampire magic just then, it's all taking its toll.

"You seem to be understanding the basics," Reilly says, circling around me. I turn with him, not wanting him behind me again. "Let's play tag."

"What?"

He darts away, his shoulder brushing against mine and knocking me off balance as he flies past.

"You're it!" he shouts from across the room.

"What are we, five?" I shout back. I run at him though; I'll be damned if I'm going to make this easy on him.

Reilly moves like he was born for this. He doesn't just run in straight lines. He seems to be able to change directions, no matter how fast he's moving like a damn gazelle. I have to pause every few seconds to conserve my energy, but he doesn't seem to tire. Every time I get close, I realize it's a feint and he twists away and ends up behind me.

Again and again, I just miss him. I'm starting to feel the strain now. If I don't finish this soon, I'll have just chased him around the room for fifteen minutes with nothing to show for it. I charge at him again, and he slips to the left.

Gritting my teeth, I lift my foot to go forward, like I have been, then launch myself blindly backward with the foot still on the ground. My back hits Reilly, and I have a moment of triumph until his arm wraps around my throat. I tuck my chin just in time to keep him from locking the choke in and twist around to jerk my head out of his grip.

We're facing each other now, and he ducks down and pushes forward, his shoulder in my stomach, and wraps his hands around the backs of my knees. He pulls his hands sharply toward him, and since I'm already tipping to the left, my right foot is jerked off the floor and I'm airborne once again.

I hit the ground hard, and Reilly pushes in-between my legs while I'm struggling to catch my breath. I have just enough experience wrestling to know I am terrible at it. I fall back on the only thing that has ever marginally worked. I flail wildly.

My elbow catches his jaw, and I get a foot in the crease of his hip. He seems to be trying to crush me under his weight, and if I couldn't pull on the vampire strength, he would. I grit my teeth and push with my feet and my hands, anywhere I can get leverage, until I'm almost lifting him off me.

Reilly shifts and spins around to my side. His arms move fast and, no matter what I do, it seems to help him. He works his way around to my back, and this time I can't tuck my chin quite well enough. He slowly but surely forces my head backward, and his arm wraps completely around my neck. The hard edge of his forearm chokes me against his bicep, which is unfairly just as solid. I struggle for a moment longer, but vampire magic or no, I need to breathe. I slap at his arm, and he drops me immediately.

I flop onto my stomach, panting. He stays glued to my back for a moment, his hand resting on my waist. My shirt has ridden up from all the wrestling. Two of his fingers brush against my skin in a momentary caress that makes me shudder before he rolls away and lays flat on the floor.

I roll over onto my back as well. I dislike not being able to see where he is and what he's doing. Even less so after he's almost choked me out.

"Where did you learn to fight?" he asks.

"The school of hard knocks," I say, wiping sweat away from my eye with the back of my hand and sitting up. "And the MMA gym Zachary's dad enrolled both of us in after he took me in."

"They didn't teach you very well."

I glare at Reilly, and he grins back, both dimples showing.

"It's been over five years, and I wasn't really interested at the time," I say I as get up to my feet in a huff. I walk over to the bench my water bottle is sitting on and take a few long swallows. "Hell, I'm not interested now. I'm just trying not to die."

"If you master your magic, you won't have to spend as much time up close and personal like this," Reilly says.

"I know that," I say, rolling my eyes.

"Not that rolling around on the floor with you is a bad time," Reilly says from right behind me.

I jump and stumble forward.

"I am seriously going to put a bell on you," I say, trying to wipe away the water I splashed all over my neck. "Personal. Space. It's not that hard."

"I don't think you want personal space," Reilly says as he closes the distance between us again.

This close, it's impossible to look anywhere but directly at him. His cheeks are warm from the exercise. It makes him seem almost human. I don't think I've ever noticed how rich of a brown his eyes are. His hair is a mess, and the muscles in his shoulders are practically begging to be traced with my—

No. I take a step back and stop those thoughts in their tracks.

"Well, I do," I say, but my face is heating up again. "Want personal space."

"Did you forget I can hear a lie?" Reilly whispers, taking another step forward.

"You know what, here's a truth. I am not doing this with you," I say, looking him in the eye.

"You think that is true," he muses, smirking at me. "But last night, you were jealous."

I roll my eyes. "Don't flatter yourself; it wasn't about you."

"You should quit lying to yourself, at the very least," Reilly says before turning and walking away. I watch him go. I can't deny it's a good view.

I put my head in my hands. I'll be glad to get out for a little while tonight and get my mind off all of this crap. Maybe I can even find someone to invite me back to their hotel room, since I obviously can't bring anyone back to mine.

I groan and grab all my stuff. I need a shower. A cold one.

13

E lise answers the door in a tight blue dress that makes her eyes stand out even more. Her makeup is half-done though, so her left eye looks twice the size of her right eye.

"I didn't realize this was going to be a dress kind of place," I say, looking down at the jeans, red shirt, and tall black boots I had put on. I hadn't even packed any dresses.

Elise looks me up and down and purses her lips. "We're about the same size. I've got something that'll work."

She waves me inside and shuts and locks the door behind us, then jogs over to her suitcase. She digs around for a moment before pulling out a black dress.

"Here," she says, tossing it at me. "Try that on."

She walks back into the bathroom, and I strip down. The dress slides on easily, but it's a good thing I didn't have a big dinner. It has long sleeves, which thankfully cover the welts on my arms, but the hem doesn't even make it halfway down my thighs. There are three black mesh strips at the narrowest point of my waist, and another bigger one right where my

123

cleavage should be. The dress is tight enough that it helps push everything into a good position.

Elise pokes her head out of the bathroom. "God, I hate you."

"What?" I ask, confused.

"I think that looks better on you than it does on me," she says with a pout.

I laugh. "I really doubt that, but it does fit all right."

I smooth my fingers through my hair and pull my boots back on, then plop down in the chair in front of the desk. I spin around lazily, and my elbow bumps the files that are spread out on the desk. I catch it before it falls, but a picture that was tucked inside slips out and flutters down to the carpet.

I reach for it and pause halfway there. The bearded man. The memory of Reilly snapping his neck flashes through my mind. I pick it up and stare at it, then glance at the bathroom doorway. Elise is still in there, bemoaning the difficulty of keeping clothes from wrinkling in a suitcase.

Before I can hesitate anymore, I flip through the file. This guy, Demeter Yagislov, apparently, had ties to one of the most powerful covens in the US. Hell, he had ties to the council itself. I close his file and open a couple of others. There is one for each of the three witches who attacked the clanhouse, and a couple I don't even recognize. I didn't know JHAPI was still investigating the attack at the clanhouse.

The woman's words come back to me. She kept claiming I was born for a reason not even my mother had known, which was bullshit. The words unsettled me then though, and they still bother me. What do they know that I don't?

Elise comes out of the bathroom, but I don't bother hiding that I've been snooping.

"I didn't know you were still investigating those crazy ass cult members," I say as she stops in the center of the room.

"I'm not," she says, adjusting her dress. "Zachary is."

I look up, surprised. "What?"

She shrugs. "It's not official either, just his little pet project."

"Why would he do that?" I ask, confused, and a little worried. Does he suspect something?

"That's a good question, Olivia. I ask myself every day. Why do you think he might?" she asks, giving me a knowing look.

"No," I say, dropping the file back on the desk. "That was never a thing."

She laughs. "You're kidding, right?"

I just stare at her.

"Oh my god, so you really didn't know he had a whole thing for you?" she cackles, her eyes watering from laughing so hard.

"Cook said something like that too. Zachary did not have a thing for me. Why does everyone think that? He was like my brother," I say, crossing my arms.

"Dude," Elise says. "He literally told me about the girl he loved who ran away and could never be found when we first became partners. It was a whole thing about trust issues and why he doesn't date."

I open my mouth to refute what she's just said, but if he told her that, I can't exactly argue. I close my mouth and stand up and head toward the door instead. Maybe Zachary was just messing with her.

"This is great. Tonight is going to be so entertaining," Elise says as she follows me out the door.

She catches up when I stop to press the button for the elevator.

"I'm still not sure why we're doing this," I say, my tone grumpy. "Not that I'm going to turn down a chance to drink too much tequila."

"We're in Las Vegas," Elise says, doing jazz hands.

I give her a blank stare. The elevator doors slide open, and we step inside. We head down to the parking garage in silence. My mind is caught in a loop, trying to remember if there was ever some kind of spark between me and Zachary. It never felt like flirting to me; it just felt like family.

We climb in the car, and Elise turns to look at me. "Are you going to brood about what I said all night?"

"What? No. I'm not brooding," I say, crossing my arms.

"Right," she says, turning the car on.

I roll my eyes but can't help the guilty smile that spreads across my face. She laughs at me and pulls out of the parking spot.

We're only about ten minutes from the strip. The club has valet only parking, so we hand over the car keys to a young guy in a blue jacket and get in line.

The bouncers aren't picky. If you're over twenty-one and not wearing a tank top and flip flops, they wave you inside. After a small cover charge, of course.

The club is loud, which isn't surprising. Strobe lights flash around the DJ and stage, highlighting the mass of gyrating bodies. It smells like smoke and old alcohol. Elise grabs my hands and pulls me deeper into the crowd around the bar.

"I think I see them," she shouts over her shoulder.

Hu and Corinne are standing near a table with four chairs. Not enough for everyone, but we're lucky they managed to snag a table at all. Corinne is wearing a tight little black dress that looks great on her. She looks much younger out of the suit.

"What do you want to drink?" Elise asks me.

"Tequila," I say without hesitation. "So much tequila."

She laughs. "You got it."

Elise pushes back toward the bar, leaving me alone with Hu and Corinne.

"Is anyone else coming?"

Hu shrugs, but Corinne nods.

"Zachary should be here shortly, he's riding with Cook. Is Reilly coming tonight?" she asks.

"I have no idea, to be honest." I shrug. I hope he doesn't. It'd be nice to have one night to loosen up and forget about all my adult problems.

We pass a few minutes in silence. It's not worth trying to make much conversation with the volume of music. Elise pushes her way back to the table with eight shots and a pile of limes balanced on a tray.

"Time to get this night started," she says with a grin as she sets it on the table.

I lick my hand and sprinkle the salt on liberally, then glance around the table to see if everyone else is ready. We all lift our shots and clink them together. I knock back the shot and bite down on the lime in a fluid motion. It burns just right. I grab the second shot of tequila and throw it back without waiting for the others. It's time to dance.

I push into the crush of the crowd. The bass is pounding, and I can feel each thump all the way down to my bones. There's not enough room on the dance floor to move without touching someone, so I give in to the flow and stop worrying about it. The energy is high. Everyone has a smile on their face. No one is worried about who they're dancing with. Hands are roaming, people are kissing and grinding against each other.

A hand slides across my lower back, and I glance

over my shoulder and see a man with a generically handsome face and dark brown eyes. I move into his touch, and he slips his hand around to my stomach, pulling me in close. The music speeds up, and we move together. Everything floats away as the tequila courses through me and the thrill of dancing erases all the worries that have been bouncing around my brain for weeks.

The guy spins me around and holds me chest to chest against him. His eyes stray to my lips, and I smile in invitation. His hands slide up into my hair, and he leans in, pressing his forehead to mine. The connection isn't electric, but it's enough to have warmth curling through my stomach. It's enough for a Saturday night in Vegas.

His lips press into mine. Our lips part, and the hot slide of his tongue against mine was exactly what I needed. The kiss deepens until we're not even attempting to dance anymore. We're just making out underneath the flashing lights in the midst of a crowd.

His fingers twist in my hair, and I gasp into his mouth. He breaks the kiss and leans in closer to talk into my ear.

"Want to get a drink?" he asks. Even this close, I can barely hear him over the music.

"Sure," I shout back.

He wraps our hands together and leads me toward the bar. He's able to slip into a gap and pulls me up in front of him, leaning into my back.

"What's your poison?" he asks. It's slightly quieter over here, so he doesn't have to shout.

"Tequila, always," I say, leaning my head back to smile up at him.

He gets the bartender's attention and orders two shots.

"What's your name?" he asks.

"Olivia, what's yours?"

"David. What brings you to Vegas?"

"What brings anyone to Vegas?" I ask with a laugh.

"Fair enough."

The bartender slides our shots across the bar. David hands me mine and holds my gaze as we throw them back.

I feel a hand on my elbow and look back to see Elise grinning at me.

"I see you've made a friend," she says.

"Elise, this is David. David, this is Elise," I say.

"Nice to meet you, Elise," David says, extending his hand. Elise shakes it with a smile.

"Oooh, you even found one with manners," she says, nudging me with her elbow. "Everybody is here now. Did you want to come say hi?"

"Umm, sure," I say hesitantly. I really just want to dance more. The kissing was nice too. "We can come over for a quick drink. If that's all right with you, David?"

David nods without hesitation, one arm still snug around my waist. It takes a couple of minutes, but we each get a vodka soda, then follow Elise back to the table.

Austin is leaning against Corinne's chair, laughing about something with her. Zachary is standing off to the side, nursing a beer and scanning the room like he suspects something fishy is going on.

Corinne spots David behind me and interrupts Austin.

"Who is this?" she asks with a big grin. Her eyes are a little glassy, and I suspect she's had quite a few drinks while I was dancing.

"David, this is everyone. Everyone, this is David," I

shout over the music. Most of the group nod in greeting. Austin just stares at David for a moment before looking at me like I'm dirt. His eyes linger for a moment on the neckline of my dress, then he scoffs and turns to Zachary, who is still looking over the crowd intently. I sip my drink and let David snake his arm around my waist again.

There is an awkward tension in the group. I take another drink. I want to finish this and get back to dancing. I didn't come here to stand around. Hu and Corinne seem to be in a good mood, at least. He's had a smile all night, and so has she. I don't think I've ever seen Corinne in a bad mood though.

I finish my drink and set it on the table with the other empty glasses. The table is a bit crowded now.

"Are you done with your drink?" Corinne asks, reaching across the table to grab my hands.

"I am," I say with a smile.

"Let's dance, then!" she exclaims, dragging me forward.

"Ok, hold on." I laugh as I tug my hands away. David follows me around the table, and I let Corinne grab my hands again and lead us to the dance floor.

She bounces, flipping her hair from side to side as a new song comes on. I dance with her, David a constant pressure against my back. We slowly push farther and farther into the crowd.

Someone I don't quite see spins Corinne around, and David takes that moment to turn me as well, capturing my mouth in a kiss. I kiss back, but it doesn't have the same heat as it did earlier.

I pull away. Corinne is laughing next to me, her arms linked around the neck of a girl with blonde hair and full lips. I spin around in David's arms. My lips are starting to feel bruised, and I've either had too much to drink, or he's making me nauseous. I shut my eyes and try to lose myself in the music again.

Someone slides into place in front of me. They're close enough that their legs brush against mine. A hot finger traces the line of mesh along my waist, just above David's arm. The touch makes my stomach clench and my skin heat.

I look up and find dark brown eyes and dimples staring back at me. I grit my teeth. Reilly looks smug, like he thinks he's won something. The room is spinning though, and I don't care what he thinks. I came here to dance, and to forget. He doesn't get to rile me up today.

I lean back into David's chest and grind against him, keeping my eyes locked on Reilly's. The dimples fade, and he clenches his jaw tightly. He steps in closer until I'm sandwiched between the two men. His hands find their way to my waist, and his fingers press into my skin, like he's trying hold onto me. His thumb traces the curve of my ribs.

David tries to tug me away and step backward, but I'm leaning toward Reilly. One hand leaves my waist and comes up to rest on the side of my neck.

David says something behind me, then scoffs when I don't respond. He shoves me forward and disappears back into the crowd. Reilly doesn't let me scoot back away; he holds my hips tight to his as we continue dancing. The music fades into the background. I wrap my hands around his neck. His heart is pounding just as fast as mine.

He leans in, his head just inches from mine. It's just like that moment on the porch. I hate him, but I can't ignore him. I can't ignore the heat spreading through my body either, but it doesn't have to make me weak. I lean in until I see in his eyes that he's sure I'm going to kiss him, then slide past him and push my way through the crush of bodies to get off the dance floor.

Elise isn't at the table anymore, so I turn in a circle, searching for her. Reilly didn't follow me, thank god. I head toward the back of the club and the neon sign that says 'restroom'. The bathroom isn't completely empty, but there at least isn't a line.

One girl is swaying in front of a sink washing her hands. I step up to the other sink and turn on the cold water, scooping up a handful and splashing it on my face and neck. The contrast between my hot cheeks and the cold water is exactly the slap in the face I needed.

The girl teeters out of the bathroom, slamming the door shut behind her. It sounds like she falls back against it before stumbling away. I look up in the mirror and freeze. My mother is standing behind me, finger pressed to her lips just like she had done during the raid.

She looks younger than I remember her being when she left, but I suppose all children think their parents are old. I can't take my eyes off her even though I want to look behind me to see if she's really there.

"What do you want?" I whisper. No matter what Corinne says, it feels like this is her ghost. Like she's haunting me.

My mother holds up a tattered, brown book. As she holds it out toward me, cuts and bruises begin appearing all over her body. Her mouth opens in a silent scream, and tears prick at my eyes as my fingers dig into the porcelain sink. I don't want to watch this, but I can't turn away. The book begins crumbling in her fingers. The pieces are carried away like ash on the wind. She reaches for me, and I turn around, almost expecting her to be standing there, but she's gone. The tingle of magic skates along my arms and pain shoots through the welts as I slide down the wall. I bury my face in my knees and wait for it to pass.

I don't know how to stop this. It's hard to want to, even as horrible as it is. It still feels like I might be able to find something, even if I can't find her.

## 14

The electric magic dances across my palm. I can't get it to take on any sort of shape, but I have kept it contained in my hand this time. I close my fingers around it, snuffing it out and glance at my phone. It's two hours until sunset. Reilly is dead asleep in his bed, and I know I won't have many more chances to do this.

I text Zachary to let him know I'm headed over to talk to him. Elise is doing something with Stocke, and odds are Zachary is already awake. I almost brought it up last night when Zachary drove me back to the hotel, but I couldn't get Reilly's face out of my head, and I knew I was too drunk to ask the right questions.

I crawl out of bed and tuck my room key into my pants, then slip out of the room. I'll figure out what to tell Reilly about what I was doing later. I hurry to Zachary and Elise's room and knock twice.

He opens the door and steps back to let me in.

"Is everything all right? Your text sounded kind of urgent."

"Yeah, it's fine. There's just something I need to talk to you about," I say, fidgeting with the bottom of my sleeve. "You've been looking into the cult. The one that attacked the clanhouse."

"Elise told you?" Zachary asks, irritation flashing across his face.

"I saw the files in your room and asked her if she was looking into it. She said you were."

"All right, I have been. Someone needed to," Zachary says.

"I agree. Have you found out much about them? Do you know who they are?"

Zachary sits down and flips open one of the files in question. "They're interesting. They've been around longer than most covens, and they have ties to the witch council. Did you already know that?"

"Nope. I don't know anything about them, unfortunately."

He looks at me like he's looking for the lie. "Why'd you bring this up, then?"

I roll my eyes. "Because I want to know who they are and why they targeted me. Those assholes blew up my future. They ran off Maybelle. And they tried to kill Patrick."

"Is that why you agreed to help the vampires? Because you didn't have any other choice?"

"Well, it certainly wasn't out of the goodness of my heart," I say, sarcasm dripping from my voice.

"Is he forcing you to do this somehow?" Zachary asks, leaning forward. The irritation on his face from earlier has shifted to concern.

I shake my head. "Why are you acting so concerned?"

He throws his hands in the air. "Because I care about you! I shouldn't. I should hate you, but I can't. I still worry."

"Save it for someone who needs it," I say softly. His father always had a big heart for anyone he thought might need help. It's not surprising Zachary has that as well. "I'm fine, and I can take care of myself."

"You don't always have to," he sighs.

"Can you tell me what you know, or not?" I ask.

Zachary runs his hand over his head roughly, then sits up straight and pulls one of the files closer and flips it open.

"Demeter Yagislov, Brittany Gable, and Benjamin Gable were the three witches who attacked the clanhouse. We've been calling them a cult, but that isn't really right. They're more like religious fanatics, but instead of worshipping a particular god, they believe they are in charge of killing one." He pulls a picture out of the file. An old woman with snow-white hair in a bun on top of her head stares out at us with a stern expression on her face that reminds me of a disapproving teacher. She is dressed in black robes like an old school witch. "This is the woman we have tentatively identified as their current leader."

"They want to kill a god?" I ask, confused. As far as I know, there's no such thing.

Zachary nods. "The few texts we have been able to associate with them speak of the Bound God and a prophecy of some kind that centers around the Day of Breaking. It appears they are looking for the key to the prophecy so they can kill this Bound God once and for all, and prevent the apocalypse. They've been keeping him trapped for something like two-thousand years, but it looks like he might break free soon."

The woman who had been at the hospital, and the clanhouse, had kept insisting I was special. Perhaps they wanted to recruit me to fight this alleged god.

I twist my hands together. Zachary doesn't have

all the information about what they were looking for, and why they went after Maybelle.

"I want to help you investigate this. There are some things you don't know yet, that are important, but I want you to promise you won't shut me out if I tell you," I say, staring at the floor.

"Dammit, Olivia, why didn't you tell me you had information sooner?" Zachary asks through gritted teeth. "I try to trust you, and every single time it turns out I shouldn't."

I look up at him and catch his gaze.

"Promise me, Zach. They killed my mother. I want to help you catch them, but I need to be part of it."

His eyes go wide, and he stares at me open-mouthed for a second. "They killed your mother? Why?"

"I'll explain all of that. Just—"

"All right, I promise," he interrupts, dropping his hands into his lap. "What the hell do you know?"

"Maybelle knew my mother." I hesitate, trying to decide how much to share. I'm not ready to tell him everything. The circumstances of my birth don't really make much of a difference anyhow. "Maybelle and my mother stole something from these people. Some kind of spellbook which they later sold. The coven questioned Maybelle about who she sold it to."

He's quiet for a moment, and I can see the wheels turning in his head. He saw Maybelle after she had been rescued. He knows what they did to her.

"They killed your mother when they tried to question her?" Zachary asks.

I nod, grateful I didn't have to say it out loud.

"Maybelle knew who I was, but I didn't know who she was until the day she was in the hospital. She told me everything then."

"Do you know why this spellbook is so important to them? Or what's in it?" Zachary asks, pulling the file toward him and taking out a pen.

I shake my head. "I don't know why they want it so badly. Do you have any idea where they are? Or how many of them there are?"

Zachary taps his pen against the desk. "No one knows where their headquarters are, or if they have any. Do you think Maybelle might know?"

I shrug. "She stole something from them once, so I guess she knew where it was. Do you think they would have moved it after something like that?"

"Perhaps," he nods. "And as far as how many there are, I'm just not sure. We don't know what they do, just that they have influence with the witch council. I'm not sure how they've managed that either. I've wondered a few times if the fanaticism was just a front for something else, but the more I look into it, the more sincere they seem in their beliefs."

"Could you, I don't know, subpoena the witch council to give up information on them?" I ask.

Zachary chuckles. "That's not exactly how that works. Though, we might eventually be able to question the council. However, I haven't been able to get a proper investigation opened. It's being blocked."

"Blocked? By who?" I ask, immediately angry.

"I don't know, and neither does Stocke. She was furious when the refusal came down. JHAPI is supposed to be above those kinds of politics, but of course, it isn't."

"So you started your own, off the record, investigation?"

"Yes," he says with a nod. "The refusal was a huge red flag. There's obviously something big going on, and I want to know what it is."

"How far do you think you can get investigating this under the radar?"

"I hope far enough that I can make a case they can't ignore. I'm not sure what I'll do if they continue to try and bury this."

I rub my hands down my face. "I want to find Martinez, but I'd rather be spending my time tracking down these fanatics. I want the people who killed my mother dead."

Zachary looks at me with pity in his face, and I hate it. He always got that look when I talked about her, so I eventually stopped bringing it up. His father had understood better. He had always encouraged me to keep looking for my mother. I run my thumb across a welt, not that finding her turned out to be a good thing.

"This god they want to kill, do you know why they want to kill it? Normally people worship them," I say.

"It's a god of destruction. It hasn't been clear, but they believe he intends to destroy either magic itself, or all paranormals."

"I guess I can see why they'd want to kill him. If he even exists."

Zachary laughs. "And that's a big if. Nothing like that has ever been proven to exist before."

I sit down on the end of the bed. "There are the old stories that witch children all learn. The ancient demons, beings that were made of magic itself. Aris and Izul supposedly led a war against them."

"Aren't those stories debunked as myth? Like the dragons humans supposedly fought in the dark ages?"

I shrug. "No one really believes them anymore, but I know I wished they were true as a child. It all sounded so epic."

"I hope this one doesn't exist," Zachary says, shaking his head. "Especially since it seems like this coven might have trouble containing him this time around."

I tap my thumb against my thigh, an idea forming in my head. "Would it help if I tried to Find one of these people?"

"What?" Zachary asks, sitting up straight. "I thought you couldn't use that magic because of your injury?"

"I'll get better. I've already started working with Corinne. Just answer the question."

"Of course it would help. We couldn't question anyone in an official capacity, but if we end up in the same city, we could do some surveillance. Stocke might even help us. Off the record, of course."

I nod. "Then I'm going to figure out how to Find one of them. Whatever it takes."

Zachary furrows his brows together. "Do not do anything stupid trying to use magic that hurts you. That won't help either of us."

"I know that." I roll my eyes. "I'm not trying to martyr myself, I just need to know that we have a plan besides sit around and hope we figure out who they are."

"You just have a history of acting before thinking."

"I won't try to Find them until I know I can do it, all right?"

He nods once. "All right."

"And one last request, does Reilly already know you're doing this?" I ask.

Zachary shakes his head. "No one knows but Elise and Stocke."

"Let's keep it that way. I don't want him involved in this."

"Are you sure?" Zachary asks. "He could help. He has connections we don't."

"I'm sure," I say with a decisive nod.

"All right." Zachary leans back in his chair. He looks like he wants to ask more questions, but instead he taps his pen once on the desk and turns back to the file.

I pull out my phone and text Staci, pride be damned. I need to dull the pain in these welts so I can practice using my Finding magic again. I pause, my thumb hovering over the keys. I also need to figure out a way to let go of these hallucinations. I shake the thought away. One step at a time.

15

Staci manages to sound smug even over text. I roll my eyes and shove the phone back in my pocket. Zachary has the files spread all over the desk and both beds. I think I've memorized the faces of every person that might be connected to the coven.

"I need to go see Staci about getting more of this salve. I'll talk to you about this again next time I can get away. But text me if you find anything, all right?" I ask as I walk toward the door.

Zachary nods absently and waves me away. He's chewing on the end of his pen and not really paying attention. I'll have to text him later just in case.

My phone buzzes as I step into the hallway. Reilly's number is flashing on the screen. I sigh and answer it.

"What?" I ask.

"Where are you?" he asks.

"I'm still in the hotel, but I'm on my way to see Staci. I need more of the salve. She said she could brew it and give it to me this morning," I say. It's not a lie exactly. He doesn't need to know I've been somewhere else for two hours.

He's silent for a moment. "Where is she going to be brewing?"

"At the local JHAPI offices."

"I'll drive you over," he says.

"I can get a cab," I say, and it sounds whiny even to my ears.

"I'll meet you in the parking garage." He hangs up, and I slap my phone shut. That's the only thing I like about this old piece of crap. Hanging up is more satisfying when you can slam something.

I head toward the parking garage, muttering to myself the entire way about controlling vampires and bad life choices.

Reilly is leaning against his car when I get there. He's dressed impeccably. I can't help remembering the heat of his body pressed against mine the night before, and how close I came to being an idiot. The fact that I didn't helps me keep my spine straight as I walk up to him. He lets his eyes wander, and I ignore that too.

"You smell like Brunson," he says as I tug on the door handle, which is still locked.

"And?"

"So you saw him sometime recently," Reilly says, raising one brow. "Why?"

"He's my friend, I'll talk to him if I want to," I say, tugging on the door handle again for emphasis.

Reilly sighs, frustrated, but unlocks the car, and we climb in.

"I'm sure you know the annual council summit is in just over a week," Reilly says as he pulls out of the parking spot.

"Uh, sure," I say. "I don't really pay attention to that. I know it happens every year; it just doesn't really affect me." I shrug.

He stops the car and looks at me. "The council

summit is the single most important event of the year for every single paranormal. This summit is going to be even more important than normal. Do you have any idea what's going on?"

"No," I say, crossing my arms. "I'm not in a coven. I'll glance at the news to see if any laws change that affect the brews I can sell, but other than that, it just doesn't seem to matter."

Reilly shakes his head, exasperated. "The goblins are moving to create their own council."

"What? Seriously?" I ask, suddenly interested. When all the other paranormals came out of the closet, the goblins chose to stay underground. Everyone knows they exist, but they refused to integrate with humanity. They stay hidden, refuse legal protections, and refuse to submit to any laws protecting humans. It's been a huge source of tension for decades.

"It's going to shift the balance of power within the councils. For the most part, the weres side with the witches on votes," Reilly says. "No one knows who the goblins will side with, if anyone. The votes could end up split, and we don't have any way to resolve that."

"Are the witches going to try to stop them from joining?"

Reilly nods. "They have been. They want them to submit to one of the councils that are already in place. It's one of the things the council will be voting on this time. No one has any idea which way the weres will vote; they've been silent on the topic. Some people think they may be secretly trying to get the goblins to submit to them instead of the witches. Some think they don't want them to have a vote either."

"That's all crazy, but I'm not sure why you're bringing it up now?" I ask.

"We will be attending the Summit. I have to report to the vampire council the status of our attempts to eliminate the NWR."

I dig my nails into my palm. "Are you going to have to report my existence as well?"

"You will be coming to the Summit with me, as my guest. I will introduce you to my sire, of course. He has wanted to meet you for a while. The rest has not yet been decided since your evaluation is not complete."

I pull on my vampire magic and listen very carefully to Reilly's heart. He doesn't seem upset or excited.

"Is there a chance he's going to try to kill me or anything crazy like that?" I ask. I haven't thought about that in a while, the chance that someone might try to put me down. It makes my skin crawl.

"No," Reilly says. Not a lie. "You're more valuable alive."

I huff. Of course, he's still thinking of how I can be most useful. That's all that matters to him.

The rest of the drive to the JHAPI office is silent. I think over everything I found out from Zachary. To be honest, he has very little useful information. Names and faces are a start, but there is no meaningful information on what the coven *does*. With the number of magical items they seem to have access to, I'm starting to wonder if perhaps it's just a front. Maybe they're just the paranormal version of arms dealers. They seem to be rich enough.

I wish I had a way to contact Maybelle or Gerard. If she could just tell me where they stole the spellbook from, it would give me a starting point.

Reilly pulls up near the front door.

"I will be visiting another clan with Ivy this evening. Wait for me to pick you up."

"You've made it clear that you will literally kill everyone I care about if I try to run. I'm not planning on disappearing into the desert," I say through gritted teeth.

"I know you won't," Reilly says. "However, you are still a target for the NWR and the coven that attacked the clanhouse. I'm not risking something happening to you when it's simple enough to keep you protected."

Not a lie. I push my door open and climb out. I hadn't really considered that the coven might still be looking for me. I think about texting Zachary. Perhaps that's something we can take advantage of. I wouldn't mind being used as bait.

The JHAPI building is freezing cold today. They must have forgotten to switch from air conditioning to heat after the sun went down. The building is also mostly deserted since it's almost seven and most people went home two hours ago.

I wander the empty hallways, trying to make sense of Staci's directions. All she had said was that the brewing room was near the workout room on the second floor. There are no signs for either of those rooms.

I pass an office with an open door and stop. At first I think the agent is still in the office, but I realize it's the janitor.

"Hey," I say hesitantly.

He looks up and takes one headphone out of his ear. He's a middle-aged man with unruly grey hair and a round face.

"Do you know where the, uh, brewing room is? I'm supposed to meet Agent Young there, but I can't find it."

"Yes," he says with a thick Russian accent. He hurries to the door and points in the direction I just came from. "You go back. Left, then end of hall."

"Thanks, very much," I say, hurrying back in that direction. Sure enough, there is a room at the end of the hall. The only sign on the door simply says Room 102.

I shrug and open it without knocking. Staci looks up, startled, as I walk in. I guess she expected me to be lost for a while.

The smell of bleach and some other unfamiliar chemical assaults my nose, and I grimace. There's no lingering scent of herbs or smoke. The air isn't tinged with magic. It feels like a science laboratory, not a hedgewitch's workroom.

"Do they even use this room?" I ask, still standing with one hand holding open the door. It looks like a laboratory in here too. The walls are stark white with no decoration. The cabinets and countertops are all white as well with shiny silver handles. Glass beakers and flasks are arranged by size in neat rows on a metal shelf.

"Of course. They employ a couple of hedgewitches at this location," Staci says curtly as she lifts a thick book and lays it next to her cauldron. It's the only thing in the room that looks well-used. She turns the thick, stained pages slowly scanning each one for something. She's a quarter of the way through the book when she pauses, humming to herself, and taps next to a line of writing.

"What is that?" I ask.

She looks at me and adjusts her glasses on her nose.

"I thought you were a hedgewitch?" she says with a haughty sniff.

"I am, and no part of brewing requires a book, so..." I gesture at the book and shrug.

She snorts. "Of course you're one of those."

I lean back against the counter and cross my arms.

"One of what, exactly?"

She grabs a canister out of the cabinet.

"A sloppy brewer. No recipe, no consistency, unreliable."

I laugh aloud. "You have got to be kidding me."

She simply sniffs and continues scanning her recipe.

I stare at her, completely aghast. "You have to realize how much more powerful it is. Brewing with a recipe makes the magic stale and weak."

She scoffs and turns to face me.

"Hardly. It makes it controlled, and I'm sure it isn't as fun," she sneers, "but that isn't the point. I know exactly how each brew I give the agents will act. Exactly. How," she says, jabbing her finger against the counter to emphasize each word. "Whatever you do in your personal life may not matter very much, but JHAPI requires a little bit more of its witches."

"It sounds more like they require less," I snap back. "I know exactly how my brews will act too. And I can guarantee they'd be more powerful than yours."

She turns back to her cauldron. "Just keep telling yourself that."

"What is your problem with me, exactly?" I ask, pushing off the counter.

She pulls out a knife and begins roughly chopping some herbs. The pieces are too big; a potion like this needs a finer blend.

"You are a felon," she says as she cuts. "And that's just for the crime they managed to catch you committing."

I roll my eyes. "I was nineteen."

"You're an untested, untrustworthy civilian the team has to carry because of politics. Stocke didn't want you involved, but we had to accept you at the vampire council's insistence."

I bite the inside of my cheek before I reply. "So, you're going to be passive-aggressive every time we have to work together?"

"I'm going to be polite when I have to," she says as she scoops the herbs up and tosses them into the already hot cauldron. "But if you want to be an ass, I can be one right back."

Her hair is slightly frazzled from the heat, and her glasses are sliding down her nose again. She looks like an angry mouse, and I have to press my lips together to keep from laughing at her. I can't completely hide the smile though, and two spots of color form on her cheeks.

She turns back to the cauldron and stirs angrily.

"I'll bring you the salve when it's done. I don't need you in here monitoring my spell work."

I roll my eyes but don't argue about staying. I don't want to watch her massacre this brew any longer than I have to. It's going to be absolutely useless.

"Sure, I'll just wait out in the hall," I say with fake sweetness. "But definitely let me know if you get stuck with your little recipe and need some help."

There is a perfunctory knock on the door, and Ivy steps inside. I'm not surprised she's here so late. She struck me as the workaholic type. The expression on her face makes me pause.

"One of the missing vampires has turned up, but it's a disaster. We need to go now," she says.

Staci flips the burner off, and we both hurry out of the room after Ivy.

## 16

The van is already running, Cook behind the wheel, when Staci, Ivy, and myself run into the garage. The door slides open, revealing the rest of the team, minus Zachary. He must still be at the hotel.

We pile in, and Cook speeds away as the door shuts behind me. I'm thrown sideways into Hu's lap. He grunts, his hands tightening around my waist for a moment.

"Sorry," I say as I drag myself over to his other side.

"No worries, Cook is a crazy driver," Hu says with a grin.

Reilly mutters something I can't quite hear across the van from him. I narrow my eyes at him, but he's staring up at the front of the van now, ignoring me.

Stocke leans around from the front passenger seat.

"What we know is that one of the missing vampires, Ryan Johnson, was found a couple of hours ago at a bar known to be frequented by vampires by one of his clanmates. He was brought back to the clanhouse immediately, where they attempted to revive him." Stocke pauses and shakes her head slightly, her curls bouncing. "He immediately killed the human woman they had brought down to feed him. He also killed his clanmate, who was both older and stronger, but another was able to escape the room and lock him inside."

"Has he gone feral, or was this an intentional attack?" Ivy asks.

"That isn't clear. His sire, Lee Vaughan, believes something else is going on but won't say what. He requested help from JHAPI, which is unheard of."

Reilly scratches his chin and leans forward. "Who exactly did Ryan Johnson kill? It's possible Vaughan simply doubts his ability to put this vampire down."

Stocke presses her lips tightly together. "He killed the sire's second."

Reilly stares at her. "Vaughan's second is well over two-hundred years old. There is no way a youngling caught him off guard."

"So this kid somehow overpowered him?" Elise asks. "That would be like a freshly bitten were killing an alpha. That just doesn't happen."

"No, it doesn't," Reilly agrees.

"This is what we're here for. The clan leader wants the vampire put down, and under every law we have, he has the right to request that." Stocke pauses. "However, we have a chance to find out what happened to Ryan. He is the only person that knows who took him, if anyone, and where he has been all this time. If he was somehow made stronger, I want to know why and how."

"You want to capture him," Ivy says.

Stocke nods. "If we can."

"We will need the most powerful tranquilizer you can get your hands on," Reilly says. He glances at me, and I can see the gears turning in his mind. He's excited about this.

"It's already on its way," Stocke says.

"The Sleeping Beauty brew?" Staci asks, her face lighting up. I can't help it; I'm curious to see it as well. It's one of the most tightly regulated brews in existence.

"Yes," Stocke confirms. "They had a double dose on hand in Los Angeles. It will be here in an hour and a half."

"So, we have a vampire that was able to kill someone hundreds of years older. He's going to be insanely fast," I say, leaning around Hu to look at Stocke. "How exactly are we supposed to administer this brew? Ask him nicely to drink it?"

Stocke looks at Reilly.

"Are you serious?" I exclaim. I'm not even sure why I'm upset. I couldn't care less if Reilly gets killed, but it is ridiculous to expect him to go in after this thing by himself.

"I'll help him," Elise says, cracking her knuckles.

"No way," Cook objects from the front seat. "Even shifted, you aren't as fast as a vampire."

"I'm fast enough," Elise argues back. The front of the van descends into a debate over the speed and agility of werewolves versus vampires.

I lean back and cross my arms, staring at Reilly. He's staring right back at me. I pull on my vampire magic and hone in on the beat of his heart.

"I'm going in with you," I whisper. I know he'll hear it.

"You're not fast enough," Reilly back with a shake of his head.

"Like hell I'm not. The sun is down. I can do this."

Reilly stares at me for a moment longer, then smirks, his cheek dimpling.

"If you're that eager, I won't turn down your assistance. It'll be good to test your limits."

I roll my eyes. Every time I get the impulse to help or hate him less, he reminds me that he's an ass.

"Just remember, if you overdo it, you'll have to feed again, and it won't be from me," he warns.

I turn away. I'm probably not ready for this. I've only had one day to focus on training since all of this started, but life doesn't seem to want to wait for a convenient time to test me. I'll just have to deal with it if I do use too much magic.

Elise doesn't stop arguing in favor of werewolves for the rest of the drive. Cook objects the most, to the point that I start to suspect he is just worried about her. I hadn't really paid attention to their interactions before, but it's possible he has a crush on her. Based on her reaction, I think this is the wrong way to go about seducing her. She looks furious.

The van comes to an abrupt stop, and Cook rolls down the window, shouting at someone to come open the gate. He and Stocke talk to someone, showing their badges, and then we are moving again. We don't have to drive far before Cook stops the van again and throws it into park. Ivy slides open the door, and we all pour out.

The clan house is a mix of modern and rustic desert vibes. It's three stories tall with balconies jutting out in unexpected places. The roof is flat, and while there are dozens of windows, they are all blacked out from the inside. I can't tell with what, but it looks like it might be steel of some kind.

I follow Hu toward the front door. Reilly falls into step beside me.

"I can already hear him, can you?" he asks me quietly.

I try to focus my hearing past all the chatter around us, but it's hard to both tune out what's happening around me and listen harder.

"I think I hear someone screaming," I say hesitantly.

Reilly nods.

Two EMTs come out of the building, carrying a stretcher. Whoever is on the stretcher is in a body bag. The absence of their heartbeat between the other two is almost disorienting.

A man with long, white-blond hair stands in the doorway. He's wearing a neat gray suit that happens to be smeared with blood. He waits for us to approach with his hands folded in front of him. His eyes stray to Reilly, and he nods.

"Mr. Vaughan," Agent Stocke says, showing her badge briefly. "I am Agent Stocke, with JHAPI. Can you please tell us what you know?"

"Ryan has gone feral," he says in an even tone. Not a lie. At least he doesn't believe it is one.

"He killed your second. As far as I understand, that shouldn't be possible. Feral vampires are normally sloppier, not stronger," Stocke says, tucking her thumbs into her pockets.

Vaughan looks at her blankly. "Yet, it happened. You have my permission to put Ryan down. Do I need to sign anything, or is my verbal consent enough?"

Vaughan doesn't look like he cares at all. If Javier had been in a situation like this, he would have been fighting to keep his vampire alive. I don't understand how this guy can stand here so calmly and ask for Ryan's death.

"There are some forms we need you to sign," Stocke says, looking back at Staci, who trots back to the van, I assume to grab those forms. "However, we will be attempting to take Ryan alive."

The clan leader furrows his brows, the first moment of emotion I've seen from him. "Why?"

155

"We want to know where he has been. Our investigation has suggested he was kidnapped. I think it's odd that someone would kidnap a vampire, then drop them off at a local bar. Don't you?" Stocke asks, tilting her head to one side as she scans his face.

Vaughan smooths out his expression once again. "I don't presume to understand anything the NWR does."

"So you know it was the NWR that took him?" she prods.

He shakes his head once. "I simply assumed. I have never heard of anyone else kidnapping paranormals of any kind."

Stocke smiles. "I've never heard of them letting paranormals go. So I'm sure you can understand why this whole thing has piqued my curiosity. Ryan has answers, and I would like the chance to learn them."

"Whatever you think is best," Vaughan says, bowing slightly from the waist.

Staci jogs back up, forms in hand. Stocke flips through them, then takes them to Vaughan and points out each place he needs to sign.

---

I check the time again. There are still twenty minutes before the brew we need will be here. The entire clan has been sent out of the house. They are gathered in front of the small parking lot next to the garage, watching us.

Reilly appears out of nowhere from behind me and grabs my elbow.

"Come with me," he whispers.

I hurry after him as he heads inside through the front door. I glance back at Agent Stocke and the others, but they aren't paying attention.

It's dark inside the house, but my eyes adjust quickly. Reilly is turning down a hallway just past the winding staircase that dominates the entryway. I stop staring and run to catch up. I don't have to go far though; I almost run into Reilly as soon as I round the corner.

Vaughan looks at me and narrows his eyes. "I asked to speak with you alone."

"She is mine. You can trust her," Reilly says. "What do you want?"

Vaughan sniffs but doesn't object further. "I want Ryan killed."

I flinch and look at Reilly, but he doesn't seem surprised at all.

"Of course," Reilly says. "And he will be, but JHAPI needs a chance to get their answers first."

"If Ryan walks out of here alive, I will be a laughing stock in front of the council and the other clans," Vaughan hisses, his lips curling back over his fangs.

"The council wants to know why and how this happened. You will be repaid for any damage done to your reputation, and you will earn the council's gratefulness," Reilly says, slipping into that tone I only now understand means whoever he is talking to is about to get played. I've certainly heard it often enough.

"Gratefulness? That is a poor currency," Vaughan says, pacing in front of Reilly.

"I can also tell the council that you attempted to interfere with their direct request," Reilly says calmly. "You can accept what you are offered, or you can find out what it means to face their displeasure. The choice is yours."

Vaughan stills and straightens his back. "I want

my new member allotment doubled for the next two years to replace what I have lost."

"I will submit your request."

Vaughan clenches his jaw tightly. He has no leverage here, and he's starting to realize that Reilly knows that, and that Reilly will use it ruthlessly.

"However," Reilly says. "I will guarantee it if you let Olivia feed from you, right now."

Vaughan looks at me, his anger shifting to confusion. "What?"

Reilly tilts his head to the side. "You heard me. Take it or leave it."

Vaughan licks his lips, looking at me with interest for the first time. "That does not seem like a fair trade for you. What are you not telling me?"

Reilly smiles. "You know what a feeding involves. There is nothing more to tell."

I take a step back. Why is Reilly doing this? I told him I wasn't going to feed from someone unwilling again.

"No," I say, finally finding my voice. "Absolutely not."

Vaughan looks at Reilly, then at me. "Yes."

Reilly turns to face me. "You heard him, he said yes."

"He doesn't—" I stumble over my thoughts. I'm not sure what to say. He doesn't really understand. He's still being manipulated.

"You don't get to withdraw this offer," Vaughan says, stepping up next to Reilly and glaring at me. "If I'm going to get shit on by the council, I want something out of it."

Reilly looks at me, satisfaction written across his face. He's so sure, as always, that he has the upper hand. There is a constant hunger in me that I do my best to ignore, but it's flaring up now with this easy temptation.

Vaughan jerks off his jacket and drops it on the floor, then pulls his sleeve up. I can't look at him. I stare at Reilly instead, my heart pounding angrily in my chest.

Vaughan holds his wrist out toward me, but I don't move. He glances at Reilly, then lifts his wrist to his own mouth and bites into it. With my senses already enhanced by the vampire magic, it's impossible to ignore the warm, bright scent of blood.

I squeeze my eyes shut but realize that was a mistake when a hand wraps around the back of my head and Vaughan's wet wrist is pressed against my mouth. My fangs descend, and I bite down purely on instinct. Blood pours into my mouth, and my hands wrap around his forearm.

It only takes two long pulls before I realize what I'm doing. I reach for his magic but stop as I brush against it. Vaughan didn't agree to this. I grind my teeth into his wrist as I struggle for control. I want this, I want it so much, but Vaughan didn't understand what he was agreeing to. He might be an awful person, he definitely seems to lack empathy, but I'm not. I refuse to be.

I look back at Reilly, who is watching intently, and pull my magic back into myself. Vaughan's blood is powerful on its own. It's feeding the hunger of the vampire magic within me. Whatever I can take from this alone will have to be enough.

My hands are shaking, and a small, dark part of me keeps insisting I take a just a little of the magic. I keep my eyes on Reilly. As long as I focus on him, it's easy to remember that I can't. I swallow one last time, then shove Vaughan's wrist away from me.

I'm still hungry in a way the blood couldn't satisfy, and I suppose I always will be. If that's the worst thing I have to endure to keep from turning into a devil, then I'll learn to live with it.

I spin on my heel and walk away from them both. The tranquilizer should be here. Reilly and Vaughan can keep playing politics if they want to; I'm done.

I hear the thrum of the helicopter and look over in the direction of the noise, but I don't see it yet.

"I can hear it too," Elise says, coming up to stand next to me. "It's still a couple of minutes out."

"You're determined to go in there with Reilly, aren't you?" I ask. I won't say it aloud and piss her off, but I'm a little worried she isn't fast enough as well.

She nods decisively and rolls her shoulders in a movement that looks more wolf than human. "He's going to need help. I've fought vampires before. Old ones. This is something I can handle."

"I'm going in there too," I say, uncrossing my arms and tapping my fingers against my leg.

She glances at me. "The way you moved in that last raid was different. That's not something a hedge-witch or a Finder or a healer can do."

"Sure isn't," I agree.

"Are you going to explain how you can do it?" Elise asks.

"I'm not supposed to talk about it," I deflect.

Elise rolls her eyes and punches me in the shoulder. "Your super-secret hidden talents better not get us killed."

"They won't," I say, punching her back and letting a little of my vampire strength slip through to make my point. She winces and glares at me.

"You passed out last time," she says, rubbing at the place I punched.

"Not until *after*," I say. "Whatever happens in there is going to be over quickly anyhow. Either we subdue him within a few minutes, or he kills us all."

Elise chuckles. "Such positive thinking."

"Realistic thinking," I correct.

The helicopter finally comes into view. It circles the house once, then chooses a point off the west corner of the house to land.

Staci hurries off toward the helicopter, and Reilly finally walks out of the house. He heads straight for Agent Stocke. Elise and I walk in that direction as well. I can't hear what they're talking about over the noise of the helicopter, but Stocke glances at me, her brows raised, and shakes her head. Reilly says something else, waving his hand through the air. She rolls her eyes but finally nods.

Elise and I approach, and Stocke walks over to me.

"I don't need you dying the first two weeks on the job," Stocke says, arms crossed.

"I'm not suicidal, Agent," I say firmly. "I wouldn't go in there if I didn't think I was going to walk out."

"It's your neck," Stocke says, shaking her head, still looking unconvinced. "I think you have a better chance with three people than one, but I'd be more comfortable sending in Hu if I thought he stood a chance of being able to move out of the way of an attack."

"I can't blame you. Hu is a better offensive magic user than I am," I say with a shrug.

"Every time I turn around, there is something else

you can do that should be impossible," Stocke says, looking at me intently. "After this, we are going to sit down, and you are going to tell me exactly what you are capable of, and why, or you and Reilly are off the team. Politics be damned."

I'm taken aback for a moment by her vehemence, but I shouldn't be surprised. She is protective of her team, and as far as she is concerned, I'm a total wild card. I swallow thickly and nod.

Staci runs up behind us.

"I have it!" she says gleefully, waving a heavy metal cylinder in the air. She has two injection guns clutched in her other hand.

Reilly walks over to join us, and we scoot out into a loose circle. Stocke takes the cylinder from Staci and twists it open.

"All right," Stocke says, slipping back into her usual business mode. "There are two injectors and two full doses."

Staci hands one of the injectors to Reilly and the other to me. Elise pulls off her jacket and begins kicking off her shoes.

"You can inject the brew anywhere," Stocke explains as she lifts the slender glass tubes out of the cylinder. "If the two doses don't stop him, then nothing will. Do not die in there trying to capture him. The main priority is getting all three of you out alive; second is Ryan. Is that understood?"

We all nod.

"Vaughan has a key to the room Ryan is locked in. He is going to open the door just long enough for the three of you to get inside, then shut it and lock it behind you." Stocke grabs two earpieces out of her pocket, handing one to me and Reilly. "Stay in constant communication. Elise, howl if you need out."

"Yes, ma'am," Elise says, handing her jacket to Staci, then stripping off the rest of her clothes.

Only Elise could stand buck-ass naked in front of her boss and still act like it's just another day at work. I admire her nerve.

The shift rolls over her all at once. I grit my teeth against the noise of her bones crunching and changing. Skin gives way to fur, and her face lengthens into a snout full of sharp teeth. When she's done, she shakes like a wet dog and her thick black fur ripples.

I hadn't paid much attention to her size or appearance when I saw her shifted in the last raid. There had been too much to think about, and I had been in a lot of pain. She is beautiful though. I reach over and ruffle the fur on the top of her head. The glare she gives me would be intimidating if I didn't know her. I grin unrepentantly.

Stocke hands me one of the vials. I hold it up and inspect the brew. It's dark blue; you might think it was black if you didn't look closely. Out of the corner of my eye, I can see Staci practically drooling over it. I slip it into the injection gun and lock it in place.

Stocke looks at each of us in turn, then nods. "Let's get this over with."

Staci fetches Vaughan, and the six of us go inside. The room they have the vampire trapped in is in a building attached to the back of the house by an enclosed walkway.

The vampire has been screaming off and on since we arrived, but as we get closer, it becomes almost constant. I'm not sure if it can hear us, smell us, or both. It certainly knows we're coming.

The building is a solid, windowless block that makes me think of a tomb. I shudder internally. The door is solid metal with bars on the outside.

"The door is inlaid with silver. Neither you nor

Ryan will be able to damage it," Vaughan says. "I will leave the bars off while you are inside."

Vaughan lifts the two solid bars off the door.

I pull on the vampire magic inside of me without hesitation and hold it ready. I'm going to need the speed and strength that comes with it. The vampire magic is energized from Vaughan's blood, but the unsatisfied hunger for magic within me thinks Hawking smells like food. She has power coursing through her that is so different from anything I've ever taken before. My fangs push out of my gums, and I lean toward her.

"Olivia," Reilly whispers harshly, his eyes scanning my face. "Are you still with me?"

"I'm fine," I growl out. I need something to do with all of this power, or the hunger is going to overwhelm me.

The key slides into place, and the lock clicks open.

"Ready?" Vaughan asks.

Reilly nods and moves to the door, his shoulders relaxed and the injector gun held loosely at his side. He doesn't look like he's about to walk into a fight at all. I edge up behind him and take a deep breath. Elise presses against my leg, her muscles just as tense as mine.

Vaughan pulls on the door, and it slides to the right. Reilly lunges inside, and I run into the absolute darkness after him. The door bangs shut behind us, shaking the entire building. It's absolutely silent in here. The vampire stopped screaming as soon as the door started to move.

Elise is still close to me. I can hear her breathing and the subtle scratch of her claws against the concrete floor. I'm not sure where Reilly is. More importantly, I have no idea where Ryan is. My eyes are slowly adjusting to the pitch black of the room, but it seems that not even the vampire magic can compensate for the lack of light completely.

There is what looks like a table or bed near the center of the room. Directly in front of me is a long table with chairs set around it, half of them overturned. There are other shapes across the room I can't make out, but I think they might be cages. It's creepy now, but it makes sense if this is where they keep new vampires.

Quick footsteps vibrate along the floor, and I launch myself forward on instinct. A rush of displaced air rushes along my back as I dodge the first charge. I don't wait for the second, darting to the right and praying I don't trip over anything.

I slide to a stop, my eyes glued to the jerky silhouette I assume is Ryan. He's not large, maybe only three inches taller than I am. He's slender as well, like all the other vampires in this clan I saw outside.

Just behind him, I see a low shape creeping along the floor. Ryan twitches and tilts his head back like he's sniffing. I stomp my foot on the ground, and his head whips around to me. Elise lunges and hits his back. He shrieks and I run forward, injector ready, but Reilly beats me there.

Ryan flings Elise off him, and she flies through the air as Reilly shoves the injector against his side. There is a *hiss* and *pop* as the brew is forced through his skin in a thin stream. Ryan's elbow connects with Reilly's chest, and something cracks as Reilly is sent flying as well.

Ryan doesn't pause or slow down as he charges me again. I dart to the left, away from both Elise and Reilly. Ryan is almost as fast as Reilly though, and he's not playing tag. He swipes at my back, and his nails slash through the back of my shirt, drawing blood.

I hiss in pain and duck down before pivoting and running in another direction. I pull harder on the vampire magic for a moment, just long enough to put some space between us. When I turn around, I can't see him anywhere.

My foot nudges against something damp and cold. I jerk away and swallow down a shriek. Whatever it is, it isn't moving. I crouch down, and in the dim lighting I can make out a face, eyes wide open, mouth frozen in a scream.

I scramble backward, landing on my butt in my hurry to get away. I had forgotten somehow about the necker they said had been killed in here. I hadn't been expecting a body.

Elise growls, and the sound makes all the hairs on my neck stand on end. My head jerks up, and I look for any sign of movement. Her eyes are two bright points in the darkness across the room. Something drops from the ceiling and lands right on top of her.

I run towards her, but I can't even tell who is who anymore. They tangle together, all teeth and shrieks and fur. Reilly is running from the other corner as well, but I beat him there this time.

Ryan is on top of Elise. He has her flipped on her back and is trying to swipe at her neck and belly, but she keeps him back with quick snaps of her jaw. I shove the injector against his back and pull the trigger. The brew rushes into him as the back of his hand connects with my shoulder. I hit the wall before I can react and fall hard on my side, the empty injector clattering to the floor.

I grit my teeth against the pain and scramble to my feet. Nothing is broken at least. Elise is off her back, and both she and Reilly are circling around Ryan. She darts in every few seconds, snapping at his hands and his legs. Every time he tries to get away from her, Reilly is there, blocking him. They're driving him back toward me.

"We have to kill him," Reilly shouts over the noise of Ryan's incensed shrieks.

It makes my stomach twist, but he's right. One dose of that brew should put anything to sleep. Two doses should have been enough to kill him on its own. There's no other way to stop him.

Ryan finally realizes he is being backed toward me and decides I'm the weak link. He turns and lunges for me. I don't try to dodge this time; there's no room for it, and he's too fast. I lean just far enough to the side that he won't hit me full on and throw a punch. My fist connects with his throat, and it crumples under my knuckles.

Hunger and anger overwhelm me. I lunge forward, and my teeth sink into the meat of his shoulder. I pull on his magic viciously, taking everything I can in one short rush. He is weak compared to the others I've fed on; there is barely anything to steal. His blood tastes bitter. I would spit it out if the magic inside of him wasn't so sweet.

It's over in a matter of seconds. As soon as the last bit of his magic flows into me, Ryan crumbles into ash.

## 18

I stumble backward, spitting and coughing, but I can't get it all out of my mouth. I fall to my knees and vomit, then stay there trying to relearn how to breathe.

I wipe my hand across my mouth and realize ashy bits of Ryan are still stuck to my face. I pull up the bottom of my shirt and frantically try to wipe it away. My hands are shaking, and I feel like I might get sick all over again.

Reilly pauses next to me and brushes his hand across my shoulder. I move away from the gesture. I don't want affection or comfort from him. I wouldn't be here at all if it wasn't for him.

"Are you hurt?" he asks.

"No," I gasp out. "Is Elise hurt?"

She snorts from behind me.

I glance back. "I'll take that as a no."

Reilly walks to the door and knocks twice.

"Ryan is dead," he shouts.

I can hear some discussion from outside, then the door is pulled back and light filters in. I squint at it and realize I still have the vampire magic coursing through me like I'm still under attack. I squeeze my eyes shut for a moment and let go of it. It makes me feel weak, and I don't like being unable to hear what Reilly is saying to Agent Stocke, but I'm already at my limits.

"What the fuck did they do to him?" I mutter to myself.

"Good question," Elise says.

I flinch. I hadn't realized she had shifted.

She is standing naked, and now slightly ashy just like I am, her hands on her hips.

"Vaughan certainly seems pleased that Ryan is dead," she says bitterly. "What a great sire."

I snort. "Yeah, he seems like a real class act."

The asshole can probably hear us. I hope he's listening.

Elise extends her hand toward me. "Come on, stand up and pull yourself together."

I accept her help and let her pull me up onto shaking legs. With the magic gone, my muscles are exhausted. We head outside, and I slip around the crowd. I need a shower, and I don't really want to talk to anyone right now.

I walk through the almost empty house and back out to the front of the property. The rest of the team is talking with someone from the local police.

My phone buzzes, and I answer it without looking at the screen.

"This is Olivia," I say tiredly.

A deep chuckle sends a chill down my spine.

"Hello," he says.

My fingers tighten on the phone, and I have to bite my tongue to keep from speaking before I get my thoughts together. I have no idea how he got this cell number. It's a JHAPI-issue phone. I haven't given it to anyone. I didn't think anyone outside of the team had it at all.

"Jason," I say, my voice tight. "It's been a while."

"Not that long," he says. "You went in after the vampire, didn't you?"

I hesitate, and he takes that as an answer.

"Of course you did. I had no doubt you would. You always charge in, even when you shouldn't. You're not very good at listening to friendly advice," he says, his voice growing more heated at the end.

"You wanted me to leave my friend to be tortured and killed in your fucking basement," I snap, my fingers squeezing my phone until it creaks. The strength of the vampire magic is still coursing through me, and the anger is only making it worse.

"I wanted you to stay out of my way. I have a mission. A calling. I thought you might understand that eventually, but you are close-minded."

"You want to destroy me and everyone like me," I growl at him.

"I want to destroy the parasites and the murderers," he says, his voice shifting back into the calm tone he had always used when I thought he was just another police officer. "Witches face a great and terrible temptation, but they can be redeemed if they just reject the magic. I gave you a chance."

I hear someone walk up behind me and turn around to see Corinne. She stops at the expression on my face.

"You didn't give me shit," I say while trying to gesture at Corinne to do something, though I don't know what. "You had me arrested, and you would have thrown me in jail to stop me."

"To protect you!" he shouts.

"You tried to kill me that night."

Understanding dawns on Corinne's face, and she pulls out her phone and begins furiously texting

STEPHANIE FOXE

someone. She twirls her finger in the air, telling me
to keep talking.

"You gave me no choice. You brought those parasites to us. The dogs as well. And all for what? To
save a vampire that would suck you dry if ever given
the chance," Jason snaps.

"You're wrong about that. You didn't break him."

"He killed Novak. I watched him." His voice is almost gleeful. I don't understand how I missed this
madness. He's completely insane.

"The man who shot Novak killed him," I say quietly. The truth is that I killed Novak in the end. He
wouldn't have survived the wound and Patrick
draining him, but when his soul left his body, it was
because I had drained him of his magic.

"You would have been an excellent warrior,
Olivia," he says softly. "You walked out of that
building just now without even a scratch. Not many
can face a creature like that and survive, much less
without being injured."

"What?" I ask, my hand shaking as I spin in a circle. Can he see me right now? Is he somewhere in the
crowd gathered along the street?

"You always were so graceful. Maybe you learned
that when you were dancing. I wanted to see you
dance for me."

He sounds wistful and almost hopeful. When we
had been in that diner, the look he had given me was
pure want. My stomach twists. He still wants me. This
sick fuck still wants me even though he tried to kill me.

"Where are you?"

He laughs. "Already gone, Olivia. We'll meet again,
but not yet. Not quite yet."

The line goes dead. I stare at Corinne, horrified,
and slowly lower the phone from my ear. My heart is

racing, and I feel like I need to chase after him, but I can't. I don't know where he is.

"He saw me, Corinne. He was watching when I walked outside," I say shakily.

"Is he still here?" she asks, looking around.

"He said he is already gone, but there's no way he's out of the city yet. It's been less than ten minutes." I text Reilly, my fingers shaking as I type out the message. "I have to try to find him. Now. While we know he's still close."

"You can't, you're still injured," Corinne objects.

"I don't care. It's not going to kill me," I say, running my hands through my hair. "I have to do this. I can't let him get away again. He's going to kill people, Corinne. Every day he is free, he is hurting paranormals and helping the NWR."

She straightens her shoulders. "You can't Find him, but I can."

"We don't have a map—"

"I don't need one," she says simply.

I hesitate. "That's risky. We have time to get you a map, right? To get something."

Corinne wraps her hand around her necklace. "No, we need to Find him before he has a chance to prepare for it."

She closes her eyes, and I can feel the magic lifting off her. It laps against me in waves, burning every welt on my body as it passes by me. This is so much more raw than what I felt when she was using the map in the office that day. Her hair moves around her face in an invisible wind. The crystal is glowing in her hand, the amber light slipping out between her fingers.

I see Ivy running up behind her, Zachary close behind. They're still about ten yards away when

Corinne gasps. Her eyes fly open, and I see a glimpse of fear contort her face before she screams.

The light in the crystal goes dark. Black tendrils appear on her hand, and they rush up her arm. I move without thinking and catch her before she hits the ground. Her hand is clenched tightly around the crystal. I rip each finger away one at a time. I think I break one, but I don't care. I rip the necklace off and throw the crystal away from her.

Magic is still rolling off her in waves. It's like it's being sucked out of her. I press my hands to her cheeks and pull. As soon as I do, I know it's the right choice. It's like pulling against a tidal wave. Something is trying to suck her dry, and I don't know if I can stop it.

## 19

I shut my eyes, blocking out the hands tugging at me and the questions being shouted over and over. I reach inside and pull on her magic, letting it flow into me like a river. It's deeper than anything I've seen before. Not even Reilly has power like this. I can only hope it will be enough to save her.

Her heartbeat begins to slow and beat in an odd rhythm. I press healing magic into her. It's difficult while I'm still draining her and fighting the tug of whatever is hurting her, but I push through. It's not just her heart that's slowing down; every organ in her body seems to be dying.

I dig my nails into her skin and push and push and push. I won't let her die. I refuse. Her magic pours into me like a battery, and I push the healing magic back into her in return. The force that has been draining her is weakening.

The welts on my body are burning. It feels like fire is wrapping around my arms and creeping across my shoulders. I push the healing magic into her, doing everything I can to stall what's happening. Just enough to keep her alive.

If I wasn't taking her magic, I'd already have

passed out from trying to push my healing magic like this. I need more. Her magic is deep, but everything has its limits, and she is reaching hers just as fast as I am reaching mine.

I open my eyes and see Reilly kneeling across from me.

"I need to feed. She's dying. I can't keep healing her, and she's dying," I gasp out.

"Why is she dying?" Ivy demands, her hand on her gun like she can fight whatever is happening.

"Reilly, please," I beg.

He stares at me jaw clenched.

"I'll tell you. I'll tell you everything," I say, tears slipping down my cheeks.

His face shifts, satisfaction and sadness passing through his eyes. He holds out his wrist. I bite down and moan at the sweet taste of blood pouring down my throat. His magic leaps into me. Cold. Powerful. Intoxicating.

I push it all into Corinne. There's something else inside of her that is all curled up in what's left of her magic and in her skin. It's something strange, and I can't draw it out or heal it. It's trying to eat at her magic, but I'm getting to it first. Her magic isn't completely gone, but only the barest remnants are left. The dark thing stills and curls up. Her heartbeat steadies. It is still slow, but it isn't fading anymore.

I search and search inside of her for the source of this darkness. It's oily and malevolent, like it's somehow alive. My control is slipping. I've pushed too hard for too long, and I just can't keep going, not even with Reilly's magic. I tug my teeth out of his wrist and feel the ground spinning underneath me.

Ivy is alternately shouting for an ambulance and demanding to know what's happened. I look down at Corinne. Her face is slack, her lips parted. The black veins are still on her hands. I shove her sleeve up and see that they stop just above her elbow. I don't know what would have happened if they had made it to her heart, but my gut tells me it would have killed her.

I collapse back onto my butt and wrap my arms around myself. I don't understand. This isn't anything like what happened when I tried to Find my mother. It can't be that he was just too far away. The NWR has always had their ways of hurting paranormals. But this—this feels like magic. Like a curse.

Stocke kneels in front of me and puts her hands gently on either side of my face, turning it until I'm looking her in the eye.

"Olivia, we need to know what happened," she says, using the same tone you might to talk someone out of jumping off a bridge.

"Martinez," I gasp out. "He called me. He was here. He—he saw me."

"He did this?" Stocke asks, glancing at the person beside her and nodding.

"I don't know. She tried to Find him." I bite the inside of my cheek to keep from crying. I can't break down right now. Not in front of all of these people. Not while I still have information they need.

"She tried to Find him? Out here without a map?" Stocke asks.

I nod once. "I was going to try, but she stopped me. She said she would do it and that she didn't need a map. I shouldn't have let her—"

"You're damn right you shouldn't have let her!" Ivy shouts. "That's against policy for a reason. It's common fucking sense!"

I keep staring at Stocke. Ivy is right to hate me. If I hadn't insisted on trying to Find him right then, maybe Corinne wouldn't have tried what she did. If I had just been patient, maybe this wouldn't have happened.

"Enough, Agent Andreas," Stocke snaps at Ivy. She turns back to me. There are sirens in the distance. I hope it's the ambulance. My vision is fading, and I couldn't heal Corinne anymore right now. She needs something, and I'm terrified the black thing inside of her might start growing again.

"There's something attacking her. Something magical," I say desperately. "It's like a darkness trying to steal her light. It's hateful. I couldn't get it out."

"Magical? Like a curse?" Stocke asks, her eyes scanning my face. She shakes me gently when I don't respond right away, and I realize my eyes were slipping shut.

"I think so," I say. "It's bad. I stopped it for now, but I can't get it out."

The ambulance screeches to a stop next to us, and the paramedics run over with a stretcher.

"Anything else, Olivia? Is there anything they need to know?" Stocke asks.

I swallow, wracking my brain for anything that might make it worse. "No potions of any kind. Nothing magical until we know what's hurting her. Anything could trigger it."

Stocke stands, hurrying over to the paramedics, and I fall forward onto my hands. Zachary is comforting Ivy, and I think keeping her away from me. Reilly walks over to stand between me and everyone else and extends his hand down to me.

"Stand up," he says.

I put my hand in his and let him pull me to my feet. Everything spins, and my vision narrows to two small points, but I stay on my feet. I feel like shit, but I'm not going to pass out.

Reilly steps in close and whispers in my ear.

"We need to go, now. You aren't going to be wanted at the hospital, and if Martinez is still in this city, I don't want you exposed like this."

I nod. I don't care where I am or what I'm doing. All I can think about is the sick, dark thing that's inside of her. And that Martinez did this somehow. He taunted me, making me think he was close by. I don't know if he knows I can use Finding magic, but it feels like, maybe, this trap was meant for me.

---

I walk in a daze. It doesn't register that we're back in the hotel until Reilly is guiding me into our room. I head straight to the bathroom. My back still aches from the scratches Ryan left me with.

Cold water on my face helps wake me up a little bit, but I'm exhausted. Reilly is leaning against the doorjamb, arms crossed, face blank. I know what he wants, and that there is no backing out of the deal I made. I don't regret it though. There was no way I was going to let Corinne die when I had the power to save her.

I suppose he'd say she might not do the same for me. And perhaps she wouldn't, but I don't care. I made my decision about who I wanted to be after I fed off that vampire. Reilly might have no conscience. He might be okay with threats and manipulations and putting his ambition over what is *right*. My mother raised me better. I'll die before I see myself become like him.

"Maybelle helped my mother steal a spellbook," I begin.

Reilly uncrosses his arm and steps closer.

"I don't know what exactly was in it other than the spell they used, if anything. And I don't know

179

where it is now." I stand up straight and turn to face him. "All my mother wanted was to have a baby apparently, but she had fallen in love with a vampire."

"And vampires can't have children," Reilly says.

"They can if they use this spell. Sort of," I say with a grimace. "Maybelle was waiting in another room, but she went in when she heard my mother screaming."

Talking about this makes me sick to my stomach. Reilly doesn't push. He knows I'm not going to clam up now.

"The spell killed my father. Maybelle said he turned to ash while he was still inside my mother."

Reilly's eyes widen imperceptibly. He wasn't expecting that I think, that it would kill the vampire.

"What else?" he asks.

"That's all I really know. It worked, obviously. Maybelle sold the book. My mother did her best to disappear with me." I shrug and pace back and forth in front of the bathtub. I feel like if I don't keep moving I'll fall asleep where I stand.

"So you are half-vampire, and half-witch," Reilly muses aloud. "You can steal magic, though that doesn't guarantee you can use it well."

"The healing magic was easy to control. The rest of this," I shake my head. "The rest is harder."

"You will learn though. You already are."

I shrug. "Oh, and something else. The coven that attacked the clan back in Texas, they knew what I was and how I was conceived. They were trying to recruit me. Did you know that?"

Reilly stares at me before answering. "I suspected it."

I rub my hands over my face.

"I suppose I'm lucky they didn't find me any sooner." I pause in the middle of my pacing and laugh. "Or I'm unlucky. Maybe they would have been better to work for than you. They might be insane, but they did seem very enthusiastic about the idea of training me."

"The witch council would have eaten you up," Reilly scoffs.

I turn on him. "You say that like the vampire council won't. Like *you* won't."

"I have done everything I could to make this easy for you. You could have just cooperated, but you have fought me every step of the way."

"Cooperated with what, though? You said you wanted to see my potential. If you want to know what I can do, that means you have a plan to use me somehow. I don't want to be used by anyone," I half-shout back at him.

"Tough shit, Olivia," he shouts back. "We're all getting used. We all have our part to play."

I open my mouth to argue back, but his phone rings. He turns away and answers it.

"Reilly here," he says pleasantly. I despise that he can do that, pretend he wasn't just in the middle of an argument.

I sit down on the edge of the bathtub and wait. He needs to get off the phone so I can keep yelling at him. I have to be doing something while I wait to hear about Corinne.

"He's dead?" Reilly asks, shock apparent in his tone.

I try to pull on my vampire magic so I can hear the other side of the conversation, but that makes the room swim and my skin ache, so I let it go.

"And we know for sure that he will be taking his place?"

Another pause.

"Yes. Just do it." Reilly hangs up the phone and stares out of the bathroom door, not moving.

"I would ask if everything is all right, but if someone has died, I guess it isn't," I say quietly. I can't tell if he is angry or upset. His shoulders are a tight line of tension, and his hands are white-knuckled around his phone.

"One of the council members has died. My sire is taking his place." He turns around and faces me. His jaw is clenched just as tightly as his hands.

"Who will be taking over as clan leader now?" I ask.

"His second will be doing that, I assume," Reilly says, his fingers tapping absently against the phone still gripped in his hand.

"Were you hoping for the promotion?" I ask, confused at his reaction. He seems distressed.

"I knew I was not going to be considered for the position. There is a clear hierarchy," Reilly says.

"Were you close to this council member?" I ask.

Reilly shakes his head.

"Is this bad news somehow?" I ask. I don't really care to try and comfort Reilly, but if he's this upset about whatever is happening, it could be putting me at risk as well.

"No, it's great news for our clan, and for my sire," Reilly says.

I wish I could hear his heart, because I don't believe him at all.

## 20

It's the middle of the day, but I can't go back to sleep. Elise had texted me a couple of hours ago that Corinne is still stable, but they've been unable to wake her up. The brain scans don't show any damage, so the doctors are baffled. She also promised me that the doctors haven't used any magic or brews on her, which relaxed the knot in my stomach a little.

I sit up and shove the covers off. They don't want me at the hospital, but I have to do something. I find clean clothes and put on a little extra deodorant because I don't care to take a shower right now.

I pace the room, tangling my fingers in my hair. I feel helpless. No one else felt the thing that's inside of her. The darkness. I stop in my tracks.

No one else has felt it, but I have. I've been so frustrated that I can't draw it out of her with the healing magic that I didn't even think about a brew. I was right that the doctors shouldn't give her anything because it could react unpredictably. It was feeding on her magic, and if I hadn't been able to take the magic first, it would have consumed it.

It was sentient, but it's not a human sort of consciousness. It's more primitive, like a parasite or a weed. It just wants to take all the nutrients it can. I think it stopped because it didn't want to kill its host. She still had magic in her, just not enough for it to grow.

I race over to pull my shoes on. As her magic starts returning, the curse is going to start growing again. It has to be stopped before that, and if I can't heal it, then I have to find an antidote.

Normally, curses are irreversible. An object that has been cursed has to be destroyed. Curses that affect the body though, those can be reversed. They can be cured. The only trick to it is making the right brew. Curse-ending is somewhat of a dying art. I blame witches like Staci with their bullshit recipes. The only way to brew for a curse is to do it from scratch. Nothing but you and your magic.

Reilly's things are on his nightstand. I grab his keys and flip through his wallet, taking everything that looks like a credit card. The things I need are going to be expensive. Hopefully, he waits to kill me until after I'm done brewing.

I haven't turned on my personal phone since we left Texas. At least ten messages pop up when the screen comes on. I dismiss them all and open the map. There are dozens of brewing supply shops in the city. I click on the one most likely to have what I need and speed out of the parking garage.

I call Elise, putting it on speakerphone so I can keep an eye on the map. She answers on the second ring.

"She's still fine—" Elise begins.

"I think I know how to fix this," I interrupt. "Or at least part of it. How to get the curse out of her."

"Whoa, slow down," Elise says. "You know how to end the curse?"

Someone talking in the background, almost trying to shout over Elise.

"I think so. I felt it, and I understand it. It's like a weed almost. It wants to feed on her magic, but since I took most of it, the curse went dormant. Her magic will recover though, and then the curse will start growing again."

Elise is silent for a moment. I hear a door open and close, and the background noise cuts off.

"Olivia, you're not making sense," she says quietly. "You took her magic?"

I bite the inside of my cheek. I don't want to have to explain all of this, but these secrets aren't protecting me anymore. They're pointless.

"I wasn't born with the ability to use all these different kinds of magic. I was only born with the ability to steal it. I stole my mother's hedgewitch magic. I stole healing magic. I stole the electric magic from a detective that was killed in the NWR attack in my hometown. I stole something different from the clan leader I worked for. It changed me, but that's— that's not important right now," I say breathlessly. "I can brew something to end the curse."

"I don't—" Elise sighs. "I don't know if they'll let you."

"Then don't tell them," I say immediately. "I'm going to brew it. I'll find a way to get it to her."

"I don't know if I'm going to let you," she says quietly.

My heart drops. I hadn't expected that. I should have.

"Olivia, curse-ending is advanced magic. It's hardly done anymore; hell, curses are almost unheard of. Especially one like this. Her coven is going to find a specialist, they're already making calls. They said there's someone in Europe who might be able to help."

"There isn't time," I plead. Corinne is too powerful, her magic is probably already recovering.

"You giving her some brew you can't prove will work could kill her."

"You didn't feel it, Elise. I know I can do this."

"You thought it was a good idea to try to Find Martinez too, and look how that turned out," Elise says, all semblance of patience gone from her tone. "We're all scared, and we're all worried. You can't do something else reckless trying to fix this."

I grit my teeth. I can't talk her into agreeing with me, but I refuse to give up when Corinne's life is on the line.

"Whatever you say." I hang up the call. I should have just done this without talking to anyone about it. It's too late for that now, but I can't give up.

The first shop has the cauldron I need, but not all of the herbs. I swipe Reilly's black credit card and let out a little sigh of relief when it isn't declined. I hope it's the type that doesn't have a credit limit.

I have to visit three more shops before I get all of the ingredients I think I might need. It's hard to predict beforehand, but I'm letting my intuition guide me. This magic is something I know. It's the one thing I was trained to use, and it's always been as natural as breathing. My mother was talented, and this magic inside of me is still part of her as well.

I put the last bag in the trunk and slide into the driver's seat. I'm not sure where the best place is to brew. It has to be somewhere I won't be interrupted, so the JHAPI offices are out. I tap the card against the steering wheel. A hotel, it is.

I pull out of the parking lot and drive toward the strip. I'm sure I can find something near there. Las

Vegas is not lacking in hotels, and I know some of them rent by the hour.

I stop at the first one I see with a sign out front that is blinking the number of vacancies. It's run-down, and there are people loitering in front of some of the rooms. Half are obviously prostitutes. The rest either have the cocky walk of a pimp, or they're pretending they aren't looking at the girls while unable to take their eyes off them.

I park in front of the main entrance and hurry inside. The receptionist, her name tag says Glenda in glittery pink letters, is a middle-aged woman with thinning hair and a pockmarked face. She has a cigarette hanging out of her thin lips.

"I need a room," I say, holding up the card. "Any non-smoking, by chance?"

She laughs, but it turns into a cough.

"They're all non-smoking, but nobody gives a fuck and smokes anyhow," she says, tapping her cigarette against the no smoking sign sitting on her desk.

"All right, whatever, I'll take a room anyhow."

She turns around and digs out a key attached to a little wooden handle with a number written on it.

"How long you want it for?" she asks.

"I'll take it for two days." I don't know how long this is going to take, and I don't want to have to worry about getting all my stuff out of it right away.

She raises a brow but slowly types it into her computer regardless. She takes a long drag on her cigarette and blows the smoke up toward the ceiling, then puts a card reader up on the counter. She doesn't mention a price, and I don't care how much it is. I swipe the card and sign the receipt she gives me.

She hands over the key.

"It's around back, first floor," she croaks.

"Thanks," I say, already halfway to the door.

I drive around to the back. The prostitute's eyes follow my car, but when they catch a glimpse of me inside, they turn back to the men still milling around.

Glenda was right about the room, it's definitely been smoked in recently. It takes three trips to the car, but I get everything inside. There isn't much to work with in here. There's one desk and the narrow shelf the television is sitting on.

I move the television to the floor and pull the desk closer. I set up the propane stove on the desk and begin lining up the ingredients on the shelf. I haven't wanted to admit it, but I am nervous. Elise's comments have only made that worse. I pause and take a steadying breath. There's no time for self-doubt.

I unbox the cauldron reverently. The circumstances aren't great, but I can't help the thrill of excitement that runs through me at the chance to use this cauldron. It's something I don't think I'd ever have had the money to buy, but I've always lusted after it.

The four most common types of cauldrons are copper, pewter, iron, and steel. This cauldron, however, is made of leaded glass. The same stuff used to make those decorative crystal trinkets people buy and then don't know what to do with. I saw one of these when I was a child, and I thought the cauldron was somehow carved from a diamond. I fell in love instantly.

It's a quirky cauldron to use. You can't brew too hot with it, and you can't brew anything that's overly flammable, or you could shatter the whole thing if something went wrong.

I fold back the lids of the box and lift the cauldron out slowly. It sparkles even in the dim lighting of the motel room. It was carved with hundreds of facets on the outer edges that catch the light. They'll catch my magic too. Brewing with one of these is like watching a fireworks show.

I set it carefully on the burner and look over my ingredients one last time. I have one shot to do this right. It isn't going to take Reilly all that long to find me, and I doubt he's willing to fund another round of this. Hell, he didn't willingly fund this attempt.

I pull up music on my phone, turn up the volume as loud as it will go and drop it next to the cauldron. It's instrumental, which I would never normally listen to, but it makes me feel classy and this cauldron deserves a little class. Or as much as it can get in a pay-by-the-hour motel in Las Vegas at three in the afternoon.

I lay the cutting board on the left side of the cauldron and grab the single, large sunflower I bought. I pluck the petals carefully and set them in a pile in one corner of the cutting board. The hedgewitch magic is already tingling at my fingertips as I work. The petals perk up, taking on a kind of glow as I pluck them.

Once they are all removed, I slice each one into long slivers. I light the fire under the cauldron and grab the bottle of carbonated water. It fizzes happily as I pour it in, and it doesn't stop. I won't be able to boil anything. My magic will have to provide the heat to bind the ingredients together. The carbonation will keep it all moving.

I sprinkle the petals in, and they dance across the surface, bending and twisting and shimmering. They won't sink in just yet, I realize. They won't do that until the end.

I cut the lemon in half and squeeze each half over the cauldron. The juice runs down my wrist too, but most of it drips into the bubbling liquid. The bright, fresh scent spreads throughout the room in a rush. It reminds me of summer days on the front porch, when the only thing that could cool me down was ice cold lemonade made fresh from the lemons we grew in the back yard.

Next are the dragonfly wings. They're arranged carefully in the little plastic box I bought them in. I crack it open and lift them out. They're colorless, lacy things that could crumble at any moment. I cradle them in the palm of my hand and lower them to just above the surface of the brew before I let them slip into the cauldron. They flutter down and dissolve in a swirl of light.

The brew pulls on my magic, and I let it. I expected the magic to be bright, and it is, but it's also colorful. It pours out of every part of me. My hands, my arms, my face, my chest. Anywhere it can escape from. It bounces off the facets of the cauldron casting light all over the room like a prism.

The door crashes open with a bang that almost makes me lose my grip on the magic. I'm immediately struck by Reilly's scent, so I don't even bother turning around. He did find me sooner than I expected, but I'll deal with that in a minute.

"What the fuck are you doing?" he shouts.

I ignore him and grab the final ingredient. The most important one. This is going to carry the light, to ensure that my magic can shine inside of Corinne so brightly, the dark thing that is trying to eat her magic will have to get out of her or die.

"Olivia, do not ignore me," Reilly says with a low growl.

I glance back and hold my finger to my lips, then tip the diamond powder into the cauldron. He sounds angry, but he looks like he's in awe as he watches the magic dancing around both of us. I'm sure he can feel it. Even a human could feel all of this.

The diamond powder hits the liquid, and the brew begins to sing. It's not audible, but I can feel it down to my bones. This is why the crystal cauldron is so beautiful. None of the metal cauldrons can sing like this. It's so perfectly clear. My magic rushes into the cauldron, and I throw my head back and raise my arms. This brew doesn't need to be stirred or prodded; it only needs my full attention and my full effort.

I feel like a conductor, and the magic is my orchestra. My fingers dance through the air, tugging on invisible strings of magic. I lean over the cauldron and watch as the bright petals twist down into the shimmering liquid one by one. Each petal makes the brew brighter until it's like looking into the sun itself.

I push the magic to its crescendo, higher and higher and higher until it's just right. I bring my hands together, and the clap thunders around the room. The brew stills instantly, but the brilliant light of the brew only grows stronger.

I'm panting like I've just run a mile, but I could keep going for hours if I needed to. I missed brewing; no other magic has ever made me feel so alive.

I turn to Reilly slowly. "Sorry, I think you asked what the fuck I was doing?"

The look of awe disappears from Reilly's face, and he clenches his jaw. "You stole my car and my credit cards and disappeared. So yes, I would like to know what the fuck you are doing."

I gesture at the cauldron. "I needed to brew this."

"And what, exactly, is that?" he demands.

"It's going to end the curse affecting Corinne," I say, crossing my arms and waiting for the inevitable objection.

Reilly stays silent though, considering. "Curse-ending is advanced magic."

"You're not the first person to tell me that today," I say, straightening my shoulders and squaring my jaw.

"Why do you think you can brew something like that?" he asks.

I drop my arms and throw my hands in the air. "Everyone misunderstands brewing. I'm sure you think most hedgewitches follow a recipe?"

Reilly nods.

"Well, that's crap. Brewing is *magic*. It's my magic. If you think about what you need, about what ingredients can give you what you're looking for, the magic will do the rest. You just have to trust your intuition and trust the magic." I point at the cauldron. "You need the right equipment, and you can't always get it. But when you have it, I mean look at this brew. You can feel it, can't you? It's perfect."

Reilly nods again, but slower.

"It is—magnificent," he says. "But that doesn't mean it can end a curse."

I rub my hands down my face. "I felt the curse. I understand it. I know this will end it. No one is going to believe that, apparently, but I know it."

Reilly stares at the cauldron for a few moments. "I'm starting to think you might be a bit unstable."

I roll my eyes and turn back to my makeshift workstation and flip off the burner. I need to get this in the vials before it cools.

"How'd you find me?" I ask as I ladle the brew into the first vial.

"My car has a GPS tracker on it. Not that I ever expected to have to use it," he says, his tone more exasperated than angry now. "What the hell were you thinking?"

"I thought I'd have more time before you found

me," I say with a shrug. "Did you wake up before sunset or something?"

"Yes," Reilly says tiredly. "Something felt off."

"So, are you going to try to stop me from giving this to Corinne?" I ask.

"No."

I look up, surprised. "Really?"

He raises a brow at me. "Did you want me to?"

"No, of course not." I stopper the vial and grab the next. "You just said you didn't believe me and that I seem unstable though."

"You're most likely insane," Reilly reiterates. "But I want to see if this works."

"And you're willing to risk Corinne's life to do that?" I ask, annoyed. He's letting me get my way, and he's still finding a way to piss me off while doing it.

Reilly shrugs. "I doubt it will kill her. There's certainly a chance it will fail, but that's not the same thing."

I turn back to the cauldron and fill the final two vials. Corinne should only need one, but I'm bringing all of it just in case.

"If you want to see if this works, I might need some help getting to Corinne," I say hesitantly.

"Why? Ivy is angry with you, but you aren't banned from the hospital."

"I called Elise and told her what I was planning on doing on the way here. She said she wouldn't allow it, so I assume she has also told everyone else in case I come try," I say with a grimace.

Reilly puts his face in his hands and takes a deep breath. "You are painfully honest when you should lie, and yet you keep secrets that could get you killed."

"Does that mean you're going to help me, or not?"

21

I press my back against the wall and wait, listening intently to Reilly's footsteps as he walks down the hall. It's only Cook in her room right now. I can't hear what Reilly says, but after just a few moments, both of them leave the room and the door clicks shut behind them.

I hurry to the door and open it just far enough to peek in, just in case. The room is empty except for the figure lying on the hospital bed.

Corinne is pale as death. She has a cannula under her nose and IVs in both arms. I think it's the first time I've ever seen her face without even the hint of a smile on it.

I glance down the hall one last time, which is still empty, and pull the door quietly shut behind me. I have the vial unstoppered before I reach her bed. I have to walk around to the left side because of the machine they have set up on the right by her head. I can see her steady heartbeat on the screen, which calms my nerves some.

I remove the pillow from behind her head and lower it gently onto the bed. I've given brews to dozens of unconscious neckers, so I have the technique down pat. As long as she can breathe, she can swallow. Even in her sleep. I tilt her head back, tug her mouth open, and hold it, which is a little tricky to do one-handed.

I move the vial over her mouth, letting the lip rest on her bottom teeth. I don't want to spill a single drop.

"Get the fuck away from her."

I jerk and look up, almost spilling the brew. I hadn't even heard the door open.

Ivy is standing in front of me, her gun drawn and pointed at my face. Her lips curl back, baring her teeth. She is furious.

She is also going to shoot me. There's no way around that. I pull on my vampire magic and pour the potion into Corinne's mouth. Everything goes slow. The crack of gunfire, my hand clamping over Corinne's mouth and nose to force her body to swallow, the hot pain of the bullet hitting my shoulder because I can't quite dodge it.

Corinne swallows, and I barely have time to lift my hand from her face before the magic explodes out of her in a violent, bright burst. Ivy and I are both thrown back. I hit the window and it cracks. I can't see anything but spots; I didn't shut my eyes in time.

All of my other senses swim into focus. Corinne's heart is still beating, faster now than it was before. Ivy is groaning and pulling herself back onto her feet. I press back against the window and blink rapidly, trying to see again. My left arm doesn't want to move, but the pain in my shoulder hasn't hit me yet, so I try not to think about it.

I hear something else though, something I can't identify. The hair on my arms stands on end, and I throw myself to one side away from the wall. Something slithers past me and hits the window with a wet smack. It reeks of decay and emanates a dark, oily magic.

My vision begins filtering back as I crab walk backward away from the undulating mass of darkness that is hugging close to the window. Thick snake-like protrusions are waving in the air and creeping toward me.

Gunfire cracks behind me, and I flinch, thinking for a split second that I must be the target again, but the window shatters and the black *thing* screeches in indignation as it falls onto the floor.

I scramble for another of the vials in my pocket. I don't know if my brew can completely kill this thing, but I'm hoping it can slow it down.

"Eyes!" I shout as I throw the vial at the curse. Even with my eyes shut the flare of light is painful. Magic fills the room until the air is thick with it.

I open my eyes and search the room, but I don't see the creature. I stand hesitantly, glancing at Ivy. She's searching for it as well. I pull the third vial out of my pocket and sniff carefully. The same oily scent is still there, underneath the smell of lemon and flowers.

"It's not dead yet," I whisper.

A black mass flies out from under the bed, headed straight for me. Water splashes against the creature and cuts through it like a knife. It falls to the ground in pieces, each of them writhing and flailing.

Ivy runs over and empties another container of holy water on the pieces. Each one shrivels under the assault until it dissolves into a coagulated mess.

I stumble back until my I hit the wall and try to catch my breath. It's dead. I look over at Corinne. She's still unconscious, but her heartbeat is perfect, and she's breathing without struggling.

"Holy water, huh?" I ask.

"I always carry it on me. Turns out, the main threat today was just you," Ivy says angrily.

"I knew I was right," I say through gritted teeth as I slide down the wall with my hand on my bloody shoulder.

Ivy stares at me, gun still in her hand, the empty container in the other.

"I don't trust you. You are reckless. You could have been wrong today, and you could have killed her," she says coldly. "You weren't prepared to fight that—thing."

I push healing magic into my shoulder, forcing the bullet out slowly and painfully. Once it's poking out of my shoulder, I grab it and pull it the rest of the way out. It's still hot from the gun, or perhaps just from my blood.

"I don't care what you think of me," I say through the harsh breaths I'm taking. "Corinne will live."

Ivy glances at her. "She's still not waking up."

"She won't until her magic recovers more. I took almost all of it." I take a deep breath and work on healing my shoulder again. I've lost a lot of blood, and I need to stop the bleeding before I pass out and end up admitted to the hospital. The healing magic is warm and soothing, but it can't dull the pain of the wound.

Ivy finally puts her gun back in its holster and walks over to Corinne and inspects her hands and arms.

"All the black is gone," she says.

The last of my worry slips away at her confirmation. My shoulder finally stops bleeding, and I let my hand fall into my lap. It still needs healing, but that's enough for now.

The door opens, and two hospital security officers enter with their guns drawn.

Ivy raises her hands, saying something about being a federal agent. I don't bother moving, I just let my head fall back against the wall and try to appear non-threatening. They argue back and forth for a few minutes, but Stocke arrives before long and the officers are sent away.

She looks at me, obviously shot, the missing window, and Ivy, who is unrepentant with her arms crossed as she stands next to Corinne.

"What the hell happened?" Stocke demands.

22

---

The chair I'm sitting in squeaks if I move, so I'm trying to hold very still. Stocke is pacing at the front of the conference room table. Her suit is wrinkled, and she can't seem to stop fidgeting with her hair. She pauses, opens her mouth to say something, then shuts it and begins pacing again.

The door opens, and Reilly walks in. He takes the seat to my right and folds his hands comfortably in his lap. Everyone else is still at the hospital with Corinne. Stocke had insisted they stay with her, just in case she woke up. She had dragged me back to the JHAPI building to yell at me though. Considering Ivy was still eyeing me like she was considering shooting me again, I didn't really object.

"I have worked for JHAPI since its inception," Stocke says, crossing her arms and staring out of the window. "I was the first team lead ever appointed and the first choice for this assignment. And in twenty-four hours, one person has compromised the entire thing not once, but twice."

She turns and presses her fists to the table, her eyes boring into me. I resist the urge to slump down in my chair or look away. I'll accept that the first choice, the one that got Corinne hurt, was reckless. I won't apologize for giving her the brew though. I've said all of that to Stocke already, so I keep my mouth shut.

"It's hardly compromised," Reilly says. "Your team is still intact, and we're closer to finding Martinez than ever."

Stocke glares at him. "She almost got our Finder, one of only three who work with the entire organization, killed."

"She didn't force Corinne to violate policy. That was her decision," Reilly says, leaning forward. "Olivia then saved her life, despite resistance from your other agents."

"I am going to do everything in my power to have both of you removed from this team," Stocke says, her lip curling up like an animal baring its teeth.

"You won't succeed," Reilly says, leaning back in his chair. "But I can arrange for you to be removed if you'd like."

Stocke shifts back onto her heels. I think she would kill Reilly right now if she thought she could get away with it.

"I don't think it would have mattered when Corinne tried to Find him," I say. No matter how angry she is, I need to get this out.

"Excuse me?" Stocke snaps.

"That curse was going to activate no matter who tried to find him, and no matter when," I say.

"So now you're an expert in curses? Are you an enchanter as well? Is there any branch of magic you can't use?" Stocke gets louder and louder with each question until she's shouting at me.

I stand up and shove my chair back. If she wants to shout, we can shout.

"I know you can't prevent a curse from activating

unless you know what triggers it. I know a curse that doesn't require physical contact is insanely rare. It's ancient magic that has been banned for centuries because it was blood magic."

Stocke crosses her arms. "Blood magic, meaning blood sacrifice?"

I nod. "All magic, but especially enchantments, are limited by what the witch can do. I don't know how blood magic works; they don't teach anyone about it anymore for obvious reasons, but we all learned about the horrible weapons it was used to create. Those things are supposed to have been destroyed, but they weren't. Not all of them."

"So, you're suggesting that Martinez is using some kind of a cursed object to keep himself from being Found?" Stocke asks.

"Yes," I say, pulling my chair back in close and sitting down heavily.

Stocke begins pacing again.

"How many times can this curse be triggered?" Reilly asks.

"What?" I ask, turning to face him.

"Corinne tried to Find him, and she was cursed. Can this object, or whatever he has, protect him forever? Or will it eventually be used up?"

"I have no idea," I say. "It's possible it could trigger more than once, but I don't know that for sure."

"That's not something we can risk happening again," Stocke says. "Finding Martinez is off limits."

"I do think he was close by," I say quietly. "Maybe not close enough to actually see me, but he was watching somehow. I think he wants to watch me die if he can't, uh, have me."

Reilly stiffens behind me.

"Have you?" Stocke asks, brows pinching together. "Like he has a crush on you?"

I rub hands over my face. "The way he was talking to me, it was like he was flirting with me again. He said he wanted to see me dance, and he keeps trying to convince me to quit trying to stop him and join him instead."

"He knows you're a witch. Why would he try to recruit you?" Stocke asks.

"The first time, when we were in that basement, he said I could still be redeemed if I stopped using magic," I say, picking at a chip on surface of the table.

"That's odd," Reilly says thoughtfully. "I've never heard the NWR use language like that before. They've always spoken of paranormals as abominations."

I shrug. "I've never heard it before either. I think he might just be insane though."

"Who have you given that phone number to?" Stocke asks. "Your JHAPI-issue phone."

"No one," I say, shaking my head. "I've barely used the thing. I haven't even talked to anyone other than the team since I left Texas."

Stocke glances at Reilly, then back at me.

"If you are lying about this, you could be putting everyone in jeopardy."

I turn to Reilly and throw my hands up. "Tell her I'm not lying."

"She's not lying," Reilly says drily.

Stocke rolls her eyes. "You'll have to pardon me if I don't take him at his word where you are concerned."

"How else could he have gotten my number?" I ask. "Is there some kind of database? Is it public information?"

Stocke purses her lips and thinks. "There is a directory. It wouldn't be all that difficult to access if someone really wanted it."

"Well, there you go," I say sarcastically. "I have no interest in chatting with Martinez on the phone. I did not somehow secretly slip him my phone number."

Reilly taps his fingers on the table. "This is an opportunity."

"For what?" I ask.

"Martinez made a play for Olivia. He set a trap, and he almost succeeded in getting her to walk right into it," Reilly explains. "However, his failure gives us the advantage. We know what he wants most of all now."

Stocke turns to me, and I bite the inside of my cheek.

"You want to use me as bait?" I ask. He could have passed the plan by me before bringing it up in front of Stocke.

Reilly nods.

"How exactly do you suggest we do that? Should I just go outside and wave around a sign that says 'come and get me'?" I ask.

Reilly shrugs. "I don't think you need the sign, but yes, something similar to that. The plan doesn't need to be complicated."

"Why didn't he take me this afternoon? I was out in broad daylight, alone. I drove all over the city," I say, crossing my arms and leaning back in my chair.

"You weren't actually alone. I've had someone following you when you aren't with one of the agents," Reilly says. "As a matter of protection, of course. The threat from the coven that attacked the clanhouse is still high."

I dig my nails into my palm and grind my teeth together to keep from saying something because whatever might come out right now would be ugly.

"If the threat is so great that you needed to assign a protective detail to Olivia, I should have been informed of it," Stocke says, leaning forward with both hands flat on the table.

"I did mention that I believed they were still searching for her," Reilly says. "And having one body-guard stay close is hardly a protective detail. He wouldn't have been able to stop a kidnapping most likely, but if you were taken, I would have been noti-fied immediately."

"Maybe you should have just installed a GPS tracker in me, and then you wouldn't have had to bother having me followed," I bite out. "I can't believe you did that without telling me."

"Yet I did, and it most likely kept you from being kidnapped yesterday when you went out by yourself, despite repeated warnings about your safety. Despite the obvious threat that Martinez and the NWR pose," Reilly snaps, losing the cool he has maintained up to this point. "Stocke is right that you are reckless."

My cheeks burn, and I want to slap Reilly across the face. Electricity sparks across my fingertips where they are still curled into the palm of my hand.

"I did what I had to, and I won't apologize for it," I growl back.

"I've gathered that apologies aren't really your thing," he sneers.

"Enough," Stocke says. "Whatever lover's spat you're having can wait until you're alone."

"We are not—" I begin.

"I do not care," she reiterates, dismissing me with a wave of her hand. "Reilly, what exactly is your plan?"

"I think it's time Olivia tried to run away," he says, putting his hands behind his head and relaxing back into his chair. "Is your shoulder completely, healed by the way?"

I cover it with my hand. It isn't, but I wasn't going

to say anything because I didn't want them trying to get me medical attention.

"No, but I can heal it later."

Reilly grins. "Perhaps we can explore installing a GPS tracker in you first."

---

My palms are sweating. I wipe them against my pants and glance over my shoulder, which still aches thanks to Reilly's stupid plan. I'm less than a block from the car rental place, but I've been walking for over an hour.

It took thirty minutes to give Reilly's tail the slip, and another fifteen to make sure he was actually gone. Both Reilly and Stocke had agreed it was necessary to make this seem real. I hadn't disagreed, but it was still a pain in the ass.

The farther I get from the Strip, the fewer pedestrians there are, which makes me breathe a little easier. I'd like to see Martinez coming if he does try to take me. I'm starting to doubt he will though. This whole thing might be a little too obvious of a trap.

I adjust my backpack again, it's awkward and heavy with all my things stuffed in it. I wonder how far Reilly will let me get before he decides this whole thing just isn't working.

I pause at the corner of the parking lot at the car rental place and scan the area. I don't think anyone is following me, and the tail Reilly had put on me is definitely gone. I head inside, and luckily, the place is dead.

There is one employee at the counter. She has a piece of gum wrapped around the tip of her finger that she's currently sucking back into her mouth. Her eyes are glued to her phone, she doesn't even look up as the door rings to alert her to my entrance.

I walk up to the counter and drop my backpack on the floor next to my feet.

"Hey," I say, but she still doesn't budge. "I need to rent a car."

She sighs and sucks the gum off her finger, finally looking up at me. "You have a reservation or anything?"

"No, and I'd like to pay cash."

"No can do," she says, popping the gum. "We've gotta have a card in case you do something stupid. Like steal the car or wreck it or whatever."

"Fine." I pull out my personal credit card. Reilly's stupid plan is going to make me broke.

She snatches the card, plops back on her stool and starts typing into the computer.

"What kinda car?" she asks.

I shrug. "Whatever is cheap."

"Uh huh," she says as she scans the screen. "We've got one compact car left. That's the cheapest."

"I'll take it."

"How many days?" she asks, popping her gum again.

"Um, three," I say, tapping my fingers against the counter impatiently.

"Will you drop it off here or somewhere else?"

"Here."

She clicks a few more things, then the printer next to her hums and prints off a couple of sheets of paperwork.

"Sign here," she says, pointing to the bottom of the first page. "There and there."

I sign both pages, agreeing to return the car with a full tank of gas and accepting the insurance. She takes a set of keys off the row of hooks behind her and hands them to me.

"It's in row D," she says, pointing toward the parking lot. "Just use the clicker to find it or whatever."

"Thanks," I say, grabbing my backpack and hurrying back outside.

The parking lot is half-empty, so it's not hard to find the car. It's tiny, but it'll do. I toss my backpack in the passenger seat as I climb inside.

I start it up and whip out of the parking spot. Stocke had suggested I drive out of the city, rather than further into it, to prevent the chance of bystanders getting hurt. I have no idea where I'm going, but I know the highway near this place leads north, and that's good enough for now.

I turn on the radio and flip through several channels before I come across a classic rock station. I don't recognize the song, but it's catchy and has a fast beat. I turn it up and speed down the highway.

About ten minutes outside of the city I notice a van behind me. I'm not sure when exactly it showed up, and there are quite a few cars on this road, but I can't help suspect it might be him. I shift uneasily in my seat, my eyes flicking to the rearview mirror every few seconds.

The van starts to slow and turns down a side road. I sigh and rub my eyes. It wasn't them. They may not come at all. This could all be a huge waste of time.

I round a turn and see something glinting on the road. I take my foot off the accelerator, but there's no time to slow down or swerve. All four of my tires blow out at once, and the car jerks violently to the right. I yank the steering wheel to the left, but I overcorrect and the car fishtails wildly. I hit the edge of the road, and the tires are jerked out onto the rough ground.

There is no shoulder, only a steep incline I can't keep the car from barreling toward. The car tips and rolls. My hands fly off the wheel. I don't know how many times it flips, but when it comes to a stop, I'm hanging awkwardly with the airbag in my face and nothing but the seatbelt keeping me from falling into the front windshield. All I can think is that I'm glad I went ahead and paid for the extra insurance.

I slap at the airbag until it deflates, then brace my knees on the steering wheel. Whatever I hit was put in the middle of the road intentionally. I don't think I have much time to get out of here. I summon some vampire strength and rip the seatbelt out of the buckle.

I catch myself awkwardly, my foot breaking the windshield further. The door is jammed shut, but two solid shoves push it open. I tumble out and see the van first, then a man I don't recognize standing a few yards away.

There's a quick pinch of pain on my arm. I flinch and look down; a dart is sticking out of my arm. I yank it out and stumble forward, but on my third step, I find myself falling forward. This wasn't part of the plan. My body is completely numb, and I can feel consciousness leaving me as everything goes black. I see a glimpse of someone else I hadn't noticed standing near the front of the car.

That was stupid, I should have looked. I should have—

## 23

Something is rocking. My head hurts, and I don't remember why I'm lying on the floor. I rub my cheek against the rough carpet to get the itch I can't seem to move my hands to scratch. My hair keeps tickling it though. Someone brushes my hair back gently, and I hum in contentment.

"They say the devil is beautiful. I always imagined the devil was a woman too," a voice whispers. "So that she can look innocent when she comes to tempt you into giving your soul to her."

I regret waking up intensely. I try to scoot away from the hand threading through my hair, but I'm backed up against something wooden. I drag my eye-lids open, but it is a struggle. I think one of them might be swollen. I'm in the back of some kind of a van. There are weapons mounted on the walls and several cases of ammo that are strapped down so they don't shift around. The back of the van must be separated from the front because it's dark back here other than the glow from a single overhead light set into the roof of the van.

"Olivia," he says. "Look at me."

Martinez crouches down in front of me. I look up at

him and bite down on the inside of my cheek to keep my face straight. He looks like something out of a nightmare. The left side of his face is red and twisted from the burns I gave him. His eye is milky white, and the skin around it is stretched down like melted candle wax.

"I don't tempt you at all, do I? Not looking like this," he whispers. "You liked me before though. I saw the way you stared at me."

I lift my head so I can see him more clearly. I let my eyes wander, I want him to have no doubt that I'm looking at the scars I left him with.

"Now the outside matches the inside," I choke out. My throat is sore and dry.

He slaps me. The smack of his hand against my cheek stings, but it's the way my face smashes back into the floor of the van that really hurts. I pull on my electric magic. I don't need my hands to kill him.

My body tenses suddenly and violently, and the metal around my wrists burns. I can't breathe. I can't even blink. Everything fades into gray, and the taste of blood fills my mouth as my teeth cut into my tongue. I don't understand what's happening, or why. I didn't think he would kill me this fast. I thought I would have more time.

The team has to be on their way, but Reilly had said it would be at least ten minutes from the moment I was taken. I don't know how long I was unconscious. I don't know if I'll last ten minutes.

There is a painful shock on my arm, and I scream, then gasp as I can suddenly breathe. I choke on the blood in my mouth and struggle to spit it out while panting. Martinez's smug face swims into view. Only the right side of his mouth seems to be able to move, while the left side is stuck.

"Did you really think I would get this close to you

if I didn't have a way to stop you from flinging your magic at me?" He leans his head back and laughs loudly.

"What the fuck did you do to me?" I gasp out.

He tilts his head to the side, still grinning.

"It's what your kind did to you," he says, tapping on the shackles holding my hands behind my back. "These were made by a very talented enchanter. She made all sorts of interesting things she wasn't supposed to. All of them one of a kind, like shackles that turn a witch's magic against them."

He grins like it's all a joke. I suppose it is to him.

"There was some resistance at first to using these things after we took them from her, but I made the others understand the beauty of it." He pulls a necklace out of his shirt. A solid gold medallion hangs from the chain, and even from here I can feel the hungry, oily darkness that emanates from it. "You know what this does, don't you?"

I don't want to be anywhere near that thing.

"It was amazing to watch it take her. I had hoped it would be you, of course, but the look on your face was almost worth my trap failing."

"You weren't there. We looked," I grind out.

"I was watching from the skies," he says. "You think magic is the only way to do wondrous things. It's so easy for paranormals to forget that there's a reason humans have survived all this time, despite not having magic."

He tucks the medallion back into his shirt and pats the side of my face.

"Perhaps I'll show you the video later. I'm sure you'll make the same face again, and it will be so much more interesting in person."

I jerk away and spit at him, my saliva still tinged

with blood. He glances at the stain on the sleeve of his shirt but doesn't seem bothered.

"You'll never win," I snarl at him. "People can see that paranormals aren't monsters."

He grabs my jaw, his fingers biting into my skin.

"That's where you're wrong," he hisses. "They are violent, deviant monsters. Their true nature will be revealed soon enough. They can't hide behind their masks forever."

The van jerks to a stop, and Martinez stands up, his back still hunched because of the height of the van, and raps twice on the doors. The doors are flung open, and I blink against the sunlight. The sun is hovering just above the horizon.

Martinez steps out of the van and walks off with the other man I haven't gotten a good look at yet. We're on some kind of wide, paved road that looks familiar in a way. I push up on my elbow awkwardly, leaning against the wall behind me, then thump my head back in irritation. I'm such an idiot. That's an airstrip, not a road.

I crane my head around to get a look at the shackles that are keeping me from using my magic. They're solid black and appear to have something engraved on them, but I can't read it.

Martinez knows I'm a witch, and it seems like he knows I can steal magic, or at least that I can use offensive magic. I don't think he knows that I'm half-vampire. All that talk about redeeming myself seemed to be about me using magic as a witch.

I don't want to die here or get taken away to be tortured by the NWR, but the choice between the two is actually pretty easy. There's a chance this might work too. The witch who made these wouldn't have intended them to be used on a vampire, or they'd be silver.

I slide back down onto my shoulder and pull on the vampire magic. There's no time for the control I've been practicing. As soon as the magic spreads through me, I brace myself for the pain and tension, but nothing happens.

One of them scoffs angrily, and I focus my senses on their conversation.

"This is insanely risky," the man says. "Peterson is not pleased you decided to do this last minute without proper approval."

Martinez snorts. "The buyer has promised me eight-hundred thousand if I bring her to them alive. That is not an amount we can afford to pass up right now just because Peterson is afraid of a little risk."

Buyer? I had assumed Martinez was planning on killing me, not selling me. An engine rumbles to life, something much louder than a car.

I yank my wrists apart as hard as I can, and pain shoots through my arms, but the shackles don't even bend. At least I'm not having another magical seizure, but if I can't get out of this van before they put me on the plane, I'm still screwed.

The shackles are connected to the wall by a short chain runs through two loops that jut out of the middle of them. It looks like a normal chain instead of the same weird black metal that the shackles are made of. If it were any thicker, I'd say there was no way I could break it, but I don't have any other options. I have to try.

I roll forward, letting my arms stretch out behind me, and begin pulling. The metal in the chain creaks and bends as the shackles bite into my skin. I'm not strong enough. It's so hard to use this magic during the day.

I grit my teeth and pull more deeply on the magic. The sunlight glaring in my face starts to burn, and my eyes ache even squeezed shut. I can deal with pain if it means surviving though. Strength flows into my body slowly, and I yank sharply on the chain. Once. Twice. Hot blood slips down between my fingers as the shackles break through my skin. I yank again with all of my strength, and the chain snaps.

I roll onto my face with no way to stop myself. I'm dizzy, but I don't wait to recover or see if Martinez heard. I struggle to my feet and launch myself from the van with all the speed and strength I have left. My feet hit the pavement, and my legs almost crumple.

Martinez shouts something, and I dart to the left. The only thing I can see in front of me is desert. To my left is a metal building attached to a long covered hangar that must be as big as three football fields with other small planes lined up inside of it. I sprint in that direction, zig-zagging to make myself less of an easy target and putting on a little burst of speed every few seconds to move vampire fast.

Gunfire cracks behind me, but nothing hits me. I hope the GPS buried in my shoulder is still working, but I know it's been way longer than the ten minutes Reilly had promised me. I have no idea if anyone is coming to rescue me, and I can't assume they will be.

I glance over my shoulder and see the van careening toward me. Martinez is hanging out of the passenger window with a gun pressed against his shoulder. I put on another burst of speed and slip behind the back corner of the metal building.

There are no doors, no way in, and nothing to hide behind. I keep running along the back of the building and skid to a stop behind one of the planes. The van skids around the corner of the building and bumps along the rough ground.

I hunch down, my arms aching from being held behind my back for so long, and scurry toward another plane. It's a hideous mustard yellow thing with a lightning bolt that extends from the nose to the tail. I crouch behind the wheel, but it doesn't hide me completely.

The van stops at the back of the hangar, a cloud of dirt kicking up around it. Martinez and the other man jump out, guns ready, as they search for me. I lean against the wheel and try not to breathe.

Their boots crunch against the rocky ground, then scrape almost silently against the concrete floor of the hangar. Martinez heads diagonally away from me, but the other guy with the mountain man beard is walking straight toward me.

I tense to run again, but a familiar noise makes me hesitate. The *whomp-whomp* of helicopter blades is unmistakable. I'm not sure if that is someone coming to help me, or if it's backup for them. Showing up in a helicopter wasn't part of the plan, but none of this was. I have no idea if the NWR has access to a helicopter, and I'm not sure why they'd use one now when they obviously have an airplane.

Mountain Man pauses, tilting his head to one side. He must hear it too. He gestures at Martinez, who jogs to the other side of the hangar and looks out at the sky.

"Time to go," Martinez shouts. Mountain Man sprints toward him, but Martinez stays where he is. I try to scoot around the wheel, but there's hardly anything between us.

Martinez lifts his gun, pointing it in my direction. I shove to the left and barely catch myself as I half-run, half-stumble. Bullets strike the plane I'm running next to. The gunfire echoes painfully against the concrete and metal all around us. I wince, my ears ringing so badly I can't even hear the helicopter anymore.

I spot the door that leads into the building attached to the hangar and put on a burst of speed. I crash through the door, little splinters of wood digging into my shoulder as the door disintegrates under the force of my body hitting it. It's dark in here, and this room is small. There is a short hall with one open door at the end that reveals a bathroom.

Another shot echoes behind me, and I duck and roll to the right. I can't go far. There isn't anywhere to hide in here, and there isn't another exit. This was a bad plan.

I grit my teeth and pull at the shackles again. I want them off. I need to be able to use my magic. The metal bites into the already sore cuts, and I have to bite down hard on the inside of my cheek to stay silent. After a few seconds of absolutely futile struggling, I realize that Martinez hasn't come in the building yet.

I press back into the corner and try to listen again, but my ears are still ringing, drowning out everything but my own labored breathing. I struggle back up to my feet and edge toward the door I busted through.

I peek out, and my eyes go wide. Hu is standing between me and Martinez, whose rifle is laying bent and half-melted in front of his feet. I'm not sure where Mountain Man is.

"You're under arrest. Get down on your knees and put your hands behind your head," Hu shouts.

Martinez grins and pulls a collapsible baton off his belt. He flings it open with a flick of his wrist, and the end sparks with electricity.

"You'll have to make me, demon."

Hu shifts his feet carefully, and fire erupts from his shoulders and chest. It wraps around him like armor, and his shirt burns away, the pieces scattering around him. His skin glistens with sweat, and the phoenix tattoo on his back glows and shifts under the magic. I've seen fire witches use their magic before, but I've never seen anything like this. Flames appear above his head, twisting into two horns.

"If it's a demon you want, I can accommodate," Hu says with a smirk.

A howl goes up, and I see Elise, fully shifted, step into the hangar a few yards behind Martinez. Following closely behind her is the last person I expected to see. Reilly's face is drawn and tired. The sun may be setting soon, but it's obvious he has been awake for a while.

Hu charges Martinez, the flames leaping out in front of him like a whip. Martinez dodges and rolls behind a plane. I dart out of the building and run toward Elise and Reilly, staying as far away from Martinez and Hu as I can. My legs are faltering, and I'm running almost human slow. I've used too much of the vampire magic, and I think the shackles might be hurting me in more ways than the obvious too. I can't keep this up.

An explosion rocks the entire hangar, and I find myself face down on the concrete. A fireball shoots up to the ceiling of the hangar, and a wave of heat rolls over me. My ears are ringing again, and the smell of smoke and burning metal fills my nose.

Elise is running toward the fight, but it takes me a moment to spot Reilly. He is headed my way, but his focus is on the fight as well. He's only a few yards away now. I struggle to my knees and get one foot on the ground. If I can just get to him, maybe he can get these shackles off me.

The other man, the one I had lost track of, steps out from behind a plane about fifteen yards away. His gun is trained on Reilly, but Reilly is focused completely on Martinez, who is shouting something at Hu I can't quite hear.

A million things fly through my head in a moment. I know the NWR have silver bullets. I know not even Reilly could survive a shot to the head at this range. The man steadies his gun, bracing it against his shoulder. I'm going to regret this.

I shove off the ground, my foot barely able to get traction. My shoulder slams into Reilly's side as the crack of the rifle reverberates through the hangar. We are both airborne for less than a second before Reilly shifts midair and wraps his arms around me, dragging me around and landing on his feet.

Reilly drops me and is standing behind the man with the rifle before he has a chance to blink. He wraps his hands and around the man's neck and twists. There is a sickening crack, and the man falls to the ground, limp.

I roll onto my stomach with a groan. That is going to leave another bruise. Reilly doesn't run to me like I expected; he runs toward the fight. I crane my neck to watch. Hu unleashes another barrage at Martinez, with Elise snarling behind him. Reilly is holding the same injector we used when we were trying to knock out Ryan.

Hu pulls the flames back, and in the same breath Reilly darts in. He is still slow with the sun up, almost human slow, and Martinez is fast. He jabs the baton into Reilly's stomach at the same time Reilly presses the injector against his neck. They drop in unison, Reilly jerking from the jolt of electricity. Martinez is absolutely still.

24

I don't bother trying to get up. Hu pulls a pair of cuffs off his belt and immediately detains Martinez. Elise shifts and helps him search Martinez for any more weapons.

I feel the sun set, but it doesn't give me energy like it has been. I'm beyond exhausted. I'm starving and I'm angry and I wish I had the strength to get to Hu or Elise. I can smell the magic in them, and I want it, desperately.

Reilly sits up, dusting off the shoulders of his jacket, then standing. He looks for me and sees I'm lying exactly where he left me. There are sirens in the distance. It's about time the rest of them showed up.

One second Reilly is on the other side of the hangar, the next he is crouched next to me, helping me sit up.

"Does Martinez have a key for these?" he asks.

"I hope so," I say shakily. I hadn't even thought he might not have the key.

"Did you find any keys?" Reilly shouts.

Hu nods and holds up a key ring.

"Make sure they take the medallion off him too. It's cursed. It's what hurt Corinne," I say.

In a blink, Reilly is there and back again, keys in hand. The quick movements are making me dizzy.

"They have the medallion," he says as he rolls me onto my stomach and starts trying keys in the lock. "What are these?"

"Some enchanted bullshit," I mutter into the concrete. "Couldn't use most of my magic. It didn't stop the vampire magic, I guess it's different somehow."

"It's blocking your magic?" Reilly asks before cursing at the keys.

"No," I say, shaking my head. "It was more like it gave me a seizure. I couldn't breathe, couldn't move. It would have killed me."

There is a click, and the shackles fall off. I groan as my arms fall forward and relief floods through me. My magic is quivering inside of me, freed as well.

"Don't try to walk," he says, scooping me up.

I turn my face into his chest and take a deep breath. He smells like magic and blood and fire. I'm so hungry. There is a brief gust of wind on my face, and when I lift my head, we're outside.

There is a line of cop cars following behind the black JHAPI SUVs. They spread out. Two stop in front of the plane, which is still running, while the other heads straight for us, coming to an abrupt stop just a few yards away. Stocke leaps out, gun drawn.

"Is there anyone left?"

Reilly shakes his head. "No, there were only two of them. Martinez has been captured alive, but the other is dead."

Stocke nods and runs past us toward Elise and Hu. Cook and Ivy follow her. Reilly carries me to the SUV and sets me in the passenger seat.

I pull my knees up to my chest, but my muscles won't stop trembling. I'm so hungry, and I'm so tired.

"Olivia," Reilly says, tugging my hands away from my face. "Look at me."

I shake my head.

"You have to feed," he insists.

"No," I groan. "I don't want to hurt anybody. I don't want—"

"You won't hurt me," he says, shaking me hard once.

The movement wakes me up a little bit, and I blink at him, trying to make sense of what he is saying.

"You?" I ask.

He jerks his sleeve up and presses his wrist to my mouth. "I understand what you're taking, and I'm telling you it's all right."

"Why?" I ask, my question muffled against his arm.

"You saved my life," he says, his jaw clenched tightly. "I thought you would let me die given the opportunity."

I guess I did do him a huge favor. I'm too hungry to argue with him. I want this. My fangs slide down, and I bite into his arm. Every swallow spreads the warmth of his blood through my body. I reach inside of him and pull on his magic as well, and the trembling of my muscles slows.

I should have let him die. I could have run after that, but I hadn't thought of that when that man was lifting the gun and aiming it at his head. I had a moment of regret while I was rushing toward him, but the thought of actually letting him die makes me sick even now. I guess as much as I say I hate him, I really just hate what he has forced me into. I couldn't let him die. I wouldn't have been able to live with myself.

I swallow another delicious mouthful and sigh

around his arm. Life would be so much easier without a conscience. His hand brushes a strand of hair back behind my ear, his fingers trailing along my cheek. My stomach does a flip at the touch, but I keep my eyes firmly shut and do my best to ignore it.

After another minute, Reilly tugs his wrist away from me. I lean back into the seat to keep from chasing after it, but it's a struggle. It helped, a lot, but I don't feel completely satisfied.

"Staci is here," Reilly says. "She brought healing supplies. Deal with your wounds. I need to speak with Stocke."

I nod absently. Reilly's warm presence disappears, and I let my eyes slip shut. I could sleep for days right now.

Someone clears their throat next to me. I shake off the sleepiness and sit up straight. Staci has a handful of first aid supplies she holds up for me to see.

"Thanks," I say hoarsely.

She hands me a cleansing wipe and sets a tub of healing salve on the dash for when I'm ready for it, then crosses her arms. I clean the blood off my fingers and hands, then gently dab at the area around the wound. It hurts an annoying amount.

"That brew you made for Corinne, to end the curse, how did you do it?" she asks.

I open the salve and spread it on my left wrist before I answer. Staci seems huffier than normal, like asking pains her. It's petty, but I'm going to enjoy it while it lasts.

"I felt the curse that was hurting her. With as long as I've been brewing, I've developed the ability to find the ingredients needed to enhance something, or stop it. So, I listened to my magic and simply brewed something that would cut through the darkness of the curse. It needed to be burned away," I say with a shrug.

Staci pinches her lips together. "Your intuition can't always be right. Magic is a tool. What you're talking about sounds like some kind of religious nonsense."

I laugh and start putting the salve on my other wrist.

"Your coven really did a number on you," I say with a smile. "I'm not brewing on faith. I understand what different ingredients do, and that took many hours of study. I also experimented a lot as a child. It's a skill I've cultivated because you're right, magic is a tool."

I hop off the stretcher, and she steps back. Her shoulders are hunched up, and her fingers are curled into her cardigan.

"I was looking for a recipe you know. I was going to try to help her," she says quietly.

I gnaw on the inside of my cheek and look around, hoping someone will come interrupt what is starting to feel uncomfortably like a heart to heart.

"Um, I sure you would have found something," I say, taking a step back. "If you ever want to talk brewing theory, or try something new, let me know. I have to go—find Reilly now though."

I turn and hurry away. Reilly is standing at the corner of the hangar, deep in conversation with Agent Stocke and a man in a crisp suit I haven't seen before. There are two men, bodyguards I presume, standing a few paces behind him.

I don't want to deal with strangers, especially ones who require bodyguards. I veer off toward the van the team arrived in. Maybe it will be safer to hide in there for a little while. Elise steps into my path, her hands on her hips. She's wearing a belt buckle that looks like a mouth full of teeth, with two glinting fangs extending just past the rest.

"Hey, you," she says, eyes narrowed.

"What is up with your belt buckles?" I blurt out.

She glances down and frowns. "My mom buys them for me."

A laugh bursts out of me, and I slap my hand over my mouth, but I can't seem to stop.

Elise rolls her eyes, but she's smiling too. "They're awesome, and it would hurt her feelings if I didn't wear them."

"That's great," I say, wiping tears from my eyes.

She watches me, the smile slowly sliding from her face.

"I'm glad you didn't die today," she says. "But if you are going to stay with the team, I need you to promise me something."

All the tension the laughter momentarily erased comes back with a vengeance. I shove my hands in my pockets.

"What do you want?" I ask.

"You follow the rules. You go through Stocke for big decisions. And you don't lie about anything else, like being able to steal magic. That is important, mind-boggling shit. That's the kind of thing your team needs to know," she says, jabbing her finger at me.

"I didn't want any of this, and I'm doing the best I can," I snap, suddenly angry. I'm sick of them all blaming me for Corinne getting hurt. "I didn't force Corinne to do what she did...hell, I tried to talk her out of it."

"I'm mad at her too." Elise snaps. "And I don't care if it is your best. Do better. This is temporary for you, but the rest of us are invested in seeing this through.

If you're going to run away again, just go ahead and do it."

I roll my eyes. "Now you sound like Zachary. And believe me, I would run if I could."

I brush past her. I want to be anywhere else right now. She catches my arm.

"What do you mean by that? That you would run if you could?" she demands.

I jerk my arm away. "Nothing."

I shouldn't have said that. She's perceptive, more so than the rest of the team.

"Did you forget I can hear a lie just like your vampire?" she asks.

I look over her shoulder at the person approaching and plaster a smile on my face.

"Reilly," I say. "Have they finally decided where they are taking Martinez?"

Elise stiffens and turns around slowly, stepping back so she isn't standing between us. I don't know how much he heard, or if him walking up when he did was a coincidence, but the tension is palpable.

"They have," Reilly says with a nod and a sideways glance at Elise. "They have the transport ready to take Martinez away now. It's time to go."

"Good, I need a shower and at least twelve hours of sleep," I say lightly. Elise is too busy glaring at Reilly to react.

"We'll see you back at the conference room in a couple of hours," Reilly says to Elise. "Stocke wants us all there by midnight."

I follow Reilly toward one of the SUVs. I can feel Elise's eyes on my back the entire time.

## 2 5

It feels like it's been an eternity since I last sat in this room, but it's been less than twenty-four hours. I made sure to avoid the squeaky chair this time, but Ivy is stuck in it instead. She's a lot better at holding still than I am though, so you can hardly tell.

Zachary drove me here, and the rest of team was apparently delayed in following us. Reilly had disappeared without comment after Martinez had been hauled off. I was surprised he had left me alone, and surprised he hadn't demanded answers about everything that had happened. I can still taste his blood in my mouth, and it's distracting, to say the least.

I shift uncomfortably in my chair. I have bruises all over the place, and I don't have the energy to heal them right now. I don't think I'll have the energy or the time to brew my own salves either. Maybe Staci will bring me some without too much of an attitude after our last conversation.

"What happened with the GPS, by the way? Were you guys tracking me the whole time?" I ask, rubbing my shoulder. The tracker is still in there. I'm dreading having it removed since I'll have to actually see a doctor. Growing up with a hedgewitch for a mother, and then stealing the healing magic at a young age meant I haven't had to see human doctors. I distrust them. Everything they have to do seems kind of barbaric.

"We lost the signal for about thirty minutes," Zachary answers.

"Shit, I was out for that long?" I ask.

Ivy nods. "You were gone for an hour total. By the time we regained the signal, we were behind and headed in the wrong direction."

"Well, I'm glad I got to be unconscious for all of that," I say, leaning my head against the back of the chair.

Zachary snorts. "I think we all wanted to be. It was really tense here for a while. I thought Reilly was going to tear the tech's head off."

"Leave it to Reilly to threaten random people," I say with a snort.

"He was very concerned about you," Zachary says, nudging my chair with his foot.

I shrug. "Yeah, I'm sure he was."

The door opens, and the rest of the team files in. Except for Corinne. My stomach sinks. I want to see her soon, but there hasn't been time yet, and I'm not sure if Ivy will let me anyhow.

Reilly takes the seat next to me, and I shift uncomfortably in my seat. I haven't spoken to him since he interrupted the conversation with Elise, but I'm sure I'll be questioned about it soon.

"I spoke with the hospital staff a few minutes ago," Stocke says, taking her usual place at the head of the table. "Corinne is doing well. They expect her to wake up in a couple of days. Right now, they have her sedated to allow her magic to continue recovering at a faster pace."

A murmur of relief spreads around the table.

Something in my gut unclenches. Hearing she really will be okay is such a huge relief.

"Where is Martinez being taken?" Reilly asks.

"A maximum security prison back in Texas," Stocke says. "We'll continue hunting down every NWR member we can find, and continue looking for any evidence needed to build a case against him, but what we already have is solid. He's going to be locked up for three lifetimes at least."

"Are these two still on the team?" Cook asks. He doesn't look at me, or at Reilly, but his shoulders are held in a tight line, and his jaw is clenching and unclenching.

"Olivia and Reilly will be taking a week of leave to attend the Summit, where they will also be reporting on the progress we have made and ensuring that we receive the funding we need to continue," Stocke says, leaning back in her chair. "So yes, they are still on the team, and they will be rejoining us at our next location."

Cook glances back at Ivy. She keeps her expression blank, but she does nod. Cook sighs but apparently takes that as acceptance on her part.

Elise is staring at me, the same question on her face she had a few hours ago when Reilly interrupted our conversation. She's going to have to keep wondering. I shouldn't have let slip as much as I did.

"Any other questions or concerns about the future of this team and this assignment?" Stocke looks around the table, challenging anyone else to voice their objections now or shut up and deal with it.

I look down at my hands and wait. I don't know if I'm hoping someone else wants us gone or not. In some ways, it might be easier not to have to do this. I'm not sure what the alternative is though.

"All right, moving on, then," Stocke says. "We're

headed to Los Angeles next. It has some of the highest NWR activity in the nation. We've known for a while that they are not only recruiting, but carrying out protests, and they have recently started attacking the local packs there."

"Openly attacking them?" Elise asks, leaning forward to rest her elbows on the table.

"Yes," Stocke says. "Ambush attacks when there are one or two of them somewhere alone. There have been four deaths so far. Basically assassinations."

"How are the pack leaders handling it?" Elise asks.

"So far, they're confining everyone to pack lands as much as possible. When they do leave, it's in groups of five at a minimum." Stocke twirls her pen in her fingers. "That's not sustainable though. These people have jobs, school, and the right to live without constant threat of being murdered."

"When do we leave?" Hu asks.

"We have early afternoon flights, so in about six hours," Stocke says. "We'll go over the rest, including case details and the NWR members we already have identified, in Los Angeles. Everyone, go pack and get a few hours of sleep if you can. It's going to be a long day."

Everyone stands and gathers their things. The adrenaline of the fight has faded, and I can tell everyone else is just as tired as I feel. One thing has been bothering me though.

"The other vampires who had gone missing, were they ever found? Or is no one looking for them now?" I ask.

Stocke sighs heavily. "Their ashes were all mailed to their respective clans."

My eyes widen. "All of them?"

"Yes," Stocke confirms. "The day after Ryan was put down."

"And the werewolves?" I ask.

"Still not officially missing. There is nothing we can do to help them, and no way to justify continuing the investigation if they aren't reported missing by their packs," Stocke says, her shoulders slumping.

I put my head in my hands. Martinez just killed them all once he decided they were no longer useful. Or maybe they died while being experimented on or whatever the hell the NWR was doing to them. If the pack leaders would just talk to JHAPI, they might be able to save their people from a similar fate, but of course they won't.

"I'll see you back at the hotel room," Reilly says, putting his hand on my shoulder and startling me out of my thoughts. "I need to speak with Stocke privately."

"All right," I say.

Zachary is already leaving the room, so I jog after him.

"Zach," I say, jogging after him. "Do you have a little bit to talk? I need a ride back to the hotel, and I want to go over that case with you one last time."

"Sure," he says. "It seems like we won't get much of a chance to work on it for the next couple of weeks."

"Yeah, that's what I'm afraid of."

I glance back in the room one last time before following Zachary. Reilly is watching me. I'm sure he overheard the conversation. I sigh; that will be yet another thing for him to question me about later.

---

Zachary unlocks the hotel room door, and I follow him inside. He sets his things down on the desk, and I take my usual spot on the end of Elise's bed.

"I've been thinking about the spellbook my mother stole from this coven," I say, bouncing my leg nervously. The only possible meaning I can glean from the most recent hallucination of my mother is that the book she stole might be important somehow. If there is even any meaning to it at all. Maybe it's just a nightmare my mind is creating. "Have you found anything about that in the research you've done?"

Zachary shakes his head. "The coven deals with so many magical artifacts. Nothing about a spellbook has stood out though."

"Maybelle sold it, probably for a lot of money. It had to have been to another witch or coven, right?" I ask, leaning back in my chair.

Zachary taps his pen against his mouth. "I don't know. It's possible any paranormal could have bought it. Even a human, perhaps. People are still trying out magical things, hoping if they just believe, it will work for them, and then they'll have magic too. You know, the usual romanticized bullshit people talk about."

I nod. "Still, it would be hard to keep something like that under wraps. And Maybelle managed to buy some really powerful magical items. I thought it was impossible to enchant something to change your appearance like that. The magic never slipped at all. No one had any idea she and Gerard weren't human."

"Why is the spellbook important? We might be able to find it, but that doesn't help us build a case against this coven."

"No, but it might help us lure them out. Or figure out what exactly they're trying to do. Maybe even find out who's protecting them," I say.

Zachary sighs and steeples his fingers in front of

his face, his elbows resting on his knees. "Do you have any idea where to start?"

"I can try to contact Maybelle, but I don't think she's going to text back," I say with a snort.

"You might as well try."

I pull out my personal phone and realize it's dead. I haven't used it for days and apparently haven't charged it either.

"Do you have a charger?" I ask, waving the black screen at Zachary.

"I think Elise's phone uses that type of charger. It's plugged in over there by her bed," Zachary says, pointing behind me.

I walk over and plug my phone in, then plop back down on the bed to wait.

"It's still hard to believe we caught him," I say quietly. "I wish we had killed him so I'd know it's over."

"That wouldn't end this. The NWR only lost one member. The organization isn't even crippled."

I shrug. "I know that. It's just different. The stuff that happened between me and him."

"Did you sleep with him?" Zachary blurts out. I don't have to look at him to know he's got his face buried in his hands.

"No," I say. Zachary sighs in audible relief. "But I would have. I wanted to before I knew who he was."

Admitting that out loud makes me feel dirty. I've never had great taste in men, but this was more than just being a bad judge of character.

"I'm going to have to start finger-printing guys and have you run a background check or something," I joke. "Since I seem to attract criminals."

"And vampires," Zachary says quietly.

I sit up and shoot him a look over my shoulder. "Vampires?"

Zachary raises both brows and spreads his hands. "Reilly."

"That is not a thing. I am not sleeping with him," I say vehemently. My phone is finally at five percent battery. Close enough. I hit the power button.

"Are you sure about that?" Zachary asks.

"I think I'd know if I was having sex with him," I say slowly.

"I saw the way you danced together at that club," Zachary scoffs. "Don't lie to me because you're trying to spare my feelings or something."

"What feelings?" I ask. "We're friends, sort of. If you don't hate me anymore at least. Why would I—is this what Elise was referring to? Something about how you had a crush on me when I lived with you?"

Zachary stares at me, one hand over his mouth. My phone starts buzzing in my hand from all the messages it couldn't receive while it was off. I ignore them.

"You—" He pauses and rubs his hands over his face. "You really had no idea?"

I shake my head. "You were, are, like my brother."

"Good to know," he says, standing and walking off to the bathroom.

I can't run after him to comfort him if I'm the source of his distress, so I stay perched on the side of the bed, feeling uncomfortable. I finally look down at my phone. There are six messages from Lydia. Fifteen from Patrick. I dismiss them all.

I do open the email though. There is a deposit for ten thousand dollars from Javier that hit my bank account four days ago. I toss my phone on the bed and put my head in my hands. Not that the money does me any good now. It would have been nice a few months ago, back when I thought I had a chance at a normal future.

"So," Zachary says, startling me. "I can look into the magical artifacts JHAPI has confiscated, or has any information on, just in case this spellbook has turned up somewhere. Will you contact Gerard and Maybelle?"

He's standing in the middle of the room, arms crossed, face smoothed out to his usual expression. He doesn't look upset at all, and the only sign of tension is the slight hunch of his shoulders.

"Sure," I say casually. I can definitely get on board with pretending that conversation never happened. "I've also been thinking about what you said about Reilly having connections. I still don't know if I trust him completely, but if it comes down to it, we might have to see if he can help."

"Only if you think you can trust him," Zachary agrees with a nod.

"Speaking of, what do you know about him and his sire?" I ask, picking at the comforter on the bed. "His Sire is going to be taking the council seat that just opened up. Reilly didn't seem enthused about that."

Zachary whistles under his breath.

"I'm not sure what to make of Reilly's reaction, but I know I share the sentiment." He sits down in the chair again and shakes his head. "Cesare Sangiovanni is a well-known traditionalist."

My eyes widen. "You have got to be kidding me."

"Nope," Zachary says. "I was shocked when I found out Reilly was the vampire the council sent to work with JHAPI. Sangiovanni was vocally against JHAPI's creation from the beginning, the traditionalists don't want any kind of human oversight. He has only recently shifted to supporting the organization, and then he personally pushed for this mission to take down the NWR. The other two vampires on the council are progressive, and they were thrilled to agree."

I rub my hands together. "I'm supposed to meet him at this Summit thing Reilly is dragging me to."

"Be careful," Zachary says seriously. "He is not the type of person you want to insult."

"I'm doomed," I laugh.

Zachary cracks a smile at that too. "I'll say nice things at your funeral."

There's a knock at the door, and my senses jump into overdrive. The heartbeat is familiar, and that realization is unsettling.

"I guess it's time for me to go," I mutter as I stand and walk to the door.

Reilly doesn't make any move to enter the room, but he does nod at Zachary over my shoulder.

"Are we leaving tonight or something?" I ask.

"No, tomorrow just after sunset," Reilly says. "Staci delivered some healing salves to the room, and I thought you might want them sooner rather than later."

"Oh, you brought them?" I ask, looking around for a bag or a bulge in his pocket.

"No, they're in the room. I had to come get you in person because you never got your phone back," Reilly says.

Of course he didn't bring them. That would have been too polite. I think he doesn't like me being alone with Zachary either, probably for the same reason he interrupted that conversation with Elise.

"Thanks for your help," I say, turning back to face Zachary for a moment. "I'll see you after the Summit."

Zachary nods. "Until then."

I follow Reilly into the hall and to the elevators.

He's silent for a moment, but I can feel the questions brewing in his mind.

"What is Brunson helping you with?" Reilly asks.

"Why are you upset that your sire is being promoted to the council?" I counter. Reilly always wants to play the question game. If that's how it has to be, I might as well try to get whatever information I can in return.

He turns to me and steps closer and closer until I'm pressed against the wall. The elevator arrives, empty, but he ignores it.

"Why do you think I'm upset my sire will be on the council?"

"Why did you let me feed from you earlier?"

Reilly steps back with a huff. "I've told you before, you're an investment. It would be a waste if I let you die or completely lose control."

"You were obviously upset when you got that phone call. I don't think you trust or like your sire, though I don't know why. I hope it's because he's a piece of shit traditionalist and you don't agree with any of that. I wouldn't be surprised if you did though," I say, upholding my end of the bargain. He chose the easy question to answer, and so did I.

The other two questions hang between us, but instead of pressing the issue, Reilly simply turns and hits the elevator call button again. The same doors reopen, and he steps onto the elevator, holding the door for me when I hesitate to follow.

"When we get to the Summit, you will do exactly as I say without hesitation," he says quietly. "Or you'll find out for yourself why I'm not fond of my sire."

I swallow uncomfortably. For once, it sounds more like he's warning me rather than threatening me. I wonder what kind of person has the ability to scare Reilly Walsh.

## 26

The dress is laid out on my bed like a gift. Any goodwill I might feel at the gesture curdles in my throat. Silk makes for more comfortable shackles, but that doesn't change the fact that it's just another thing I can't escape from.

I walk forward and smooth my finger across the deep red hem. The fabric is the color of fresh blood. It's garish, not something I'd ever pick for myself. I'm going to look like a walking wound. That must be what the vampires like.

My phone buzzes twice, a text flashing on the screen. It's Reilly, of course.

*Be ready in an hour.*

I scoff and dismiss the message. My phone buzzes again.

*Or I will come dress you myself.*

. . .

241

I throw my phone with a growl. It bounces off the headboard and slides across the bed, rumpling the top of the dress. I consider, just for a moment, ripping the dress apart with my bare hands. Instead, I turn on my heel and stomp into the bathroom. Perhaps a quick shower will cool some of my anger.

The bathroom is just as gaudy as Javier's. White marble stretches across the spacious bathroom. The glass shower takes up the entire far wall. The faucets are some shiny gold material I'm sure isn't real. The sink is an iridescent blue basin set on the white marble vanity, and it is striking. It's the only splash of color in the room. The color shifts and glimmers as I walk past it. There is a stack of plush, white towels next to the shower door on a gold tray.

I drop my clothes on the floor, leaving a trail to the shower, and step inside. The water is immediately hot, and I jump back with a yelp. It's a little too hot. I adjust the temperature and ease under the spray, turning on the other shower head so everything steams up faster.

They have full-size shampoo and conditioner; this is a classy joint after all, which I use to lather up my hair. It's unscented. I wonder if that's something Reilly requested or something they did for the Summit. It'll clean my hair either way, so I don't really care.

Some of the tension leaves my shoulders as I rinse the shampoo from my hair, but I don't feel as safe in here as I had hoped. I thought I had won something when I convinced Reilly to let me have a private room, but apparently, he still has a key. He still controls my life. I'm still about to be outed to the vampire council.

Reilly had not seemed overly thrilled to hear of

his sire's imminent promotion to the council, which was unexpected. I wasn't sure what to make of his reaction. It's possible he hates his sire, but he still does everything his sire asks of him. I can't imagine someone as strong-willed as Reilly showing that kind of loyalty to someone he doesn't believe deserves it. Then again, I've been wrong about people before.

I press my forehead against the cool glass and trace my finger behind a rivulet of water. At least Martinez has been captured. Dead would be infinitely preferable, but at least if he's in jail, he won't be able to hurt anyone else. We're one step closer to seriously crippling the NWR. I sigh and push away from the shower wall and hurry to finish. As much as I don't want to do this, I don't want Reilly showing up in my room before I'm done getting ready.

I step out of the shower and wrap my hair in one of the towels, then grab another to dry my body. I leave a trail of wet footprints into the bedroom. My hairdryer is at the bottom of my bag, so half the contents end up dumped out by the time I stand triumphantly with it in my grasp. My towel starts to slip, so I re-tuck it around me and walk back into the bathroom.

There is a small vanity with a stool on the wall the bathroom shares with the bedroom. I sit down and plug in the hairdryer, then unwind my hair from its turban. A few quick strokes of the brush get rid of the remaining tangles. I sigh at the mirror, then set about making myself presentable for a ball.

I know how to do my makeup, and well. I painted it on every night for six months when I was stripping for a living, and that's just not something you forget. The makeup I wore for that isn't entirely appropriate for this event though. I go for something a little more elegant this time.

My skin is clear; I don't make all those cosmetic brews for nothing, so I keep it simple. A smoky eye, tinted brows, and a dark red lip that'll match the dress perfectly. I always tried for a sultry vibe when I was stripping, but I was young, and I tended to overdo it. I've done good tonight. I won't look out of place in the dress.

My hair, on the other hand, well, I don't have many options. Down seems too casual, so I decide to put it up. The curling iron is hot, so I begin twisting pieces around it. I only burn my fingers a few times, and the marks are easily healed. I pin the curls up, pulling a few strands down to frame my face, and drape down over my collarbone. It's not perfect, but it looks good enough. I stand and drop the towel.

The dress is still lying on the bed, taunting me. I pick up the slinky dress and unzip it, then step into it carefully. This isn't the kind of get up that allows undergarments. The silk slides sensually across my skin, reminiscent of the kind of touch I've gone so long without. I shove my feet in my heels and turn to face the tall mirror next to the bathroom door.

The dress is even more low cut than I realized. It dips down between my breasts, precariously close to reaching my belly button. The waist is tight, a piece of fabric on the bodice wraps around to the back. There is a slit on the side that comes all the way to the upper part of my thigh. The back is low as well. The zipper doesn't even reach halfway up my back.

I trace my finger over my shoulder that still has the tracker embedded in it. There isn't even a scar, thanks to my healing magic and the salves. The welts from the Finding magic are on full display like this. They look strange under the dress, like bad tattoos.

I haven't dressed up like this since...well, I guess I never have. It was never this fancy. The dresses I wore were always short. This should be a fairy tale moment, but instead it's a nightmare.

The door to my room opens behind me without so much as a knock.

"Are you—" Reilly's question dies on his lips.

I roll my eyes at his slack-jawed reflection and turn to face him.

"Am I ready? Yes, I am."

It's my turn to stare as I take in his appearance. He's wearing a sleek black tuxedo with a white bow tie that is perfectly tailored to his frame. The black fabric makes his auburn hair appear even more red. He has managed to tame it as well. He looks, dare I say it, debonair.

Reilly clears his throat, and the silent assessment ends.

"It's time to join the party," he says, extending his arm toward me.

"Grand," I say, striding past him and out the door. I have to go to this, but I don't have to take his arm. He catches up to me, and we walk in silence down the hall. A few couples of varying races step out in front of us. Reilly glances at me without turning his head.

"You look lovely, Olivia," he says quietly enough that no one else should be able to hear him.

"I look like your whore. Or a candy cane," I say, pointing at my arm.

This is the kind of get up a man puts his escort in. Not his co-worker or whatever it is we are. I didn't intend to sound so angry, but his compliment makes me want to kick him.

"An expensive whore though, at the very least," Reilly says with a smirk. "Possibly like a candy cane as well."

The elevator dings, and Reilly presses his hand to

the small of my back to encourage a little haste. We slip inside just as the doors begin to close. The other guests chat amongst themselves, but I'm distracted by the line of heat from where I am pressed against Reilly. We should have waited for the next elevator. This one is cramped, and there isn't room to turn around, much less stand apart.

The elevator swoops upward, slowing to a smooth stop, and the doors open again. I step backward and turn quickly, taking a deep breath now that I can smell something other than Reilly's scent. This area of the hotel is very different from the floors with the rooms. The walls stretch up into arches at least thirty feet high. The ceiling is painted like an old cathedral, complete with clouds and fat cherubs fluttering around dimpled women who can't seem to find a shirt and men with swords.

In the alcove between each arch are statues carved from marble. They are striking. Each one conveys some extreme emotion. The one closest to me is a woman in anguish, her hand reaching out toward me as though I could save her. I pull my eyes away and quicken my pace. Reilly keeps his hand on the small of my back, and I wrestle down the impulse to shove it away. In a place like this, his presumptuousness is a claim, and that claim is protection. I'm an unknown nobody here, but based on the glances Reilly is getting, he is not.

I get a few glances of my own, but they're all lecherous. No one thinks I'm a threat. To most people here, I'm probably not. I might have learned a few new tricks hunting terrorists, but that doesn't make up for years of inexperience. I don't have the kind of control over my stolen magic someone who was born with it would have.

The hall of arches opens into the kind of ballroom

I've only ever seen in movies. There is a wide stair-case with a plush red carpet laid down the center. The ballroom has two levels. The bar is on the top level, while tables are on the lower level. The people milling around lean against the ornate balcony that extends around the top level. There must be five hundred people here, at least. There is room for more as well.

On the lower level, there is a clear area for dancing and a stage in the center of the far wall. There are twelve chairs on the stage, though they'd be better described as thrones. Three red for the vampires, three black for the witches, three white for the werewolves. The remaining three on the far right are a stone. They must be for the goblins.

"Would you care for a drink?" Reilly asks, his breath tickling my ear.

"God, yes," I say, not resisting as he nudges me to-ward the closest bar.

As we walk, I can tell the race of most of the people we pass. Another vampire with a necker, his hand around the back of her neck, his thumb brushing up and down on the vein in her neck. A pack of werewolves barking in laughter.

The goblins are the easiest to spot, of course. Their green skin stands out as inhuman. They are huddled together in small groups, keeping to the edges. Most of them look like they want to flee. A few stride around with their bulbous noses held high, daring anyone to question their presence here.

We arrive at the bar, and I lean my hip against the edge and wait for the bartender to look up so I can catch his eye. Reilly leans past me and waves him down. I roll my eyes. He's so impatient.

"What can I get for you?" the muscled, blond bar-tender asks Reilly.

"It's for her," Reilly says, gesturing at me.

"Do you have tequila?" I ask with a bright smile, leaning forward just far enough to almost show him the goods. Reilly frowns at me, but the bartender smiles.

"We got everything," he says, spreading his hands wide. His name tag reads 'Devan'.

"Give me a double of your best stuff, Devan," I say, setting my chin in my hand.

"With pleasure," Devan says with a wink. He grabs the bottle, spinning it around with practiced ease before tipping the spout over a sparkling glass.

"You cannot get drunk tonight," Reilly hisses in my ear.

I glare at him. "You're the one who asked me if I wanted a drink."

"A cocktail, not shots. This isn't a bar in Las Vegas."

"You worry too much."

His fingers bite into my back. "I cannot watch you every second, and these people are all dangerous. Do not let your guard down just because we're at a party."

"You almost sound like you care, Reilly," I say, patting the front of his jacket.

Devan slides the glass across the bar to me, his smile fading a little as I touch Reilly.

"Enjoy, ma'am."

"Oh, I will," I say, turning my smile up a notch. I grab the tequila and throw it back, drinking down the burning liquid with relish. I drop the empty glass back on the table with a loud thunk and spin away from the bar. "So is there going to be food, or what?"

Reilly wraps his arm tightly around my shoulders.

"Quit acting like you're incapable of being a lady.

There are people I need to introduce you to. Dinner will be served in a couple of hours."

"Hours?" I gasp. My stomach growls on cue. "You could have warned me to eat a snack beforehand."

"Stop complaining."

He scans the room, and I look longingly back at the bar. I wonder if I can sneak another later when he isn't paying attention. I need something to fill my stomach if they aren't going to feed us for hours.

I spot a waiter carrying a small tray, making the rounds, and make a beeline for him. Reilly scrambles to follow me.

"What are you doing?" he demands.

"Sandwiches. Little fancy ones," I mutter, keeping my eye on the prize. He huffs out a sigh behind me but follows without further complaint.

I come up a little fast on the waiter, and he startles slightly, then extends the tray. I grab two petite sandwiches and contemplate grabbing a third, but Reilly tugs me away with a nod at the waiter who doesn't hesitate to escape.

"They're so small," I say before stuffing the first one in my mouth. A bitter taste overwhelms me, and I spit it out in my hand, trying not to vomit.

"What the fuck are you doing?" Reilly hisses, scrambling for a napkin to grab the half-chewed food out of my hand with. "When I said you needed to act like a lady, that wasn't a challenge for you to act even more ridiculous."

His eyes are snapping with genuine anger, and his jaw is clenched tight.

"Sorry, that was disgusting though, I think it's rotten or something," I say, wishing even more that I could get another drink to get that awful taste out of my mouth. My stomach is rolling.

"If you're done, I've spotted someone I need to introduce you to. Do us both a favor, and be polite. If you offend him, there is nothing I can or will do to protect you. Do you understand?"

"Yeah, yeah," I say, waving my hand at him.

He grabs it and holds it tight, grinding the bones together.

"This is not a joke."

"I understand," I say slowly, looking him in the eye.

He releases my hand, and I resist the urge to rub at the ache. He takes a deep breath, and his features smooth out to calm indifference, like a mask slipping into place. I had joked earlier about him caring, but the concern really is unexpected.

He presses his palm into my lower back and guides me down the wide staircase. We weave through the tables, passing mostly vampires in this section. A few nod at Reilly as we pass, but we don't stop.

It becomes apparent that Reilly is leading me toward a group gathered around a dining table near the stage. There are a few men who don't seem part of the group. They are facing outward, their eyes constantly scanning for anyone approaching. They tense at our approach, but visibly relax when they notice Reilly. A few people who seem to be waiting for an audience move out of our way as we step up to the table. I guess we don't have to wait in line.

Seated in one of the chairs is a man with black hair streaked at the temple with silver. There are lines around his eyes and mouth, but those are the only signs of age on his face. His eyes are sharp as steel, and the color of steel as well. He doesn't look at Reilly, only at me, taking a long breath with slightly parted lips as though he is tasting my scent. Reilly bows deeply and pushes me down into a bow as well.

The man stands, unfolding from the chair. He's taller than I expected, and while lean, every movement seems like controlled violence. He turns his cold eyes to Reilly.

"Introduce us, *passerotto mio*, or have you forgotten your manners?" the man says, his voice slipping into an accent when he uses the strange endearment. Reilly straightens, and I follow suit.

"Sire, this is Olivia Carter, the half-breed I have spoken to you about. Ms. Carter, this is Council Member Cesare Sangiovanni," Reilly says, taking my hand gently in his and extending it toward his sire.

Cesare takes it and presses cold lips to my knuckles with a short bow.

"You defy expectations, Ms. Carter. My imaginings of what you might be all revolved around a twisted creature born of some strange experiment. I am pleased to discover you are instead a beauty our Reilly here does not deserve."

I don't know how to respond. My heart is beating fast in my chest, something that won't escape Cesare's notice.

"You're too kind, though you are right. Reilly does not deserve me," I say with a smile I hope makes up for my nerves.

Cesare laughs unreservedly, throwing his head back. The people around us chuckle along. I wonder if they're obligated to, or if they just find me hilarious as well. Reilly is notably silent beside me. He's probably going to kill me later.

"I like this one Reilly," Cesare says, pointing his finger at him. "Her heart is racing like a hummingbird, but she does not cower."

"I'm not certain she knows how to cower, Sire," Reilly says in a resigned tone.

"Have a seat," Cesare says. He still has my hand,

and he leads me to the seat directly to his left. I sit down hesitantly, for once comforted that Reilly will be sitting right next to me. Cesare scoots my chair in for me, and I sit stiffly in my chair, my hands in my lap.

"The two of you have had an eventful week," Cesare comments. "I must say, from the description of your injuries, I did expect you to show up looking at least a little battered."

"Healing salves work wonders," I say with a tight smile.

He reaches over and smooths his thumb across my shoulder. "There isn't a scar from the bullet wound or the GPS tracker. Whatever brews you are using must be very well made."

"The healing magic helps prevent scars as well," I say. It takes all of my willpower not to flinch away from his touch, but again, my heart is racing. I think he likes it, or perhaps he likes testing me to see at what point I'll visibly react.

"Yet these linger?" he asks, his thumb dropping down to press into a welt just hard enough to make me grit my teeth before he moves his hand back to his lap.

"Magical injuries are different, harder to heal. I'm working on it though," I say.

"Tell me," Cesare says, leaning back in his chair. "What do you feel at the point when whoever you are draining of magic dies?"

I glance at Reilly, but he is looking at his sire, his posture relaxed and his face blank. I clear my throat and twist my fingers together. Maybe this is the reaction he was hoping for.

"I'm not sure I understand what you're asking for," I say finally.

"You killed Ryan. You didn't have enough time to

drain him in the few seconds you were latched onto his neck, so I assume you must have killed him by ripping away the magic that keeps him alive." He taps his fingers against the table, looking at me intently. "In that last moment, what do you feel?"

I square my shoulders.

"They become empty," I say. "With—with a witch, it's different. There's something I can't take in them, but I didn't feel that in Ryan. He just ended and turned to ash."

Cesare hums to himself, his expression turning thoughtful. I hope he's amused or whatever by that answer. I don't want to talk about it anymore, but I'm not sure I have a choice.

I grimace. Ryan turning to ash in my mouth was awful. I can still remember the bitter taste of his blood. I reach for my glass and freeze. This isn't just a memory; that same bitter taste is in my mouth right now. I stand abruptly and search the room for a waiter carrying a plate of hors d'oeuvres.

Cesare raises a brow and watches with interest.

"Olivia, what are you—" Reilly begins.

I spot a waiter and hurry toward him without waiting for Reilly to finish his sentence. He's following me, and I'm sure he is about to lecture me about being ladylike or polite again, but I don't care. I grab the waiter's arm, startling him into almost dropping the tray.

"Sorry, just, give me the tray," I say, reaching for it. The stunned waiter lets me take it.

"Would—would you like some more sandwiches?" he asks, his eyes flicking between me and I'm sure an enraged Reilly standing behind me.

"No, she would not like some more sandwiches," Reilly snaps. "You may leave."

The waiter scurries away as I lean over the tray

and sniff the sandwiches, pulling on my vampire magic.

"What the fuck are you doing?" Reilly hisses in my ear.

"When I bit Ryan, his blood tasted awful," I say, sniffing at a sandwich with a cucumber poking out of it. It smells suspicious, but not bitter like the other sandwich had tasted.

"What does that have to do with sandwiches? Or with you leaving the table like that? You've embarrassed me and—"

"The sandwich I had earlier, the one I spit out, it tasted exactly the same as his blood," I snap. "There is something wrong."

"What exactly are you suggesting?" Reilly asks, brows pinching tightly together.

"Ryan lost control, and we still don't know how. We don't know why they took him, or why they let him go," I say, waving a sandwich at him. "What if it was an experiment?"

"An experiment in what?"

"A weak vampire comes back to his clan, and he's out of control. So, obviously, the more highly ranked vampires in the clan step in to try to help him regain control. But he kills one of them."

I can see the wheels turning in his head. "He shouldn't have been able to."

"It was like they sent a bomb back with him. If they hadn't been able to lock him in that room, he might have killed the entire clan, or at least a lot of them."

"It's possible the NWR did something to him to make him both lose control and become stronger, but that does not mean the sandwiches are poisoned. No one else has complained about them."

I roll my eyes.

"None of the vampires are eating them, maybe they only taste bad to me. I don't know, and I don't care. When Martinez had me in that van, he said something I didn't think was important at the time because he was rambling about so much. He said that vampire's true nature would be revealed soon. Something about taking away the mask they hide behind."

"That's propaganda speak. They say that kind of thing all the time," Reilly says.

"And they're always trying to prove it. They aren't sitting around passing out flyers. They are organized, and smart, and driven."

"What are they planning, then?"

"Dinner is being served tonight, this whole big thing," I say, looking around at the tables, all set with more forks and knives than anyone should ever need. "What are the vampires eating?"

"Everyone has brought their own neckers," Reilly says. "They're waiting in the meeting rooms on a different floor."

"Are they eating these?" I ask, shoving the tray at him.

"I don't know. I've never been concerned with what they eat," he says, eyeing the tray. He rubs his hand along his jaw, then looks at me. "You think they are somehow poisoning the neckers, and then what? The vampires feed from them and lose control?"

"It's hard to poison a vampire," I say. "It's not hard to slip something into food for neckers. No one cares about them; they're just dinner themselves."

Reilly shakes his head. "This is insane, you don't have any proof. This shouldn't even be possible."

"Stocke said she thought the stuff the NWR did in Texas was an experiment, right? That they wanted to see if they could discredit a vampire clan. It was working too."

255

"Yes, I remember this," he says impatiently.

"Can you imagine the shit storm if vampires at the Summit lost control and killed a necker? Or another paranormal?" I ask. "All of this, everything the NWR has been doing, has been about finding a way to make a vampire lose control. They say you are monsters, and if they can prove it to the world, they will start an all-out war."

"That all sounds terrible, but you still can't prove any of this. I can't halt this entire thing because you have a hunch," Reilly bites out.

"Ryan was a child. What happens when someone like your sire loses control? When he is three times as powerful as he is now?" I demand.

Reilly grinds his teeth together, glaring at the sandwiches like he can blame them for my insanity.

"There is an hour until dinner. Find a way to prove this by then."

I glare at him. "How am I supposed to do that?"

"That's your problem to figure out," Reilly says, leaning in close. "I have to go explain to my sire why I can't keep you under control. Let's hope neither of us fails."

## 27

R eilly walks away, and I'm left standing with a tray of sandwiches and a huge problem. I turn and march toward the exit. I pass another waiter holding a tray and shove mine at her. She grabs it with her free hand and almost drops it, but I keep walking as fast as I can. I need to get out of here and get my phone. Maybe Zachary can help, or even Stocke if I have to talk to her.

There is a constant stream of paranormals in and out of the main room. I weave through them as quickly as I can, but I don't want to shove past anyone too roughly and start some kind of fight I don't have time to finish.

The elevator is just as busy. I manage to slip in just before the doors close, but it stops at almost every floor on the way up. I tap my foot impatiently, letting person after person slip around me to get off until it finally arrives at my floor.

I run down the hall, no longer worried about who might see me or who I might run into. My room is exactly as I left it, as is my phone. I grab it off the bed and see three missed calls, two from Zachary and one from Elise. There is a voicemail which I tap, then put the phone to my ear.

"Olivia," Zachary voicemail starts. "Martinez transport was attacked as soon as it left this morning. He's been gone for hours. We aren't even sure when exactly he escaped. Stay at the Summit with Reilly, don't try to leave, and don't go anywhere by yourself."

My hand shakes as I lower the phone. If he has escaped, he has to be coming here. He's been a part of this experiment from the beginning. It was probably all his idea.

If I can find him, I can prove something is going on, and stop him. I look down at the welts on my arms and flex my fingers. Corinne can't help me. She's still unconscious, and Stocke wouldn't let her try to Find Martinez again anyhow. I text Zachary, telling him everything I can think of. My suspicions about the food, about where Martinez is headed, and what I'm about to do.

I turn and sprint down the hall, dialing Reilly's number with shaking fingers, but he doesn't answer. I slap my hand against the elevator call button, but it doesn't light up. I hit it again. Nothing. I stare at the elevators, panic growing in my gut. It could just be malfunctioning, but what if it's something worse?

I spin around, my dress flaring out around me, and search for the entrance to the stairs. There is a small emergency exit placard on the wall that directs me down the hall and to the left. I sprint there and hit the door at a run. It flies open, hitting the wall with a bang that echoes down the stairwell.

Magic flows through my body in a cold wave as I sprint down the stairs vampire fast. I barrel out of the stairwell onto the floor the Summit is being hosted, but I'm not anywhere near the main entrance.

I don't recognize the hall I'm in. A man wearing the light blue jacket of the serving staff is standing a few paces away, looking at me with wide eyes.

"Is everything okay?" he asks hesitantly.

"No. Where are the neckers being held?" I demand as I march toward him. He visibly shrinks back, and I realize my fangs are poking out of my mouth.

"I, uh, I'm not sure," he says, trying to back away.

I grab him by his lapels and pull him close. His face pales, and sweat beads up on his forehead.

"Then find someone who is. The NWR is about to attack this place, and I can stop them, but I need to know where the neckers are," I growl.

"O-okay. I can take you t-to my supervisor."

I spin him around and shove him forward. "Go, then."

With one last glance over his shoulder, he starts jogging down the hall. I follow, doing everything I can to push down the vampire magic so I don't waste it. His heart is racing, and he stinks of fear. He's lucky I don't crave human blood.

He leads me around two turns, then through a door marked 'Staff Only' into a huge industrial kitchen. There are chefs in their white coats creating more trays of hors d'oeuvres and dozens of waiters weaving through the chaos. He taps a woman in a crisp black suit on the shoulder. She holds up her hand to the person she was in the middle of speaking with and turns to him.

"She—terrorists in the building—the neckers," he begins to stutter out. The woman raises a brow.

I grab the waiter by the back of the collar and drag him out of the way.

"I need to know where the neckers are. Their food has been poisoned, and if the vampires feed on them, they are going to lose control and murder everyone," I say, throwing my hands wide.

The woman looks at a loss for a moment. "Who are you?"

I bite the inside of my cheek before answering. Of course, the woman needs some assurance I know what I'm talking about. It would be way easier if she didn't though.

"Olivia Carter, I've been working with JHAPI at the request of the vampire council," I say as calmly as I can. "Look, I don't have a lot of time here. Do you want to die, or are you going to help me?"

The woman hesitates, evaluating me, then grabs a walkie-talkie off her belt buckle.

"Delay dinner for thirty minutes. No one goes in or out of the necker holding room until I say so, all right?" She puts the walkie-talkie back on her belt and crosses her arms. "If you are with JHAPI, where are the rest of the agents?"

"My team is in a different state," I say. "But other agents are on their way. This was a last-minute tip."

My phone starts buzzing in my hand. It's Zachary.

"Give me a minute," I say, turning away from the woman and slipping back into the hall. The door swings shut behind me.

"Zach," I say with relief as I answer the call.

"Olivia, what are you doing?" he asks.

"They've poisoned the food," I say. "I ate a sandwich, and it was bitter like Ryan's blood. I think they injected him with something that made him lose control and made him stronger. They're going to do the same thing here, and all these vampires are going to lose control in the middle of the Summit."

"How do you know this?" he asks.

I pause in my pacing. "You don't believe me?"

"I'm asking how you know," he says, his tone suggesting he's trying to keep me calm.

"Martinez has escaped. All these disappearances, they've been experiments. Stocke said they were, and she's right. They were all practice runs for this," I insist. "Zach, I can't do this alone."

He sighs. "I can have them send a team over, but if you're wrong, we're going to look like idiots. The councils will be furious."

"They're only willing to delay dinner thirty minutes. Can they test the necker's blood before then? Or the food?" I ask.

"I don't know," Zachary says. "Maybe Staci can figure out a way to prove it's contaminated, but without having an idea of what it has been poisoned with, we can't test it."

I sigh and pace back and forth across the hall.

"The elevators aren't working, by the way. I don't know what else they've done, but they may have blocked the exits somehow."

Someone is talking in the background. Zachary holds his hand over the phone for a second, drowning it out.

"All of the elevators?" Zachary asks.

"I don't know. The one that led up to my room is the only one I tried," I say.

"Stocke wants you to wait for a team to get there. It will be someone local, but she'll be on the phone with them."

"What if I can prove Martinez is here?" I ask.

"Is he there?" Zachary asks.

"I think so," I say. "And I'm going to find him."

"Olivia, you can't do that—"

"Just get people here, okay?" I hang up the phone.

The door behind me swings open again, and a waiter hurries past, but my attention is captured by a snippet of conversation. The woman I spoke to is asking for security to come upstairs and remove me.

I shove my way back into the kitchen.

"What the hell are you doing?" I demand.

"I need security up here right now," she says into the walkie-talkie before looking at me with raised hands. "Ma'am, I need you to please leave."

"You cannot send those neckers into that room—"

"I spoke to our head of security, and he told me there is no threat from the NWR. There is no tip," she says calmly.

"Just because your head of security doesn't know, doesn't mean it isn't happening," I say, stepping toward her. I want to get to Martinez, but all of this is for nothing if any of the vampires feed on these neckers.

"Ma'am—"

"What is the problem here?" Cesare asks from behind me. I didn't hear him walk up.

I turn around slowly. He doesn't look angry, merely curious. Reilly is standing a few paces behind him, as well as the two bodyguards who were at the table earlier.

"The food the neckers ate was laced with something," I say haltingly. "Their blood is poisoned now. It will make a vampire lose control."

Cesare frowns. "And how fast acting is this poison?"

"I don't know, but I don't think it takes very long to go into effect. The NWR wants everyone to lose control during the dinner."

"And you don't have a way to prove this?" Cesare asks.

"There's never been anything like this before. It's not like I can ring up a lab and have them test it in the next ten minutes," I say, glancing back at Reilly. I wish he would help.

"Reilly has assured me you are not insane and you are not simply trying to make me look like an idiot," Cesare says, extending his arm to me. "Walk with me."

I slip my hand into the crook of his arm. The magic rolling off him is intoxicating. If someone like him were to feed on one of the neckers, I don't know what would be capable of stopping him.

Cesare leads us back into the hall. I keep my eyes straight ahead and focus on putting one foot in front of the other. If I'm wrong, I have a feeling it will be the last thing I'm ever wrong about.

One of the bodyguards walks ahead of us and opens an unmarked door. We follow him inside. There must be almost a hundred neckers in here, all dressed in black. They bow in unison.

Cesare gently removes my hand from his arm and walks forward, grabbing the arm of the closest necker.

"Tony, feed from her," he says, nudging the woman toward his bodyguard.

I start to object, but a firm hand wraps around my mouth, cutting off the words. I can smell that it's Reilly. His hand stays tightly clasped over my lips as Tony leans down and bites the woman's neck. He drinks from her with long gulps while the woman goes glassy-eyed.

"That's enough," Cesare says after a couple of minutes.

Tony lowers the woman to the ground and stands up straight, awaiting his next order.

"Did she taste odd?" Cesare asks.

"No, sire. She tasted better than I've ever had," he says.

Cesare looks at his watch. "In five minutes, I'm going to give a speech accepting my position on the council. Reilly, if he loses control, put him down and come tell me Olivia was right."

Reilly lowers his hand from my mouth but stays pressed against me, his other hand wrapped tightly around my arm.

"Yes, sire," he says.

Cesare looks at me as he passes by until a strange grunt draws our attention. Tony huffs again, his fangs pushing down onto his bottom lip. A quiver passes through his body, and he looks at Cesare and growls.

"Interesting," Cesare comments.

Tony lunges toward him in a blur, arms outstretched. Reilly yanks me backward, and we slam into the wall behind us.

I don't see Cesare move. One moment he is in Tony's path, the next he's standing behind him, holding his head while Tony's body topples forward. Both crumple to ash. Cesare shakes the dust from his hands as the neckers behind him start screaming.

"Reilly, evacuate the main hall," Cesare says as he pulls out a handkerchief.

Reilly steps out from behind me and hurries out of the room. Cesare walks toward me, stopping only a foot away and carefully wiping the remains of his bodyguard from his hand.

"You have been very useful," he says, his eyes scanning my face.

"I think Martinez is here," I say shakily. "He escaped. I got a voicemail."

"Then find him if you can," Cesare says before stepping around me to address his other bodyguard. "Stay with them, make sure no one leaves. We don't want anyone feeding on one of these by mistake after this is all over."

He walks out. The neckers are all huddled as far back as they can get, their eyes on me and the bodyguard now that the others have left.

I stumble out into the hallway and take a deep breath. He just murdered one of his own men, and no one flinched. Reilly knew what was coming, and he let it happen. I press my hand to my mouth and wonder what I'm protecting. Maybe Martinez is right, maybe the mask does need to be stripped away.

Patrick's tear-streaked face flashes through my mind, and I drop my hand. Cesare might be awful, but not all vampires are. They aren't all monsters any more than all humans are. I'm going to do what I can to stop Martinez. There will be no capturing him this time. I'm going to finish it.

I look down at my shaking hands, and the Finding magic shifts inside of me. I picture Martinez, just like I did with Corinne when I was practicing this in her room. The magic moves and stretches out into the hotel, but something else moves too. I can feel *her* shift inside of me. She's always there.

I force myself to look up, and she's standing in front of me in the hallway like she's real. No mirror this time, just her.

"Mom," I say, my voice quaking.

"Olivia," she says, her face splitting into a smile. "Finally."

"Are you real?" I ask.

"I need you to find the book," she says. "I made a mistake, but you can still stop him."

"Stop who?" I ask. "Reilly?"

She shakes her head. "No, the god that is coming unbound. He wants to destroy all of us."

"What book? How is that going to stop anything?"

"Find it, Olivia," she whispers. "Only you can undo this terrible thing I did."

"Mom," I whisper, my voice shaking like I'm five years old again and waking up from a nightmare. "I don't understand."

"You were born with a burden I tried to hide from you. I'm so sorry." Her eyes fill with tears that slip down her cheeks.

"No, don't cry," I say, reaching up a trembling hand to wipe them away, but she grabs my hands and I freeze. She is real. I don't understand how this is possible.

"Find the book. Find the magic," she says urgently.

"What book?" I ask, clinging to her hands. I don't want this to end.

"Find the book. Find the magic," she repeats. "You'll need all of it."

She leans forward and wraps me in a hug, whispering the same thing over and over, but I barely hear her. I squeeze her as tightly as I can, my fingers curling into the fabric of her dress as the comforting scent of herbs surrounds me.

"You don't need me," she whispers.

"Yes, I do," I sob.

"I'm holding you back."

I shake my head viciously and squeeze her even more tightly to me. "No."

She pulls back and cradles my face in her hands.

"My girl," she says. "You can do anything. Be anything. Do what's right."

"I miss you." And I do. I miss her every day, and I'm so angry she can't be with me anymore.

She smiles, and I realize she's already fading. My fingers are sinking into her and through her. I close my eyes because I can't watch her disappear again.

"I'm so proud of you," she says.

My hands and arms tingle as the magic that was giving her form flows back into me. Some warmth I didn't realize I was missing curls back up in my chest. The constant pain that has wrapped around my arms and shoulders fades into nothing.

I blink my eyes open. I'm standing alone in the hallway, but I know where he is.

28

---

People are pouring out of the main hall. There is a sense of restrained panic as they all attempt to walk but not run. I push through, having to use my elbows to make any progress in the opposite direction of the crowd. Martinez is somewhere in there.

I make it inside and shove my way up toward the bar. I find an empty spot along the railing and close my eyes, focusing on the magic. Images flash through my mind. The mass of people pouring out the exit. Reilly near the stage on the phone. Then a woman in a red dress, her eyes shut. I look up and see Devan staring at me.

He has a bottle of tequila in one hand and an empty glass in the other. My stomach sinks. There's no way it's him, but the magic pulling me toward him knows the truth, no matter what disguise he is wearing. There is a thick gold band on his right hand, just like the one Maybelle and Gerard both wore.

He pours a shot of the tequila and drinks it, eyes still on me, then turns and disappears through a door behind the bar. I run after him and jump over the bar, my dress dragging the glass off and shattering it. I push through the door and run in the direction I can feel him headed.

Distant gunfire echoes from somewhere downstairs. I put on a burst of speed and skid around a corner. Martinez, still looking like Devan, is standing at the end of the same hallway the neckers are on, waiting for me.

"You're always forcing me to go with Plan B," he says calmly as he tugs the ring off his hand and drops it in his pocket. The handsome facade is gone in a blink.

"Whatever you're planning, it's not going to work," I say, my hands clenched at my sides.

He takes two steps back and grins, his smile twisted gruesomely. He lifts his hand, showing me a small black box with a red switch.

*Click.*

An explosion rips through the room the neckers are in, and the door flies off its hinges. A fireball billows out of the room, and I stumble backward, shielding my face from the heat. There is another explosion farther away, and then another that rocks the entire building. My head is spinning, and Martinez is getting farther and farther away.

I sprint after him. Moving this fast, I don't even feel the fire as I dash through it. Anger is building in my chest, and magic is sparking at my fingertips. There were so many innocent people in that room. Hundreds more may be dead from the other explosions as well.

I round a corner and stop. He's close, but there are people running everywhere. Two shots hit the wall next to my head, and I duck down. He slams into a group of people running down a connecting hallway, and I lose sight of him again for a moment. When he reappears, he has his arm wrapped tightly around the neck of one of the wait staff, his gun pressed firmly against her head. She screams as he drags her backward, her eyes wide and frightened.

"None of you is getting out of here alive," Martinez hisses.

"Neither are you," I growl at him. I don't think I'm fast enough to get to him before he can pull the trigger.

"You should have just walked away from it all in Texas," he shouts. "If the clan had fallen, you would have been free, and I could have shown you how to redeem yourself. We could have done this together!"

"What do I need redemption from? I'm not the one murdering innocent people!" I shout back as I take a few steps toward him. If I can close the distance a little more, I might be able to get the gun.

"I know what you did before Brunson found you. How you sold those drugs," he says, pressing the gun even harder into the girl's head. She sobs, and her feet slip as he drags her backward down the hall. "I know that vampire almost killed you. They're monsters. How can you not see that?"

"It was one vampire, and he was insane," I say through gritted teeth.

"You're just like her! Always making excuses. It's like you want to die. Why won't you let me save you?" he yells, spittle flying from his lips. "My father tried to beat it out of her, but that didn't help either."

"Let this girl go, Jason," I say, trying to calm him now. "This is between us. She doesn't have anything to do with it."

He squeezes her more tightly to him. She scrabbles at his arm, gasping for air. I take another step closer and pull on the vampire magic harshly. I need every bit of strength. I can't save anything for a counterattack; it has to be now or never.

"She let them feed from her! She's just another jezebel whore lusting after the parasites that will suck all of humanity dry!"

"You're the monster here!"

A gun goes off twice behind him, much closer than before, and for a split second his eyes leave me. It's a reflex, the kind of thing you can't help when you are startled, and it's all I need. I lunge forward and close the distance. I wrap my left hand around the gun, pushing it back into his face, and yank the girl forward, freeing her from his grasp. She runs screaming as he kicks me in the stomach.

I wrap both hands around the gun and rip it away as he pulls out the same baton he had in the hangar. I jerk almost out of reach, but he has a foot on my dress, and the end of it hits me in the stomach with a bone-aching burst of electricity. All of my muscles seize, and he punches me in the face. I fall to one knee, and he hits me again, pain from the strike and the taser burning through my arm. I roll onto my back and push electric magic in an arc from my hand to his leg. He jerks away, and I lunge forward and tackle him.

My elbow connects with his jaw, and I grab the hand with the baton and squeeze. His hand breaks, the end of the baton cracking as well, and he screams in pain. I rip it out of his hand. Rage, hunger, and pain rush through me. I sink my teeth into his neck and drink down a rush of blood. A small, stagnant pool of magic is hidden deep inside of him. I reach for it without thinking and pull it into me. He claws at my back as I rip away his pathetic magic. It's familiar and earthy, something I've stolen once before. The first kind of magic I ever took.

I rear back, my teeth ripping out of his neck, and shove off him. He lays there, twitching, as blood gurgles from the wound in his neck.

"You sick fuck," I pant, frantically trying to wipe his blood off my mouth. "You're a witch. All this time, you've been killing your own kind."

"No," he hisses, struggling to sit up, but he's too weak now that I've taken most of what little magic he had. "My mother was a hedgewitch just like you, but I rejected the magic. I am redeemed."

"You are pathetic," I growl at him.

"Take the rest of it," he says desperately, lifting his hand toward me. "Get it out of me. Get it out. I want to be clean."

I stare at his outstretched hand, then reach down and clasp it tightly with my own.

"No," I say.

I let all of the anger and betrayal and hatred burn into the electric magic that is churning inside of me. It flows out of my palm and into him like a lightning bolt. The magic crackles down his arm, searing his skin in fractured streaks. He screams, the sound tearing from his throat. The sound is inhuman and hurts my ears. Jagged cracks open across his torso and his face, light pouring out of them as the magic overwhelms his body until he bursts into flame.

I jerk my hand away and stumble backward as his body crumples forward. The sounds of the chaos around me filter back in. People are still running, trying to escape. Gunfire, which I hope is the SWAT team, is getting closer and closer.

The smell of burning flesh makes me gag. I turn away from Martinez's corpse, my vision swimming. I need to find Reilly. I need to get out of here.

I lift my hand and shut my eyes, letting the Finding magic take over. It doesn't scare me anymore, though perhaps it should. The magic spreads out of me like a net, searching for Reilly. He's not far.

I run toward the hallway I came from, but another explosion knocks me onto my back and deafens me. Plaster cracks and falls from the ceiling. I struggle to my feet and run in the other direction. The building is shaking, and smoke is pouring out of the hallway. I'm getting farther from Reilly, but there's nothing I can do about that if the building is about to collapse.

I find a door that leads into the stairwell and sprint down the stairs. Someone below me trying to get out as well, but the exit is jammed. Reilly's location shifts. He's getting closer now instead of farther away. I'm on the second floor when the door to the stairwell bursts open and Reilly runs in. He's holding the GPS tracker in his hand.

"Hurry up," he says, waving at me.

I take the last flight of stairs two at a time, and Reilly grabs my arm, yanking me through the doorway. I follow, letting him drag me as I stumble over my own feet.

"Are you okay?" he asks, looking back at me.

"Martinez is dead," I gasp out.

He stops in his tracks and turns around, grabbing me by the shoulders.

"You killed him?" he asks, inspecting me for injuries. He freezes when he sees the welts are gone. "What—"

The building shakes, something crumpling above us with a loud crash. Dust sprinkles down from the cracks in the ceiling.

Reilly reaches down and rips my dress' split even higher.

"What are you—" I begin, slapping at his hands, but he drags me onto his back and takes off at full speed.

I wrap my legs tightly around his waist and cling to the front of his jacket with my hands. The ceiling crumbles behind us, and the floor starts cracking underneath his feet. Everything turns into a blur as he charges forward faster than I thought anyone could move.

The hall is a dead end, but Reilly doesn't slow down. He sprints straight for the window, and we crash through it in a shower of glass and fire as the ceiling collapses behind us. He lands neatly on the grass but doesn't stop running. This side of the building is about to collapse completely.

Fire trucks and emergency vehicles line the street, but Reilly bypasses all of that, running along the edges of the activity. He turns down a side street that passes by the hotel and stops in front of a limo. The door opens, and Reilly sets me down, then pushes me inside, following close behind.

I collapse into the seat and wrap the pieces of my dress around my legs. Cesare is sitting opposite me, suit spotless, hands folded in his lap.

Reilly closes the door, and the limo speeds away. I look through the back window and watch as the side of the hotel crumbles, a cloud of dust and smoke billowing up from the remains.

## 29

The clanhouse is like nothing I've ever seen before. It's not just a mansion; it's a sprawling estate that covers at least an acre. Balconies jut out of the vine-covered brick along the front of the house. The windows are all obscured except for the two on either side of the front door.

The limo stops in front of the house, and the door is opened by a vampire. I'm not sure if he is a butler, bodyguard, or both. Cesare steps out, and Reilly nudges me to follow.

The front door swings outward, and we walk inside. Directly in front of us is a wide, sloping staircase that is covered in red, plush carpet. At the end is a tall, stained glass window that is lit from the outside somehow even though it's the middle of the night. The stairs split and continue up to the second story, wrapping around on either side and lined by an intricate wrought iron railing.

Two large paintings are hung on either side of the staircase. One is of some old city, perhaps somewhere in Italy. The other is the traditional Renaissance type with a woman laid back on a settee, her hair strategically covering all the fun bits while a man kneels beside her. The clan is obviously wealthy, but the decor makes it feel like a museum and not a home.

"Freshen up, and meet me in the library in an hour," Cesare says as he walks ahead of us.

Reilly leads me up the staircase to the left. The floors up here are dark wood. There are rugs every few feet that soften our footsteps. Two women walk past us, both nodding in greeting at Reilly and ignoring me.

We pass down a long hallway, through a large open room with a high ceiling that is painted to look like the sky, then up another short flight of stairs before Reilly stops at a door and pulls out a key. He unlocks what I expect to be a room but is actually an entrance to a sort of self-contained house.

To the right is a living area. There are two couches and a love seat set around a fireplace. I can see a dining room through an open door, and to the left appears to be a kitchen.

Reilly presses his hand to my lower back. "This way, we don't have time for a tour."

"Right," I say absently, still looking around as he guides me toward his rooms.

We walk through what I assume is his bedroom, though it's decorated like it could be any other room in the house, and into a small bathroom. The walls are stone, and there is a thick rug laid in the center of the room, but it still feels more like a jail cell than a nice bathroom.

There is a claw foot tub set under the window, though the shutters are closed blocking any view you might have. The shower looks recently added. It's set in the corner, but there wasn't room to make it very large.

"Take a shower. I'll have clothes laid out on the bed for you," Reilly says, turning to leave.

"How many people died?" I ask quietly.

He pauses at the doorway. "I don't know. We may not know for a couple of days, but that's not important right now. You made a good impression on Cesare, despite everything. You need to get through this meeting with him before you worry about anything else."

I turn to face him. "What does he want from me?"

"He wants you to do as he says."

"That's not an answer," I say, shaking my head.

"Take a shower," he repeats, before shutting me in the bathroom.

I strip out of the tattered dress and avoid the mirror. I'm sure I look disgusting. I turn on the water and pick out the pins that are still holding my hair up. I toss them behind me, not caring about making a mess.

Black grime from the smoke and debris trails down my legs and into the drain as I step under the hot water. I scrub viciously at my skin, catching bruises and scrapes I don't even remember getting. I force myself to slow down and heal them. I'm not as exhausted as I could be now that I'm not being constantly drained by the Finding magic. I don't want to be in pain while talking to Cesare.

I dunk my head under the water again, and despite the temptation to linger in the shower, the imminent meeting keeps me from relaxing. I wash quickly, not bothering to condition my hair. I forgot to grab a towel, so I have to walk across the chilly room to grab one off the shelf by the bathtub.

I dry off and wrap the towel around me before padding into the bedroom. As promised, there are clothes laid out on the bed for me. They're not something I'd ever pick out though. Reilly even thought of underwear and a bra, which makes me grimace, but I'd rather have it than not.

I pull on the shirt and realize a tag is still attached. I rip it off and toss it back on the bed. My wet hair leaves wet spots on the white blouse, but I don't have anything to tie it back with. The black slacks mostly fit, but they're uncomfortably high waisted. I pull at them, but there's no making them less tight.

I glance at the full-length mirror next to the bed and sigh. I look like some kind of soccer mom on her first job interview since she had kids.

There is a single knock at the door, and Reilly walks in. His hair is also still wet, and he is dressed in one of his usual suits. It's not awkward on him like it is on me.

He stops near the end of the bed.

"You look like an adult," he says.

"I look stuffy," I retort, crossing my arms.

He walks closer and brushes a strand of wet hair back behind my ear. I keep my eyes fixed on his chest; I'm too tired to play these games with him right now.

"It would be wise for you to be able to hear and smell everything you can while we are here," Reilly says, dropping his hand.

"You make it sound like we're walking into a raid or something," I say.

"This is more dangerous," Reilly says, turning away.

"Why do you not trust your sire?" I ask, my voice just above a whisper.

Reilly stands still, his back to me and sighs. "You already know why. Let's not keep him waiting."

I furrow my brows, not sure what he means unless he did hear everything Zachary and I talked about in our last conversation. Reilly glances back and holds out his arm. I step up beside him and slip my hand into the crook of his elbow.

There is a familiar tattooed face waiting in the living room.

"Ihaka," Reilly says with a grin, removing my hand from his arm to greet his clanmate.

"It's good to see you again, brother," Ihaka says with a grin.

"And you," Reilly says as they press their foreheads together briefly. "How is Leslie?"

"Restless, but well," Ihaka says before looking over at me.

"Olivia, this is Ihaka, a longtime friend," Reilly says, waving me forward. "I'm sure you remember him from Javier's."

"Nice to officially meet you," I say as I shake Ihaka's hand.

"Our Sire waits impatiently for the two of you," Ihaka says.

Reilly nods. "We'll talk after the meeting, then."

"Yes, there is a lot to discuss," Ihaka says seriously.

"Soon," Reilly says before turning back to me. "Let's go."

I follow him back out into the winding hallways. We take so many turns, there's no way I'd be able to find my way back alone. This place is huge.

The library has two guards standing outside. The one on the right knocks on the door once. I hear Cesare's command to enter, and the guard opens the door for us.

The room is lit only by the fireplace and a tall lamp near the doorway. Cesare is sitting in a high back chair behind a desk, but he stands and walks around it as we enter. The door is shut, and locked, behind us.

STEPHANIE FOXE

"You did good today, Olivia," Cesare says. "I was not entirely convinced that allowing you and Reilly to work with JHAPI was the right call, but it has paid off quite nicely."

His voice is soft, almost pleasant. Goosebumps creep up my arms.

"I'm glad it paid off," I say hesitantly.

"Yes, I have learned to be patient throughout my life. In fact, twenty-five years ago I bought a book. Much to my chagrin, the spell I thought was within it could not be performed again for many years," he says, spreading his hands wide and shrugging. "How delightful it was to discover recently that the spell had already been cast by someone else. It was also quite interesting to discover what the witches left out of the book."

He walks closer, stopping right in front of me, the tips of his shoes only inches from mine.

"I suppose they did not consider the death of the vampire involved in the spell important enough to mention. That wasn't very polite of them, don't you agree?"

"It was kind of a dick move," I say, my voice steady even though my heart is racing. "I doubt my father appreciated it."

Cesare laughs.

"No, I doubt he did. I'm sure we can find a way around that eventually," he says, placing his cold hand on my shoulder. "All magic requires balance, a price to be paid. Sometimes you can give the spell something of equal value to avoid paying too high a price."

I look at Reilly, unable to reply. Reilly doesn't meet my eyes though; his gaze is focused on his sire's hand on my shoulder. His heart is beating faster than normal, almost like he's afraid.

"So you want to create more like me?" I ask, finding my voice again. "Half-witch, half-vampire?"

"Perhaps," Cesare says. "It's interesting what you can do. We still haven't found your limits, I think."

"I don't know about that, I seem to be able to exhaust myself pretty easily," I say, struggling to not lean away.

"Reilly said he thought your injury was limiting you, and that is gone now," he says, dragging his fingers down the outside of my arm.

"That was holding me back," I agree. "I still need to work on control though. The electric magic is new and hard to use. It's not like the rest."

"Another way JHAPI is going to be useful. Learn what you can from that fire witch," Cesare says, as he lifts his hand away, finally, and strolls toward the table. "The witch council has been angling to steal you away from us; of course, we won't let them."

"Of course," I say.

"JHAPI will eventually outgrow its usefulness as an organization, but I think it best that we continue to work with them while we still can. They not only trust us right now, they rely on us."

"We made them look good," Reilly comments.

"And we need to keep it that way," Cesare agrees. "I don't want to hear any more rumors that the team lead is attempting to have either of you removed."

"I will make sure that doesn't happen again, Sire," Reilly says, walking up to stand next to me.

Cesare sits down behind his desk and looks at the two of us over his clasped hands.

"Learn everything you can, Olivia. There will come a time when you will have to use it, and failing me will not be an option."

"Yes—sire," I say, not sure how to address him.

"Go and rejoin your team tomorrow," Cesare says,

sitting down and crossing his legs. "I'll call you back when I need you, but until then, we can keep picking away at the NWR. They'll be desperate after the failure here."

Reilly tugs on my arm, and I follow him out of the room. He is silent as we walk through the clanhouse. We pass dozens of other vampires, but no one stops us.

It's not as quiet as it was when we arrived. I can hear conversations floating up from downstairs. The quiet moans of feedings as we pass by closed doors. I can even smell someone cooking, so they must house some of the neckers here.

Reilly pauses in a quiet alcove halfway back to his rooms but doesn't look directly at me.

"I'm sorry."

I stare at him, confused. Never in my wildest dreams did I expect an apology, and I'm not sure what he's apologizing for anyhow. He's not lying either. His heartbeat is still fast, but it's also steady. He means it.

"For what?" I ask, glancing over my shoulder to make sure no one is approaching.

"He touched you because he knows I want you," Reilly whispers, staring straight ahead. "He was toying with me, not you."

I open my mouth to try to respond, but I don't know what to say. I can't deny that Reilly and I have chemistry, but I didn't think it meant anything to him other than the thrill of the chase. Reilly had seemed bothered in the room, but I hadn't understood why.

"Let's not linger," Reilly says.

I shut my mouth and follow him, my head spinning from everything that has happened. The rest of the walk is silent and uncomfortable.

When we arrive back at his rooms, Reilly opens

the door and ushers me in ahead of him. As the door shuts behind us all, the sounds from the rest of the house go silent. These rooms must be sound-proofed.

The Viking, whose name I still don't know, Ihaka, and a person I've been both dreading and waiting to see are in the living area. Leslie is sitting on the couch, her legs curled up underneath her, looking bustier than ever. She smiles when she sees me.

"Olivia Carter," she says. "This is some crazy shit, huh?"

I laugh. I can't help it.

"I'm glad to see you somewhat alive," I say with a smile.

"How is Javier doing without me?" she asks, tilting her head to the side.

"I'm not sure," I say, the smile slipping off my face. "I haven't spoken to him since I left a couple of weeks ago."

"Ihaka won't let me contact him at all," Leslie says with a pout. "He won't let me see anyone really."

"So I've heard," I say, walking over to sit on the couch opposite her.

"Does she know now?" Ihaka asks.

Reilly nods. "She knows enough."

"Knows enough about what?" I ask, looking at everyone in turn.

"You know about the Bound God," Reilly says. "And the coven Zachary has been investigating, off the record."

I tense, so he had overheard at least part of our conversation. "Yes, so what?"

"Cesare believes he is real," Reilly says, walking around the back of the couch to stand behind Leslie. "And he thinks that this god is the key to overthrowing the council and propelling vampires back into a place of power in the world."

"I'm sorry," I say, leaning forward to rest my elbows on my knees. "He what?"

"Whether you believe this thing is a god or not, there is something that has been held back by a spell for several centuries. The thing Aris and Izul stopped," Reilly says.

I look at Ihaka, then at the Viking, and at Leslie, but no one is laughing.

"That's not just a myth?" I ask.

"No," Ihaka says. "Though most have forgotten it is true, except for the coven that still guards it."

"The one that killed my mother." I lean back and cross my arms. "What is this thing going to do if it breaks free anyhow?"

"It wants to destroy paranormals. Anything that has or uses magic," Reilly says.

"Then why does Cesare think it can help him?"

"He wants the vampires to go into hiding once it is released. After the witches, goblins, and weres are decimated, he intends to have you kill it," Reilly explains. "After that, he believes his rise to power will be fairly easy."

I bust out laughing, but it's clear no one else thinks it's a joke.

"He thinks I can kill this thing? Aris and Izul had an army behind them if the stories are true. I'm one person, and I barely know how to use half the magic I have."

"That's why I've pushed you. If you're going to stop this thing before it wipes out half the paranormal population, you need to be stronger," Reilly says.

"Why you've pushed me?" I ask, getting angry.

"You threatened me and manipulated me. You destroyed my entire life."

"This is more important than your life," Reilly says, snapping back.

"You could have told me why you wanted my help!" I shout, jumping up to my feet. "You threatened everyone I care about. You destroyed my friendships!"

"I did what I had to do to get you to a point where you would understand what we're facing. Neither of us has any choice here. Cesare ordered me to find you and prepare you for this," Reilly says, skirting around the couch and advancing on me. His eyes are flashing with anger.

"You didn't have to do what you did. You used me. You're still using me," I say through gritted teeth.

"I found out early on that I had to use people if I was going to survive, much less succeed. Grow up," Reilly snaps.

Leslie leans around from behind Reilly's back.

"Just for the record, he wasn't going to actually follow through on his threat to wipe out the clan. If that makes you feel any better," she says with a shrug.

"What?" I ask, anger being replaced with confusion.

Reilly rubs his hands over his face. "If you find the right leverage, and you're just scary enough to be convincing, you don't ever have to follow through on your threats."

I stare at Reilly for a moment, and he stares back, jaw clenched tight. Ihaka is smiling behind him.

"Leslie makes Reilly sound like a soft-hearted man," Ihaka chuckles. "He is not, but he tries to not kill people unnecessarily."

I plop back down on the couch and put my head

in my hands. "Say I trust you lunatics. What exactly are you planning?"

"We have to contact the coven without Cesare finding out and figure out how to stop this thing from being released," Reilly says, his voice tired.

I stare at the floor, the vision of my mother replaying in my mind.

"I think we might also need to steal that spellbook Cesare has," I say, looking up at Reilly.

"Why?" he asks, brows pinching together.

I lean back against the couch.

"It turns out what I thought were hallucinations were something more," I say. "I don't know exactly what she meant, but I think my mother knew this was coming."

"Your mother?" Reilly asks.

"Yeah," I say. "It turns out you can Find the dead."

Reilly sits down next to Leslie, and I take a deep breath, then start at the beginning.

## 30

Corinne is sitting up in the hospital bed reading a book when I walk in. She looks up with a smile, and while she's still a little too pale, her eyes are bright.

"Olivia, I'm so glad you finally came to visit," she says, putting her book down.

I walk over and sit down in the chair next to her bed.

"It has been a long week," I say. "And I wasn't sure if you wanted to see me."

Corinne twists her mouth up ruefully. "Everyone has been just as angry at me as they have at you. We both know you're not to blame though."

I look down at my hands, twisting them together. "If I had been calmer, we might have waited."

"And then the same thing would have happened," Corinne says, leaning over to put her hand on my shoulder. "The trap was set, and we had no way of knowing Martinez would be using magic against us like that. It's completely unheard of. No amount of safety measures could have prevented it."

I sigh. She's right, but I still feel guilty about the whole thing.

"Honestly, if it had happened in any other way, I think I'd be dead because you might not have been there to drain my magic and stop the curse," she says.

"I'm glad you didn't die."

"Me too." She pats me on the shoulder and leans back into the pillows. "The welts on your arms are gone."

I brush my thumb over my forearm. It's almost weird to be able to wear short-sleeved shirts again.

"Yeah, I let go, like you said, but—" I hesitate.

"But what?" she prompts.

"I spoke to her. She didn't seem like a memory. She talked about things I didn't know, and she asked me to do something. It wasn't just an echo or whatever you called it," I say quietly.

"It wouldn't be the first time I've been wrong," Corinne says with a shrug. "It should be impossible, but you should be too. I believe, for what it's worth, that you Found her ghost somehow."

"It does make me feel a little less crazy to hear you say that," I say with a laugh.

"Magic never follows the rules we try to set on it," she says.

"No, it really doesn't."

"Are you staying with the team?" Corinne asks.

"Yes," I nod. "The vampire council still wants Reilly and me on this assignment, especially after the Summit attack."

"That was insane. Ivy came and filled me in on it. We're lucky there weren't more casualties," Corinne says, shaking her head.

"Just over a hundred neckers were killed. Dozens of paranormals. It feels like we lost." I put my head in my hands. "It doesn't feel like we stopped anything."

"You stopped a war," Corinne says, placing her hand on the back of my head. "If the councils had been wiped out, and the vampires had been made to look like monsters, this country would have been thrown into chaos. Thousands would have died instead of hundreds. It may not feel like enough, but you did everything you could."

"Sure," I say, staring at my hands. I clear my throat and sit up. "I shouldn't stay long, but I wanted to see how you were."

"I'll be out of here tomorrow," Corinne says as I stand. "I'm glad you came by though."

"Me too," I say with a smile. "I'll see you again soon."

"See you soon," Corinne agrees.

I leave and close the door quietly behind me. Zachary is waiting outside.

"Did it go all right?" he asks.

"Yeah." I nod.

"Are you sure you want to do this?"

I take a deep breath. "I want to find the people who killed my mother."

"And you're sure about Reilly?" he asks.

"As sure as I can be. He wants to stop Cesare, and I'm willing to help him do that if it gets me what I want," I say.

"I still don't think this god is real," Zachary says.

"I hope he isn't," I say, shaking my head. "But whatever this coven is trying to stop, Cesare is trying to release. Maybe we can take them both down at once."

Zachary nods, and I follow him down the hall. Reilly is waiting for me in the car, perhaps as an ally, perhaps still as my enemy. I'm willing to risk it if it means finally tracking down the people responsible for my mother's death. I had given up on finding them, and on finding out why she died.

I dig my nails into my palm. I know where the

book is. I can get it, somehow, and I can figure out what I'm meant to do. I'll do it for her.

# MESSAGE TO THE READER

Thank you so much for buying my book. I really hope you have enjoyed the story as much as I did writing it. Being an author is not an easy task, so your support means a lot to me. I do my best to make sure books come out error free.

However, I am the worst with commas. They are my nemesis. I deeply apologize if my comma usage bothered you. Going forward, I am hiring a professional editor to review the books before publication. Eventually, I will be able to have previously published books edited as well. If you found any errors, please feel free to reach out to me so I can correct them!

If you loved this book, the best way to find out about new releases and updates is to join my Facebook group, The Foxehole. Amazon does a very poor job about notifying readers of new book releases. Joining the group can be an alternative to newsletters if you feel your inbox is getting a little crowded. Both options are linked below :)

Facebook Group:
https://www.facebook.com/groups/Thefoxehole
Newsletter:

https://stephaniefoxe.com/newsletter-wb/

Reviews are very important to indie authors, and help other readers that would be interested in a series like this find it. I also love reading your thoughts on the book.

To review the book simply go to the website below.

https://readerlinks.com/mybooks/764/1/1237

# FOLLOW ME

Thank you so much for buying my book. I really hope you have enjoyed the story as much as I did writing it. Being an author is not an easy task, so your support means a lot to me. I do my best to make sure books come out error free. However, if you found any errors, please feel free to reach out to me so I can correct them!

If you loved this book, the best way to find out about new releases and updates is to join my Facebook group, The Foxehole. Amazon does a very poor job about notifying readers of new book releases. Joining the group can be an alternative to newsletters if you feel your inbox is getting a little crowded.

Facebook Group:
https://www.facebook.com/groups/TheFoxehole
Goodreads:
http://goodreads.com/Stephanie_Foxe
BookBub:
https://www.bookbub.com/authors/stephanie-foxe

**Misfit Pack** is the first book in a new series by Stephanie Foxe –

**Everything changed in a flash of pain and blood.**

All because she had to play hero.

Amber finds herself tied to two strangers, her humanity stripped from her, and a heavy responsibility laid on her shoulders.

Haunted by guilt and loss, she struggles to understand what it means to be a werewolf – and an alpha.

Magic is commonplace, but there is a divide between humans and supernaturals. There are rules. Expectations.

The title of alpha isn't given lightly, it's earned through a

Trial that will test her in ways she never expected.

Left with no choice but to fight for her new status as alpha, Amber must pull together her fledgling pack of werewolves that never wanted to be more than human. Time is ticking as they prepare for the night that could tear them apart. If Amber fails the Alpha Trials, they'll lose a lot more than their humanity.

They'll lose their freedom.

www.stephaniefoxe.com

Printed in July 2019
by Rotomail Italia S.p.A., Vignate (MI) - Italy